She looked str[...]
Slate Walker's [...]

Cassidy's legs turn[...] eased herself down [...] the day she'd meet [...] and she wasn't ready.

Her daughter had no such problem. Lindsey stared up at the big cowboy and smiled. "I fell down," she explained.

"You sure did." He sat by Cassidy and pulled Lindsey onto his lap. "Let's see if there's any damage."

Watching them, Cassidy felt her heart would stop. Lindsey looked at Slate with open affection, and he returned her gaze with a look that was both confused and clearly warm. As if something between the two of them had connected.

"Would you like to stay with us and train our horses?" Lindsey asked him.

"Lindsey, we have to go home," Cassidy said abruptly.

Before her daughter could say more, Cassidy scooped her off Slate's lap and hustled her away. Lindsey's instant trust in Slate unsettled her.

It was almost as if Lindsey had sensed Slate was her father.

ABOUT THE AUTHOR

As a young girl Caroline Burnes traveled through Texas with her parents. They stopped for lunch at a small café, and Caroline decided it was the end of the trip for her. She'd always wanted to be a cowgirl—and Texas was the perfect place to be one. She would stay. Although her parents did eventually convince her to leave the café, to this day the Lone Star state continues to have special memories for her—and a special place in her heart.

Books by Caroline Burnes

Remember Me, Cowboy
Caroline Burnes

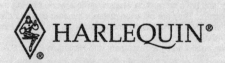

TORONTO • NEW YORK • LONDON
AMSTERDAM • PARIS • SYDNEY • HAMBURG
STOCKHOLM • ATHENS • TOKYO • MILAN • MADRID
PRAGUE • WARSAW • BUDAPEST • AUCKLAND

To all my rowdy Hill Country friends—Bill, Liz and Nancy—thanks for introducing me to Texas.

ISBN 0-373-22485-0

REMEMBER ME, COWBOY

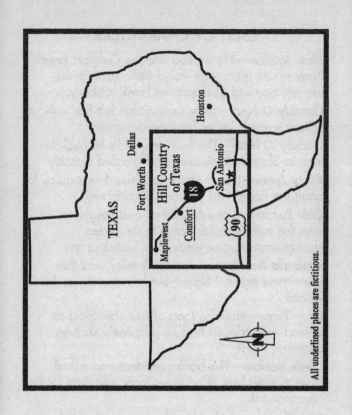

All underlined places are fictitious.

CAST OF CHARACTERS

Slate Walker—He walked into the Comfort Ranch Bank to ask for a loan—and woke up with no money, accused of attempted bank robbery.

Cassidy O'Neal—Slate's conviction left her without a fiancé—or a father for their daughter.

Lindsey O'Neal—The four-year-old's immediate trust in Slate both pleased and worried Cassidy.

Rusty Jones—Slate's childhood friend was quick to point the finger—as prosecuting attorney.

Cole Benson—Cassidy's friend and neighbor won the million-dollar purse in the rodeo championships, one week after Slate's arrest.

Amanda Best Tyree—The bank teller was the eyewitness against Slate—but how good was her vision?

Dray Tyree—Had the loan officer shot Slate to protect Amanda, or had he purposely shot an unarmed man?

Clyde Barlow—The bank president had asked Slate to meet him at noon—a *very* odd time for an appointment.

Sheriff Owens—Had his blindness to the truth put an innocent man behind bars?

Lucky Hill—Cassidy's foreman knew his job—but was he working for Cassidy, or someone else?

Joker—The renegade stallion could be a million-dollar horse—if Slate could catch him before someone else shot him.

Prologue

At high noon, the parking lot of the bank was empty. Slate Walker pulled his dusty pickup truck into a space and got out. Standing beside the truck, he tucked his shirttail into his jeans and glanced down at his hand-tooled boots. They were well worn but polished and neat. He removed his Stetson and smoothed back his light brown hair. He'd been in the Comfort Ranch Bank a thousand times before, but never, literally, with his hat in his hand.

Borrowing money was a hard thing to do. Begging for it was even harder. But if he didn't find some cash, fast, the Three Sisters Ranch would be sold on the courthouse steps in a matter of days. His mother, Mary Walker, was the last living sister, and though the doctors didn't give her much longer to live, Slate was determined that she would die in her own bed on the ranch that she had worked and loved since birth.

Whatever it took, Slate would get the money to keep his mother in doctors and on her ranch.

After she was dead, he'd settle accounts the best way he could.

His boot heels thudded against the newly laid asphalt of the parking lot as he walked toward the bank, which had once been an old general store. He'd had dealings with Clyde Barlow in the past and had found him to be a rea-

sonable man. A cautious man when it came to loaning out
money, but Slate was certain he could put up his cow-horse,
truck and trailer and get a loan for enough to keep the
creditors at bay. At least until the national rodeo finals.

Slate pictured the big stallion, Mr. Twist, in his mind. If
he could hang on to the blood bay bronco for an eight-
second ride, he'd walk out of the arena with a million dollar
purse, not to mention the side money that came with ce-
lebrity.

Slate was certain he could do it—he didn't have a choice.

Mary Walker wasn't the only person counting on him.
He thought of Cassidy O'Neal, and his face flushed with
pride. They were getting married on Sunday. He'd decided
to ask Barlow for a loan large enough to cover a small
honeymoon, even though Cassidy had assured him she
didn't mind waiting until they had money to spend on "lux-
uries." To him, the thought of a weekend alone with Cassidy wasn't a luxury, it was a downright necessity.

The bank door opened and Hook'em Billings walked out,
cheek bulging with a plug of tobacco. "If you want money,
you'll have to pull a gun on 'em," Hook'em said before
he spat, the ends of his waxed mustache twitching.

Hook'em had gotten his name as a bull rider in his youth.
He'd been one helluva rodeo rider in the days when per-
formers risked injury and death without a chance at the big
money. But Hook'em had never seemed bitter. He'd always
been like a father to Slate.

"What's wrong?" Slate asked, set to hear one of
Hook'em's famous yarns.

"Clyde acts like I'm asking to borrow *his* money,"
Hook'em grumbled. "I need a little to carry me over until
the calf crop comes in next spring." He spat again.

Slate felt a tug of concern. In the past, Clyde Barlow had
always been generous in loaning money to the ranchers and
cowboys. But the past two years had been hard on every-

one, including the bank. "Can you cull your herd?" he asked.

Hook'em gave him a sour look. "I don't guess I have a choice. You want to come over Saturday and help me round 'em up?"

"Sure," Slate answered. Helping with a herd was something that all of the ranchers did for one another.

"I'll make sure you don't get bruised or too tired, what with your wedding comin' up on Sunday." His good spirits restored, Hook'em grinned.

"There's not a cow on your ranch that could wear me out," Slate said with an answering grin.

"That's big talk for a man who's walking down the aisle."

"A happy man," Slate emphasized.

Hook'em chuckled. "A *lucky* man. Cassidy's the prettiest woman in Texas. I can't figure why she's gone on a man like you."

Smiling, Slate stepped past him and entered the bank. The lobby was empty, and he glanced to the right to find Clyde Barlow's office door open, but he couldn't get a clear view to see if the bank president was in or not. Karlie Mason, Clyde's secretary, was not at her desk. Slate checked his watch. It was 11:57. He was three minutes early.

He took two steps forward and caught sight of Dray Tyree in his office. Dray was a part-time rodeo rider who served as the bank's loan officer and who would sympathize with Slate's plight. Dray knew how hard it was to make a living on the rodeo circuit. His solution had been to deploy his college business degree and finally accept a full-time job. Slate was both envious and sorry for Dray— Slate wanted the security of a job, but he couldn't stand the idea of working for anyone other than himself.

He started over to talk with his old high school friend

but realized there was someone in Dray's office. Slate could only catch sight of the back of the visitor's head.

"Can I help you?" a pretty bank teller asked.

Slate advanced toward the teller window where Amanda Best stood behind the old-fashioned black iron bars. She'd been behind Slate in school, and he didn't know her well, but Amanda and Cassidy had resumed their childhood friendship when Cassidy had moved back to Comfort from Houston. In contrast to Cassidy, with her lithe blond looks, Amanda was dark and small. She had a quick smile that now flickered nervously and disappeared.

"I have an appointment with Mr. Barlow," Slate said.

Amanda nodded. "I have to get some change." She left her station and walked over to another counter. Ducking down, she disappeared.

Slate eased over to a display that showed the different interest rates for savings accounts. He glanced at his watch. It was 11:59. Lunch was an odd time for a banker to make an appointment, he thought for the third or fourth time. But he was glad. Cassidy was meeting him at Dobie's Barbecue for lunch, a luxury that they seldom had time for.

A movement by the counter caught his eye, and he looked up. Amanda's face was wide-eyed with horror. She held up both hands, staring at him as if he were a snake. "Don't hurt me," she said. "Please, Slate, don't hurt me!" She pushed a cloth bag across the counter at him. "Take the money, just don't hurt anyone."

Slate started toward her, confused. "What are you—"

Amanda's scream echoed off the old wood of the bank.

Slate felt as if he were in thick, wet sand. His limbs seemed weighted. He lifted his hand, a gesture of help, only to see Amanda's fear heighten, and now he had no doubt that she was terrified of him.

"Amanda?" he said, but his question was lost in the shrill of her scream.

"Drop it, Slate!" Before he could react, he heard the report of the gun. He felt the bullet as it slammed into his head, and he felt himself fall. It seemed to take forever, his body in a free fall to the right side. The familiar decor of the bank was a kaleidoscope of colors and shapes as he went down. And when he struck the floor, it was with a final thud that brought the release of darkness.

Chapter One

As the chain-link gates topped with razor wire slowly swung open, Slate took a last lungful of prison air. He did not expect to feel anything when he walked through the gates of Huntsville Prison, but he did. Something in his chest was both painful and sweet. After four and a half years, he was once again a free man.

"I don't want to see your sorry ass back here," the guard called after him as he stepped through the gate to freedom.

Slate lifted a hand in farewell but didn't turn around to look. He'd done his time, and if he could, he intended to put it behind him. His sentence to Huntsville Prison hadn't been as hard as it might have been. From the very first, Slate had found a niche. He'd done his work and minded his own business, and he'd somehow managed to earn the respect of the prison officials as well as the other inmates. The Texas penal system had made a lot of money on the rodeos he'd organized and managed. He'd been one inmate who hadn't cost the state a dime.

He looked for the red pickup truck Hook'em Billings said he would be driving and was surprised to see the old cowboy sitting in a comfortable sedan. The car pulled up to him, and Hook'em gave him a friendly wave. "Hop in, Slate. Time's a'wastin'."

When it came time for him to leave prison, there'd been

no one else for Slate to call. His mother had died while he was behind bars. When the warden told him of her passing, Slate had tried to attach emotion to the image of the frail, gray-haired woman who had sat behind the rails of the courtroom during his trial. He'd felt regret at the death of a woman who was obviously devoted to him, a woman acknowledged as good by everyone who spoke her name. But all efforts to *feel* the past were futile.

Bitterly, he'd realized that he wouldn't have remembered he had a mother if someone hadn't told him.

That day, five years before, when he'd stepped into the Comfort Ranch Bank, he'd lost not only his freedom but his memory. He had not recognized a single person, and he could not remember any of his past.

"Where to?" Hook'em asked as he spun the sedan out of the parking lot and headed for open highway.

Slate was taken aback. He hadn't thought about what he would do once he was released. The only thing that had been on his mind was figuring out if he really had attempted to rob the Comfort Ranch Bank. All the trial evidence painted him guilty, but Slate simply couldn't justify the evidence with this own feelings.

"Why don't you come to my place?" Hook'em suggested.

Slate nodded. There wasn't any other choice. He had forty dollars in his pocket, no transportation and no destination.

"Things around Comfort are pretty much the same," Hook'em said, putting the car in drive. "I'm a little older, but that's about it. Cassidy's as pretty as ever."

Slate turned to look at him, no expression in his green eyes. He knew who Hook'em meant—the striking blond woman who'd sat beside the woman identified as his mother in the courtroom. Once again, the void of the past rose in front of him.

The old cowboy reddened and pressed harder on the gas.
"None of my business, anyway," he mumbled. "Hey, why
don't we stop by Dobie's and get some barbecue? That
used to be your favorite hangout. Maybe if you see some
of the local places, it'll jog your memory. Never mind if
some folks around town are a little stiff-actin' at first."

Slate didn't answer. He had no memory of a favorite
place to eat, and no interest in food. In prison he'd eaten
whatever was served.

"Your mother had a beautiful funeral service, Slate.
Cas— It was fitting. She's buried out on that ridge that she
loved. We can drive out there later if you'd like."

Slate swallowed. "No, thanks." He didn't want to visit
his mother's grave until he had some memory of her. He'd
spent the first year in prison trying to force the memories.
He'd thought that if he tried hard enough, he could make
them come back. But the harder he tried, the more elusive
the past had grown. It was as if he'd started his life in the
county jail, awakening full-grown to the realization that he
had walked into a bank, pulled a gun and tried to steal
money.

The horror and desperation of his actions had been
brought home to him at his trial. He had nearly frightened
a bank teller to death, not to mention threatening the lives
of several other bank employees. Based on the testimony,
he had been a real desperado.

"I got a little surprise for you," Hook'em said. He
glanced toward Slate.

"You do?" Slate didn't know if he wanted any surprises
thrown at him. This freedom thing was enough of one. In
prison, he hadn't needed a memory. He'd walked in and
made his reputation. But in the outside world, he was at a
complete loss. The man sitting behind the wheel of the car
knew more about him than he knew about himself.

Of course, he'd read the newspaper stories. He'd been a

bronc rider with a little talent and a lot of luck. His had been the rising star on the national rodeo circuit before the attempted bank robbery. He was the son of Mary Walker of the Three Sisters Ranch, a woman highly respected for her ranching techniques and kindness. He'd been a good student in high school and had shown promise as a horse trainer. He knew the facts, but he didn't own them.

"I been keeping this a surprise." Hook'em grinned at him. "You want the surprise or the barbecue?"

Slate actually wanted to go somewhere quiet and be left alone. "Whatever you decide," he answered.

"Let's decide when we get to Comfort." Hook'em pushed the car up to the maximum speed allowed as the wide open vista of the Texas countryside began to develop a gentle swelling as they headed west. "Why don't you put the seat back and take a little nap? We'll be home in no time."

Slate was not tired, and he was far too keyed up to sleep, but he leaned the seat back and closed his eyes. The truth was he had nothing to say. The man beside him was obviously an old friend, but Slate didn't have a clue what their past relationship had been like. He was as vulnerable as a newborn baby.

"Slate," Hook'em said.

"Yeah." He kept his eyes closed. It gave him a small sense of protection.

"There's something been troublin' me."

"Yeah?"

"I saw you goin' into the bank that mornin', remember?"

Slate eased his eyes open. He tried hard to remember. "No, Hook'em, I don't."

"Well, damn!" Hook'em hit the steering wheel with his palm. "That was the problem at the trial. Whatever anybody said, you couldn't put up a defense because you didn't remember. If you'd had the money to hire yourself one of those Dallas lawyers, you coulda beat the rap. The gun was the only real evidence against you."

Slate's mouth turned up in a wry smile. "The gun and the eyewitness testimony. I can remember the trial. It seems pretty obvious that I did it. I mean, those people were friends of mine, or that's what they said. That woman…"

"Amanda Best," Hook'em prompted.

"Yes, Ms. Best cried on the stand. She seemed upset to have to testify against me." Slate felt a dagger of pain at the memory. The trial had been hard on him, but it had seemed to be just as hard on the people who testified against him.

"She sure did," Hook'em agreed. "Whatever happened, it was a terrible thing for her. But I saw you goin' into the bank. I know you don't remember, but I was comin' out and you were goin' in. We talked a minute and I drove off."

"I remember that you testified to that." Almost every second of the trial was etched in Slate's brain. The whole experience had been a nightmare. People swore that he'd done things he had no memory of and couldn't understand.

"What I tried to tell all of them was that when I saw you out on the porch, you didn't have a gun."

Slate was fully alert. "They found the gun. It was my *father's* gun. It had to have come from me."

"You coulda had it tucked in the back of your belt, I suppose, but you didn't have it where I saw it." Hook'em scowled over at him. "I may be old, but I'm not senile. If you'da had a gun in your hand, I would have seen it. You never were the type to stick one in the back of your pants. Too sissy for you."

Slate pondered this. The gun had been the thing that had hamstrung him in his own defense. Its hand-carved grip had apparently been his father's pride and joy. Mary Walker had positively identified the pistol. "If I didn't have the gun, where did it come from?" he asked.

"That's what we have to find out." Hook'em's face was grim. "I know everybody in that bank, and they were all friends of yours. They all seemed as shocked and hurt as you were. Still..." He let the sentence fade away. "Slate, do you remember the pretty blond woman who sat behind you in court?"

Slate did remember her. Cassidy O'Neal. Long blond hair, sad blue eyes and composure that held her back erect even though he refused to see her when she came for jail visits. She had stared at him in the courtroom as if she expected something from him. He was certain that somehow his actions had hurt her deeply. "She came to the trial every day," he said. He didn't mention the jail visits he'd rejected. "Was she related to someone who worked in the bank?"

Hook'em took a breath. "No." He worried his bottom lip. "She worked for your mother. She's... Damn it all to hell, I can't go against my word and I promised I wouldn't do this."

Slate felt the relentless pressure of no memory. This woman was someone he should know. And chances were he'd done some wrong to her and she had attended the trial to see that justice was served. Another load of guilt. "What did I do to her?" he asked.

"Just take a nap," Hook'em responded.

Slate closed his eyes again and felt himself being tugged back into the squirrel cage of his thoughts. He had lost nearly five years of his life because he'd done something he didn't remember doing.

In the bank he'd been shot, the bullet grazing his head. The doctors had said his memory loss was due to the fall. When he had gone down, he'd struck his head against the counter. The prognosis was that his memory might return, intact and complete, or it might not. He might recover bits and pieces, or he might get nothing. Dr. Janeway had explained that his particular injury *could* account for the memory loss, or it could simply be that Slate *didn't want* to remember. That he was repressing the things he'd done because he knew they were wrong.

He'd been over this ground a million times in the years he'd spent in prison. There were no answers. He tried to relax his neck and back and let the gentle lull of the car push him into a light sleep. He liked the feeling of going— of being on the move. He liked glancing out the window and seeing the Texas countryside flash by. And he found that he liked the idea of being free.

That was a start.

THE TELEPHONE POLE was as tough as a mesquite trunk, but Cassidy O'Neal hammered the nail that would support her broadsheet. She stepped back to survey her work, reaching for the little blond girl who sat at the curb on the nearly deserted street.

"Are you finished?" Lindsey asked, staring up at her mother with blue eyes as big and wide as the one's that looked back.

"Three more. Then we'll get that milkshake I promised."

"And barbecue?" Lindsey's eyes sparkled with anticipation.

Cassidy found she could not deny her. "And barbecue." It was a simple-enough thing to give to make her daughter happy.

"When will the horse trainer come?" Lindsey asked.

"Oh, maybe in a day or two. He has to read one of these advertisements first, and then apply. You know I can't hire just anyone. I don't want my horses manhandled. We're looking for someone very special. Someone with a gentle touch and a respect for animals.'' Cassidy found, to her distress, that the words caught in her throat. She'd known a man like that. Once.

SLATE RAN HIS HAND over the fender of the old truck. In the back was a saddle and tack, all freshly cleaned and oiled. "I thought my belongings were sold," he said.

"They were. You owe me ten grand. You can pay me or work it off," Hook'em said. "There's another surprise waiting for you out at the ranch."

Slate lifted his gaze from the saddle. "What?"

"Your horse, you fool. How can you work cattle without a horse? And Stargazer was the best in the business. Since you don't remember, I ought to switch horses on you and keep him for myself."

"Stargazer." Slate felt a whisper of something familiar. "A chestnut?"

Hook'em stared at him with sympathy. "A dun."

Slate nodded. The name had only seemed familiar. The past was lost. "If you've got a place for me to put up, I'll work off what I owe you."

"That's a deal. Right about the time you went to…away, things got better for me. I came out ahead with the cattle, and I had enough to keep Stargazer from going to the knacker."

Slate didn't remember the horse, or the past, but he felt a deep debt of gratitude to the old cowpoke who'd done his best to hang on to Slate's past for him. "Thank you, Hook'em."

"Don't go gettin' sentimental on me," Hook'em said, walking away. "I drew you a map out to my place. It's on the seat. Maybe you ought to drive around Comfort and see if there's anything you remember."

"What about the barbecue?" Slate asked.

"Get it yourself. I don't want you lookin' to me to see

what you ought to remember or not.'' He glanced down the street where the blond woman was nailing broadsheets to a telephone post. A smile tugged briefly at the corner of his mouth. ''Just meet folks and see what happens.''

''Thanks,'' Slate said as he got behind the wheel. The truck started like a charm, and he noticed that the gas tank was full.

''MAMA, LOOK!'' Lindsey pointed across the empty street to a multicolored ball that was rolling along the gutter. She was up and running before Cassidy could grab her.

''Lindsey!'' Cassidy saw the old truck four car lengths away just as Lindsey dashed into the street in front of it.

''Lindsey!'' she yelled.

Her daughter turned to look at her, oblivious to the vehicle rushing at her.

There was the squeal of brakes and the truck slued dangerously into the other lane. Cassidy was moving, but too slowly, while her daughter stood frozen in the middle of the street. As Cassidy watched, the gleaming bumper inched into her daughter, nudging her backward and down onto the asphalt. Lindsey seemed to disappear beneath the truck, which screeched to a stop.

''Lindsey!'' Cassidy flew into the middle of the street. She saw her daughter lying on the pavement, her blond hair blowing beside the truck tire. ''Lindsey!'' She thought her chest would burst.

The tall man got out of the truck and lifted the little girl into his arms just as Cassidy got there. Not bothering to look at him, she touched her daughter's face. Lindsey turned wide blue eyes on her. ''Mama,'' she said, holding out her arms.

Cassidy clutched the child to her chest, feeling her daughter's small body sob with fear.

''Are you hurt?'' Cassidy knew she had to examine her,

but she didn't want to let her go. Not for a second. "Thank you," she said, finally looking at the man. "Thank you…" The rest of the sentence died on her lips. Slate Walker stared down at her, green eyes furrowed with worry and fear.

"Is she hurt?" he asked, recognition plain on his face.

Cassidy opened her mouth, but nothing came out. Slate remembered her, but she was willing to bet it was only from the trial. He took her arm and moved her out of the street.

"Let me see her," he urged, his hands already untangling the sobbing child from her arms and pulling Lindsey onto his lap as he sat on the curb.

"Hey," Slate said softly. "Let me see if there's any damage." He spoke to Lindsey, his hands moving over her back and arms and legs. "You scared me pretty good, little lady. Does it hurt anywhere?"

Lindsey stared into his face as if mesmerized. Her sobs had tempered to a few ragged breaths. "I went under the truck," she said.

"You sure did." His hands calmed and comforted the child as he spoke.

"I fell down," Lindsey explained, looking at her mother. "I'm not supposed to run into the street," she offered, tucking her chin.

"Oh, Lindsey." Cassidy knelt beside the little girl. "Are you okay?" Concern for her daughter pushed everything else from her mind. Even the painful knowledge that Slate's prison term was finished.

Lindsey nodded. "Are you mad at me?"

Cassidy caught her daughter's face in both hands. "I should be, but I'm not. I'm just so glad you're okay. But don't ever run into the street again, do you understand?"

"The truck could have smushed me." Lindsey looked

from her mother to the man who still held her loosely on his lap. "It was a bad noise when the truck stopped."

"It's okay," he said. "No harm done as long as you're not hurt." His hand smoothed her blond hair.

Cassidy felt the reaction in her legs. They were rubbery and weak, and she eased herself down to the curb before she collapsed. When Slate had first been convicted and Lindsey was born, she'd marked the years of his prison term in her heart and dreamed of the day they'd first meet— father and daughter. Now it was happening, and she was unprepared. Every maternal instinct she had urged her to protect Lindsey, no matter the cost. She felt Slate's curious gaze on her, and she looked down at the toes of her cowboy boots.

"Are you okay?" he asked.

"I'll be fine," she said, still staring at her boots, hating the lie she was prepared to tell. She took a deep breath and choked it out. "Seeing her disappear under your truck scared the life out of me. It's tough raising a child alone, and Lindsey's all the family I have. Her father is dead to us." She finally looked up at him, uncertain what his expression meant. "That's the way it has to be."

"I remember you from the courtroom," he said at last. "You came to the prison. Several times. Whatever I did to you, I'm sorry."

Cassidy felt a rush of sympathy, and her own pain. It had to be hell, feeling the need to apologize for something even if you didn't remember doing it. "There's no need for apologies," she said softly. "What are you going to do now that you're free?" The question slipped out, and for a moment she was afraid he would sense the lingering intimacy that it revealed. Once, they'd shared everything. Every plan, every dream.

"I'm going out to work for Hook'em Billings. I owe

him a bit of money, and he says I'm good at working cattle."

"You're better at horses." Cassidy forced her gaze down. "You had quite a reputation before you went...away."

"Mama, can he train our horses?" Lindsey asked. She readjusted herself to a more comfortable position in his lap. "I like him."

Startled, Cassidy finally looked up. When she did, she thought her heart would stop. Lindsey was looking up at the man with open affection, and the glance he was giving her was filled with confusion and what was clearly warmth. Something between the two of them had connected, and her gut reaction was concern. She would protect Lindsey at all cost.

"Honey, Sla—Mr. Walker has made other arrangements." She forced strength into her legs and stood, her arms open for her daughter.

Lindsey snuggled deeper into his lap. "He'd be able to catch Joker."

Slate frowned. "Who's Joker?"

"He's the stallion Mama needs to make the horses happy. He's beautiful, but he's so wild and smart that nobody can catch him. And some bad men have been trying to kill him." Lindsey looked at her mother. "Tell him, Mama."

Cassidy leaned down and eased her daughter out of Slate's lap. She watched as the tall cowboy rose easily to his feet with the same grace and strength she'd always found so breathtaking.

"Joker's a million-dollar horse," Lindsey said. "Nobody can get a rope on him."

"Is that right?" Slate spoke to Lindsey, but his gaze had settled on Cassidy. His brow was furrowed, as if he was concentrating.

She felt as if time had turned backward. She'd seen that look on Slate Walker's face a thousand times through the two years that they'd been lovers. "We have to go home, darling." She stumbled over the words she spoke to her daughter.

"What about my milkshake?"

"Another time." She had to get away.

"But you promised," Lindsey said, a tremor in her voice. "I was bad to run in the street, but I'm sorry."

"We have to feed the horses." Cassidy resettled her daughter in her arms and forced herself to meet Slate's green stare. "Thank you...Mr. Walker."

"Slate."

"Thank you, Slate." She managed it without mangling his name.

"How old is Lindsey?" Slate asked, smiling at the child.

"She's just old enough for kindergarten." She felt as if she were opening the door on danger and tried to be vague.

"I'd better get my truck out of the street." He looked at the lone car waiting patiently behind the vehicle.

"Thank you again," Cassidy said. She put Lindsey on the sidewalk and caught her hand tightly. Before her daughter could say anything else, she hustled her across the street to the stack of broadsheets she'd left beside the telephone pole.

"Why didn't you like that man?" Lindsey asked, as Cassidy gathered her things. "He was nice."

"We can't take up with strangers, honey. We don't know anything about him." The lie was bitter, but it was better than the fear that Slate evoked.

"I liked him."

Cassidy didn't say anything else. She picked up the sheets and reached again for her daughter's hand, then hurried toward the truck she'd left on a side street. Lindsey's instant attraction for Slate terrified her. It was almost as if her daughter had somehow known that Slate was her father.

SLATE WATCHED THE TWO of them hurry down a side street. He put the truck in gear and found a parking space. In five long strides he was across the street and standing beside the telephone pole that held the broadsheet.

Double O Ranch. Horse trainer wanted. Must respect horses. No abuse tolerated. Job comes with room and board. Call 555-5454.

Slate pulled the flyer free of the nail and slowly folded it into a square that would fit into his pocket.

"THIS IS THE LAST ONE," Cassidy assured her daughter. She now regretted not going to Dobie's and getting something to eat. Her stomach was growling, and she knew Lindsey was miserable. But the job was finished. The flyers were up, and with any luck, they'd have a new trainer at the Double O Ranch in a matter of days. She had to keep herself focused on business and not the emotions Slate Walker stirred in her.

"We'll be home…" She leaned in the truck window and found her daughter asleep. Lindsey had given in—her fatigue had overridden even her hunger. "Excellent," she said sarcastically under her breath. "You let your daughter go to sleep without eating after she's had a traumatic day. That's good, Cass. Real good." She was sliding behind the wheel when she heard a vehicle slowly pull up beside her.

"Morning, Cassidy," Cole Benson said, tipping his hat. "I've got a question for you."

"What's that, Cole?" Cassidy had recently been seeing more and more of the rancher. In the past three years, since she'd bought the Double O, he'd been a good neighbor.

Lately, he'd let her know he was interested in a deeper relationship.

"How exactly can you tell if a prospective trainer respects a horse?" His wide grin was filled with good-natured teasing.

Cassidy smiled. "I'll be able to tell."

"One day you're going to get killed by one of those spirited animals that you've let run all over you. The only thing horses really understand is who's boss. The quicker you let them know who's running the show, the easier it is on them in the long run."

Cassidy had grown up with men who viewed their relationship with a horse as a battle of domination. She'd long ago learned that the worst thing she could do was to argue about training techniques. What counted was results—and her horses were winning everything they were entered in.

"My horses know who's boss, Cole. The difference is, they work for me because they *like* it." She wanted to add "and not because they're afraid," but that would only start a range war. Cole was not cruel to his animals. He simply didn't know any better, and he refused to try and learn.

"Slate Walker, with his crazy Indian notions, was the worst thing that ever happened to you."

Cole's statement, with an edge of anger, caught her by surprise. Her own temper kicked in. "That's not for you to judge, Cole. My past is my business."

"Slate is the one who put those crazy horse ideas in your head."

Cassidy couldn't ignore that, and she didn't have to try. What she fully intended to do was keep the conversation away from Slate. The shock of seeing him was too fresh, too sore, and Cole would find out soon enough that Slate was back. "I know you don't like the way I train, but you can't deny my success. So let's just leave this conversation here, before we make each other mad." She smiled at him.

"I count on you, Cole. You've been a good friend. Let's not argue."

Cole turned off his engine and got out of the truck. He walked slowly up to Cassidy's window, and his smile was warm. "That sounds like a deal. In fact, let me take you to the dance. I was headed out to the Double O to ask you."

Cassidy had forgotten about the summer dance that was held each year at Stubby Olman's ranch. It was one of the social events of the season for the area ranchers—a time for them to get together and brag about calves and foals and hay crops. It was always a good time, and a rare chance for her to visit with friends who were as busy as she was. "I don't know...."

"Don't tell me you have a date?" Cole asked.

"No, I haven't. I actually forgot. My mind has been on weaning the foals and putting up better fencing in the pasture that borders the creek." She shook her head. "I really have too much to do, Cole, but I thank you for the invitation."

"I won't take no for an answer. You need to have a little fun. And if you need some help with fencing, I'll send a few of the men over. Things are kind of slack at Vista Blue. I can come and help with the horses."

Cassidy took a breath. "You've been a good neighbor, but I won't take advantage of you. I'll have a trainer soon, and the horses will be weaned in plenty of time."

"Then, the fencing?"

To refuse both offers would make her seem ungrateful. "Thanks. That would be nice. We can get the fence up in a matter of hours."

"And that'll clear you for the dance. Hook'em Billings is doing the barbecue."

There was no graceful way to refuse. "Thanks, Cole." She smiled. "That sounds like fun."

"I'll pick you up at seven Saturday. And by the way, if

you have any horses out on the west range, you might want to bring them in. That stallion's been running over there." Cole's mouth hardened. "But he won't terrorize us for much longer."

Cassidy felt her stomach knot, and she looked over to find that Lindsey had awakened and was listening, her blue eyes alarmed by the hard tone in Cole's voice.

"He's not really bothering anyone," Cassidy offered.

"He stole four of my best cow ponies, and when my men went to bring them back, he tried to kill them."

"Having your stock bred by that devil isn't the worst thing that could happen. He throws some fine babies." Cassidy tried to keep her voice light, but she could feel the anxiety.

"He's a menace. I've tolerated him long enough."

"What are you going to do?" Cassidy hardly dared to ask.

"If we can't catch him, then we'll kill him."

It took every ounce of control not to argue, and luckily Lindsey unbuckled her safety belt and stood on the seat.

"You better not hurt him," the child said, her eyes narrowed in anger.

"Well, well," Cole said, laughing. "You've got your mother's temper. When she was in the first grade she punched me in the jaw."

Lindsey, diverted for the moment from the horse, looked at her mother. "Did you?"

Cassidy couldn't help but laugh. "I did. He was trying to make me eat dirt."

Lindsey whirled to the man. "You were?"

"She had put a big handful of dirt down my pants."

Lindsey slowly turned to her mother. "That wasn't very nice."

Cole laughed. "Now, that's an understatement, Lindsey." He tipped his hat at Cassidy. "I'd better get busy.

The men will be over to mend the fence tomorrow, and I'll
pick you up Saturday.''

"When are you going after that stud?" she asked.

"Next week. I found a ravine that might work as a trap,
but it's going to take some work to disguise it. If I can
catch him, I can make a lot of money selling him to the
rodeo. If not…" He shrugged.

"See you Saturday," Cassidy said, buckling Lindsey's
seat belt and heading home as fast as she could.

"Is he going to kill Joker?" Lindsey asked.

"No way, baby. We're going to catch him first." She
only hoped that she would not have to go to her daughter
and tell her that she'd lied. She'd do everything in her
power to catch Joker and protect Lindsey from getting hurt.

Even if it meant keeping Slate Walker out of their lives.

Chapter Two

As the rolling Hill Country of west Texas slid by, Slate was aware more than ever of the intricacies of memory. Gazing out the window of his old truck as he sped along the highway, he felt strangely at ease. The truck responded in a way that teased his memory, and the roll of the land to the left and right was more than simply beautiful—it was home. He knew this in a way he could not fathom or explain.

The Guadelupe River wound through the area, and Slate found that he was fascinated by the green depths of the fast-moving water. He knew the river's color came from limestone deposits that were the foundation for the rugged land. And it was that same limestone that was the bedrock of the pasture where he saw a herd of beautiful mares and foals grazing.

He continued down the road, looping back and following the sign to Center Point. As he read the name of the town, he knew that more Texas rangers had been killed in Center Point than any other place in Texas. He didn't know how he knew these things, he simply did. Like he knew how to drive, or how to saddle up Stargazer and cut a cow from Hook'em's herd. How was it possible that he knew trivial facts, but he couldn't recall his mother's face or remember a single incident of his past at will? Perhaps the psychiatrist was right—maybe he was repressing his memories because he didn't want to confront the type of man he was. Or why he'd been so deeply affected by Cassidy and her daughter.

He drove slowly down the main street of Center Point, crossed the Guadelupe and headed toward Comfort. He knew the route to take without having to ask directions. What he didn't know was if his trip to the county prosecutor would do any good.

RUSTY JONES LEANED his head back against his leather chair, but his gaze never left Slate's. His dark eyes seemed emotionless.

"Are you accusing me of tampering with evidence and setting you up?" he asked softly.

Slate shook his head. "No." The problem was that he didn't know what he was doing.

"You come in here and say you *think* you're innocent." Rusty slowly sat up. "You want to see the evidence. You want to see the police reports. Let me ask you, Slate, why didn't your lawyer obtain these things for you when it might have made a difference? You've done the time. My advice to you is to put the past as far behind you as you can. You grew up here. You were respected and well liked in the community before the attempted robbery. If you show folks here that you're sorry for what you did and looking for a decent life, they'll give you a second chance." Rusty's voice grew harder. "Just don't keep rubbing their noses in the past."

Slate kept his mouth shut and nodded. The words that threatened to spill out would only make it harder—on him. He forced a civil tone into his voice. "I appreciate the advice, Mr. Jones, and I want to make it clear that I'm not accusing anyone of any wrongdoing. I'm simply looking for the truth."

"Memory can be a convenient thing, Slate. Maybe you

don't remember because you don't want to have to face your own actions." He stood up. "I have an appointment with Judge Brisko."

That was the judge who'd presided at his trial, but Slate kept a poker face. He'd tried to make an appointment with the judge but had been told that Frank Brisko was too busy to see him. "Even though you don't feel it's necessary, would you do me the favor of getting those reports released for me? I'd like to take a look at them, to satisfy my own mind."

"Suit yourself." Rusty put on his coat. "But you'd do a lot better to spend your time in a round pen with a horse. You have a talent for working with animals." He smiled. "Take the advice. It's free. This time."

Slate rose to his feet. He didn't remember Rusty Jones, but he had the distinct impression they had a past. "Is my father's gun still being held as evidence?"

Rusty was on his way out the door, but he stopped and turned around. "It's been nearly five years, Slate."

"Once a trial is over, the evidence should be held or returned to the owner. Unless that gun went to my mother, it should be in the safekeeping of the county. At this point, I believe it's legally mine."

"I'll check on it." Rusty started out the door.

"My mother identified the gun. But she was a very sick woman. Are you certain, in your mind, that the gun belonged to my father?"

"Mary Walker, sick or well, knew her own mind." Rusty turned to him. "But I didn't need her to identify the gun. Most everyone in town knew what it looked like. I knew it, too. I remember the day when we were fourteen and we took it from your father's holster and went out to the cattle tank to shoot cans. And I remember the trouble we both got into. The handle was carved teak, an intricate pattern of a wolf. A shaman carved it for your father. It was one of his most prized possessions.''

Slate saw that the other man was breathing light and fast, his response emotional. It made him wonder if Rusty Jones had something to hide. ''The gun was in my hand?''

''In your hand.'' Rusty walked toward him. ''I would have preferred to convict someone other than you. You claim you don't remember, and I have to believe you, but we were friends once. Good friends. It gave me no pleasure seeing you go to prison. But the past is over, Slate. If you don't put it behind you, it will destroy you. And you've got a lot to live for if you'll only look for it.''

Slate swallowed. ''I'll keep that in mind.''

CASSIDY WALKED UP the steps of the Comfort Ranch Bank and found that she had to draw an extra breath and steady herself with the handrail. Seeing Slate had reopened all of her old fears. After the trial, it had taken her a long time to be able to walk into the bank without feeling as if she were going to burst into tears. Time had passed, and she'd put the nightmare behind her. And now, once again, she was an emotional mess. All because she'd seen Slate on the street. He hadn't even recognized her. He hadn't felt a thing for her.

She pushed through the door and stopped, in her mind seeing Slate lying on the floor, blood oozing from his head and a gun in his hand, a sack of money at his side. Thank goodness Dray Tyree's shot had been off, or Slate would have been dead.

She walked to the teller's window and spoke to the young blonde, Betty Brown, a woman she didn't know very well. ''Is Amanda in?''

Betty smiled. ''You haven't heard? She quit.''

''This is obviously good news,'' Cassidy said, judging Betty's wide smile.

"She'd wanted to quit for a long time, and Dray finally told her that she could." Betty leaned forward and lifted her eyebrows. "I think she may be pregnant," she whispered. "And it's about time. They've been wanting a baby for a long time."

"Well, congratulations are in order, then." Cassidy tried not to show her surprise. She and Amanda Best, now Amanda Tyree, had been best friends. Over the past three years, since Cassidy had bought the Double O, their friendship had cooled—partly because Cassidy didn't have time, and partly because of Amanda's role in Slate's conviction. But a pregnancy? It hurt her that Amanda hadn't told her.

"Don't tell her I said so," Betty urged. "She acts like she's afraid to tell anyone or it will go away."

"I'll keep it a secret." Cassidy looked around. "Is Mr. Barlow in?"

"I'll buzz him. Karlie ran down to the store to pick up something." She rang the bank president's desk. "Miss O'Neal is here to see you." She nodded at Cassidy. "He said to go right in."

Cassidy passed Karlie's empty desk and entered Clyde's private office. His bald head gleamed in the light from the window, and he steepled his hands in front of a paunch that strained at the buttons of his vest. "It's good to see you, Cassidy. You know you're one of my best success stories."

"Thanks." She had done well since she bought the Double O. In three years, she was way ahead on her notes and looking at another profitable year. "I've been lucky."

"Lucky and smart. An asset to our community. The day you came back to Comfort from the big city was our lucky day. What can I do for you?"

She hesitated. "Slate's back in town."

Clyde sat forward, his hands moving to the arms of his chair. "I'll never know what possessed that man. I would have loaned him the money. He didn't even ask." He looked out the window.

"Clyde, is there a chance Slate didn't do it?"

The bank president didn't answer immediately. He got up and went to close his office door. When he returned, his face was expressionless. "I was busy. I didn't see any of it until I heard the shot and rushed out there. What I saw was Slate on the floor, bleeding, with the gun and the money. Dray held a gun in his hand and had obviously shot Slate. I testified to what I knew."

Cassidy felt her hopes drop further. "I know. It's just that…you helped raise money for his defense. And you paid for the psychiatrist to examine Slate about the amnesia."

"Slate's mother was a valued customer of the bank, and she was also my wife's dear friend. What I did was for Mary more than Slate. Put the past behind you, Cassidy. Slate isn't the man for you. There's too much baggage there. If he's smart, he won't stay in Comfort." He placed his manicured hands on the desk. "If you want to help him, urge him to move along."

"I saw him…." She broke off and shook her head. "You're right. It would be best for everyone if he moved away."

"Especially best for Lindsey."

Cassidy's gaze snapped to him. "She doesn't know, and I don't want anyone telling her."

"Then encourage Slate to leave. He never was a stupid man, and if he finds out about the two of you, it won't take him long to put the facts together and figure out that Lindsey is his daughter." Clyde's eyes narrowed. "She'll have to grow up knowing her father was a convicted felon. That's something you should spare her if you can."

Cassidy wanted to protest that statement, but not even she could deny facts. Slate had been tried and convicted.

And it didn't matter that she'd never really believed him guilty.

There was a soft tap on the door and a feminine giggle. "Oh, Clyde..." Karlie Mason hurried in and then started with surprise. "I didn't know you were here, Cassidy," she said, glancing at Clyde. "Cly—Mr. Barlow...I didn't mean to intrude." She fidgeted nervously.

"I was just leaving." Cassidy rose. She was out the door before she remembered that she'd come to pay off her truck and get the title. She turned around abruptly and started back, but she halted. Both Karlie and Clyde were staring after her, and both of them looked worried. She changed her mind about the truck and quickly left the bank.

THE ROAD TO THE DOUBLE O RANCH wasn't exactly familiar, but Slate knew exactly the way it would wind up the slopes, meandering through live oaks and outcroppings of rock. He stopped his truck and finally got out. Even though the day was hot, the wind pushed through the dry grass and leaves of the trees with a gentle rustling sound. Slate turned so that the breeze struck his back, sticky from the leather of the truck seat.

On impulse, he walked along the edge of the ridge until he saw the sparkle of the creek below. The laughter of young boys floated to him on the wind, and he strained to see them, finally realizing that the sound was in his mind. He had played in a place like this. He knew it, though he couldn't remember where.

There had been an old rope and a deep swimming hole worn into the bedrock of the creek. The water had been icy, and he had played there with his friend...Rusty Jones? He clearly saw the snaggle-toothed face of his friend grinning at him. It had been Rusty. And the power of the memory was so strong that Slate wanted to simply sit and think a moment.

He started down to the creek, his boot heels catching in the tall grass and his toes tumbling small rocks that clattered before him. The sun was hot on his back, and the gurgle of the creek promised cool relief. Slate forgot that he had driven to the Double O to apply for a job. He forgot that he was on another's property.

As the ground leveled out, he started to jog. The cypress trees in the creek bottom were huge. The bed of the creek was scattered with rocks as large as potatoes washed smooth by the rapid current. Slate went directly to the deep hole, worn into the creek bed. An old rope dangled above the creek. It was exactly as he knew it would be.

He stripped off his boots and jeans, unbuttoned his shirt, letting it fall to the ground, and dove into the water. For a split second, he thought the shock would drive the air out of his lungs. But once he got his breath, he wanted to shout with the simple joy of a cold dip on a hot summer day.

A red-winged blackbird perched on a cypress bough just above his head and watched him with open curiosity. Slate whistled at the bird, imitating its call. The bird answered, then turned its head from side to side. Slate swam across the creek and pulled himself out on a large, flat rock. In the heat of the day, it wouldn't take him long to dry. He stretched out on the rock and closed his eyes.

The memory of Rusty was something of a breakthrough. It was his first memory of childhood. And if one came, there would be more. Eventually, he might recover everything he'd lost.

And he would have the truth about the bank robbery.

The rush of the creek and the hot sun on his chilled body was the most wonderful sensation he could remember. This was freedom. This was what he's given up for nearly five years. What had been taken from him. He swallowed back the sudden anger and forced his body to relax. He would rest until he was dry, and then he would continue to the

Double O and apply for the job of horse trainer. If respect of the animal was the only qualification Cassidy O'Neal required, then he might get the job.

SLATE AWOKE to the sensation of someone breathing on him. It was a prison nightmare, and he forced his body not to react. In prison, the worst thing a man could do was show fear. Even in his sleep. He opened his eyes slowly, stunned to find it was broad daylight and to see the boughs of the cypress trees fluttering in a steady wind.

He sat up slowly, instantly focusing on the huge bay horse that stood not three feet from him.

It had been the horse's warm breath that awakened him.

The animal was better than sixteen hands, with the long back and wide chest of a Thoroughbred. But there was mustang in his eyes and in the tangled mane that hung far below his neck.

"Well, well," Slate said, edging around slowly so that he gave the horse his shoulder. The stallion blew and snorted but didn't attempt to leave.

"Where did you come from?" Slate asked softly. He glanced around but didn't see the herd. Apparently the stallion was on a stealing spree. He'd come alone to see if he could find more mares to add to his harem. "Good idea, but Mrs. O'Neal seems to have all of her stock up at the barns." Even as he spoke he noticed the fence a hundred yards to the west. Several of the boards had been splintered—as if they'd deliberately been knocked down.

Slate knew exactly who the culprit was. He eased to his feet. "I wonder if you're Joker."

The horse backed away from him a step or two and was poised for flight. "So, you've been chased. I'll just bet you have." He remembered what the little blond girl had called the horse—a million-dollar stallion. Slate was a good judge of horseflesh, and he knew that the animal that stood before him was either extremely valuable or totally worthless. It all depended on how he took to people.

"I'll be seeing you later," Slate said softly. He reached for his clothes and drew them on. He felt the horse watching each move. "You don't know what to think because I haven't tried to catch you." He laughed. "That's good."

He walked away from the creek and never turned back to look. He didn't have to. He knew the stallion was watching him with intense interest.

When he got to the truck, he allowed himself to turn and look, but there was no sign of the big mahogany bay. He was sure that Mrs. O'Neal would have a lot of questions for him to answer, but he had one for her. Where did such a horse come from? Joker, and he had no doubt that was Joker, wasn't a wild range animal. He was a refined horse, one with deliberate breeding. It would be interesting to find out how such an animal had been left to go wild.

He followed the winding drive that continued up the steep incline until he saw the outline of the ranch house set among the live oaks. It was a new house, its wood and glass blending into the rocky terrain. As he drew closer, he realized it was the kind of house he would one day like to build.

Before he'd stopped the truck he saw the blond woman pause at the screened door. She started toward him, but she was passed by a blond blur that ran with the abandon of childhood.

"Lindsey!" Cassidy called.

"I won't run under the truck," she answered, stopping five feet from the bumper. She looked up at Slate and smiled. "I knew you'd come," she said.

Slate found that he could not look away from the little girl. She was a handful, but it seemed that sunshine danced in her eyes. "How did you know?" he asked, despite himself.

"Because if you don't catch Joker, Mr. Benson's going to kill him."

Slate looked up to find another pair of blue eyes riveted on him, but these were filled with worry and what might have been fear. That he was an ex-con, a man to be feared, was like a kick in his gut.

"What can we do for you?" Cassidy asked, her hand grasping her daughter's shoulder and moving her back to her side.

"I came about the advertisement."

Cassidy bent down to tie her daughter's shoe. When she looked up, the confusion was gone from her eyes. "I know your reputation."

"Are you referring to my horse training or my time in Huntsville Prison?" There was no point beating around the bush. He might as well confront the issue head-on.

"Both. But it was the horses I was referring to."

"I'm an ex-con, and that's a fact I can't change." He could see his directness caused her pain, though she hid it well.

"I know that."

"I need the job, and I'm good with horses."

"You used to be the best."

He looked up to find that she was sincere. "I saw that stallion your daughter was talking about."

"Joker?" Cassidy's interest was immediate. "Where?"

"Down at the creek bottom. He came up on me. As your daughter pointed out, he's a valuable animal, if he takes to people."

"Joker was here?"

Cassidy's mouth parted, and Slate found that he was suddenly focused on her lips. She was a beautiful woman, and she had one of the most sensuous mouths... He forced his thoughts back on the horse. "Not fifteen minutes ago."

"Yesterday he was on the north range." Cassidy took a

quick breath. "If he's this close, maybe we can get him." She started walking toward the barns, signaling Slate to follow. Lindsey skipped along at her heels.

"He's out looking for mares," Slate said. "I wouldn't be surprised if he came up here to visit."

He could see the enthusiasm on Cassidy's face. "Do you think we can get him in the barn?"

Slate shook his head. "He's too smart for that. But give me a few weeks and I'll get him for you."

Cassidy shook her head, her blond hair tumbling over her shoulders. "You don't understand. We don't have a few weeks. Cole Benson is going to catch him or kill him."

Slate's forehead wrinkled. The name Cole Benson rang a bell. "Who is he?"

"My neighbor and one of your old—" She stopped, eyes narrowing. "He was a bronc rider."

"Cole Benson." Slate nodded. "I remember him. Or I remember the name from some of the newspaper articles I read. He was a good bronc rider."

"Still is," Cassidy said as she picked up a halter and lead rope. "Excuse me, but I've got a horse to catch."

"You won't get him by riding up on him and trying to drive him into a trap."

She stopped in midstride. "Do you have a better idea?"

Slate wanted to smile. Cassidy O'Neal had that impact on him. "I do." He did smile when he saw her hands go to her hips.

"Are you going to tell me or just stand there grinning?" she asked.

Her exasperation made him smile wider. "I came up here looking for a job. Now, I promise you, I can do this job. But you have to hire me first."

"You always had a reputation as a good bargainer," Cassidy said. She tossed him a bridle. "You're hired, and your first job is to catch that stallion. You can ride Cutter."

Slate walked to the stall she indicated and began to tack up the gelding. "We aren't going to catch him. My idea is to make him want to be caught."

"And how do you suggest doing that?" Cassidy lifted Lindsey and set her on the stall door. "You're staying here. And no guff. Nita will help you color some pictures."

Slate gave the little girl a sympathetic look but picked up with the conversation. "We offer him more and better of what he already has." He brushed the gelding down and lifted a saddle from the rail. In a matter of seconds, he was tacked up, and he led the horse out of the stall.

"More and better what?" Cassidy asked, gathering the reins for her mount.

"More mares, better feed, a kind word. He struck me as a smart horse. It's a bargain he's likely to accept if it's put to him the right way."

"And that's your job," Cassidy said. "Yours—" she looked at Lindsey "—is to head for the house. And no complaining." She waited until the little girl started up the walk toward the house.

"Let's ride out and take a look." Slate swung into the saddle, knowing that the ride was more for a chance to be with the blond woman than to check out the stallion.

Cassidy led the way and Slate followed. Instead of heading for the creek bed, Cassidy chose a trail that hung on the lip of the incline where the house sat. It was a high point that eventually gave a view of sloping green pastures.

"This is a pretty place." Slate liked the way the trees were so varied in their shades of green. The grass was plentiful and good quality. His respect for Cassidy's skills as a horsewoman rose.

"It was part of an old ranch called Three Sisters."

He felt her staring at him and knew why. "My mother's place," he said. "Don't worry, I'm not territorial. I don't remember any of it. Except..." He thought of the creek.

"Maybe I do remember. When I was down by the creek, for just a moment, I knew I'd been there as a child."

The sudden hope in Cassidy's face that was quickly replaced by caution left him wondering.

"Look," she said, pointing toward the bottom of a long, narrow pasture. At the very end was a band of seven or eight horses. Out of the trees Joker surged, running around them and packing them into a herd.

Slate was struck by the beauty of the horse's movements. He was one of the finest animals he'd ever seen. "Where did he come from?"

"There are lots of stories, but no one knows the truth. Several people have tried to claim him, but it didn't do any good because they couldn't catch him."

"What about a helicopter?"

Cassidy sighed. "So far, they haven't taken it to that level yet, but it's coming. My neighbor is mad. Joker's been raiding his mares, and Cole is a man who likes to keep what he owns under lock and fence. He says if he can't catch him, he's going to kill him. Hunting him down with a helicopter would be the most expedient method. That's why we have to get him before they do."

Slate couldn't have agreed more. "Let's ride down to the bottom and see how close he'll let us come. He knows my scent."

He took the lead and heard her horse following behind. The slope was steep and studded with the small stones that rolled from beneath the horses feet. But the two horses were solid, dependable animals, and they made their way to the bottom safely.

Cassidy pointed up to an overhang of rock. "Every winter, some of this comes down. The ice freezes and breaks the rock. It's beautiful in a way, but it's dangerous."

"Nature seems to blend beauty and danger in equal measure," Slate said. He urged his horse beneath the outcropping and into the sunshine. He turned to speak to Cassidy. Before he could utter a word, there was the sound of a sharp explosion. Slate felt the ground tremble, and as he looked up, a huge chunk of rock broke loose. It tumbled several feet, then seemed to lodge as a hail of smaller stones crashed to the ground.

He felt the thud of fear as he realized the big rock, so precariously lodged, was directly above Cassidy's head.

Chapter Three

When Cassidy felt her mare tremble, she wasn't certain if it was because of Joker's nearby presence or because of her own dislike of the narrow trail that wound beneath the overhanging rock. The ungainly formation called Big Boot, because of its shape, loomed high overhead. Cassidy thought that it might be of geological interest, but it made her nervous. Her mare, Lightning, began to prance in place and throw her head.

"Easy, Lightning," she said, soothing the flaxen mane. "We're—"

She never finished. Above her, it sounded as if the world had begun to explode, and she saw the giant outcropping of rock break free and begin falling. She dropped her heels into the mare's sides as Slate and his horse charged forward, but Lightning was paralyzed by fear. The mare's head snapped up and Cassidy could see her eyes rolling. The first rubble of sharp stones began to ping down around them.

The hail of smaller rocks subsided, and Cassidy looked up to see that the huge rock that had broken free had somehow managed to lodge against another rock. Even as she watched, it shifted and a trickle of dirt, and small stones cascaded down the bluff.

Cassidy slid from the horse's back and whipped off her

hat. Yelling and screaming, she flapped the hat against the mare's rump, trying to drive her out of the narrow ravine and to safety.

Already panicked, Lightning began backing toward her, stumbling on loose rocks and whinnying wildly as the huge boulder shifted yet again and baseball-size stones slammed into her back in another minor avalanche.

To Cassidy's horror, she saw that Slate had dismounted and was running back toward her—back to the danger that hung above her. A huge chunk of rock smashed into the path not four inches from her foot, and an orange-size stone struck her shoulder sharply, making her cry out with surprise and pain.

Ignoring the onslaught, Slate captured Lightning's reins. "Easy," he said, putting a steadying hand on the horse's shoulder. Then he yelled at Cassidy, "Get out of here! I'll bring the horse."

Instead, Cassidy flapped the hat harder, finally startling the mare forward. Once Lightning began to move forward, she was ready to run. She churned toward the mouth of the ravine, grunting as a heavy rock struck her neck.

Cassidy ran behind the horse, her gaze focused on the broad shoulders of the man in front of her. He'd risked his life and gone back for Lightning—and her. It had been a remarkable display of courage, and heart. They were almost out of the ravine, and she could see the open meadow ahead where Cutter waited for them, ears twitching and nostrils flaring.

Only twenty feet to go. Slate was almost in the clear. Small rocks continued to shower down on them, and Cassidy flinched again as one struck her foot. This would be a story to tell around the campfire—the day Big Boot nearly crushed her to death.

"Cass!"

It was the horror in Slate's voice and the use of a name

that no one had uttered in nearly five years that tingled Cassidy like an electric charge. Her blue gaze met and locked with his just as another rock struck the side of her head.

Her upper body went numb, but she felt the pain in her knees as she dropped sharply to the ground. And then there was nothing.

SLATE SAW THE ROCK strike Cassidy, and it was as if the pain was transmitted to him. Afraid if he released the mare too soon, she'd panic and run back on top of Cassidy, he led Lightning clear of the opening and sent her running free. In one smooth motion, he was dodging and weaving his way back through the narrow passage.

A cloud of dust partially obscured his vision, but he didn't need to see clearly. The image of Cassidy, blood flowing from the gash on her temple, was imprinted on his mind. He didn't wait to decide if she was alive or dead. He lifted her into his arms and turned and ran. Small stones cascaded all around him, striking viciously. But he felt only the woman in his arms, her body still warm and her limbs pliant. He couldn't be certain she was breathing.

He burst into the sunshine and staggered, nearly losing his footing. He heard a low rumble behind him, and felt the earth jar as the huge hunk of rock finally hit the ground. Dust exploded from the narrow ravine.

To his right, a cottonwood tree cast dense shade, and he eased Cassidy down. His fingers found the pulse at her neck, steady and strong, and for the first time since the landslide, he allowed himself to feel relief. She was alive.

The creek was only a hundred yards away, and once he made sure she was as comfortable as possible, he ran to it. He needed fresh water to clean the cut on her temple, cold water for the swelling that had already begun and could be serious. When he got to the creek, he used his shirt as a cloth. He was headed back when he saw the stallion.

Joker stood over Cassidy, his nose almost touching hers. When the gelding he'd been riding stepped forward, Joker laid his ears back, snaked out his head and threatened the horse. For a second, Slate stopped and watched. He couldn't be certain if Joker was standing his ground against the gelding, or if he was protecting Cassidy.

He didn't have time for more observation. He was too worried about Cassidy. As he approached, Joker gave one loud whinny that was answered by the mares at the far end of the meadow. With a whirl, he was gone.

Slate settled beside Cassidy and took her head in his lap, where he could cradle her from the hard ground. He gently used his shirt to clean her wound. A goose egg had already formed, and the skin on top of the swollen area was cut and bruised. It was a long gash, but not deep. He was as easy as he could be as he carefully worked the bits of rock and dust from the wound. Although her face was ashen, she was breathing regularly. As he dislodged a sharp bit of rock, he was glad she was unable to feel the pain.

He had barely finished when she stirred, and her lids fluttered.

"Slate?" she said, confusion in her eyes. Her hand reached up and touched his face. The faintest smile lifted the corners of her mouth. "What a wallop. What hit me, a hoof?"

"A rock," he said, taking more pleasure than he ever dreamed possible in her touch. "Don't you remember?" he asked softly.

Cassidy lowered her hand, and the gentleness in her eyes disappeared. "I'm sorry," she said, trying to get her elbows under her and push off his lap into a sitting position. "I forgot...I was confused."

His hand restrained her as he eased her back down

against his thighs. "You just took a nasty knock on the head. Give it a minute or you'll pass out."

Even as she rested back against him, he felt the tension in her. Well, he couldn't blame her. Now that she remembered he was an ex-con, she didn't want to be that close to him. But just for a split second, she'd seemed mighty glad that he was there.

What would it be like to have this woman care for him in that way? The thought was like a sharp kick, so painful that Slate wondered if he'd been shot.

Her reaction to the change in his expression was instant. "Are you hurt?" she asked.

"No," he assured her. "I thought for a few minutes that you might be seriously injured. Looks like it was a glancing blow. No serious damage."

"Lightning has never frozen like that. If you hadn't..." She licked her dry lips. "You saved my horse, and then you risked your life again to save me." She turned to look at the narrow opening, now filled with rocks. "What caused the landslide?"

"I don't know." But he had some suspicions. "When you feel like it, we should take a look."

Cassidy took a breath and sat up. "I'm fine, Slate." She looked at the pass. "Thank you. That was brave—"

He shook his head. "Thanks aren't necessary. Anybody would have done the same thing."

This time her smile lingered. "Not many people would have gone back in that ravine with half a ton of rock falling to save another person, much less a horse."

Slate felt his own lips tugging into a reluctant smile. He'd gone back for her—and he knew she'd never leave her horse. "Lightning seems to be a really *nice* horse."

Cassidy couldn't help the laughter.

Slate laughed, too, glad to see that she'd caught his dry humor. He looked down at her hand and felt again the brush of her fingertips on his cheek. Some man would be very lucky to have this woman. Very lucky.

"Let's see if we can discover what happened," she said, rising slowly to her feet.

"While you were out, Joker came and paid you a visit. He was quite taken with you," Slate said as he, too, stood.

"Really?" Cassidy's blue eyes snapped to life.

"He came right up to you and seemed to be guarding you. It was something to see."

She turned to him and stopped abruptly, eyes widening as they dropped to his bare chest. They lingered there, and before she turned away, Slate caught something wistful in her gaze.

He felt a twinge of self-consciousness and picked up his shirt from the ground, shook it out and put it on. "It'll dry in no time," he said.

"Yes." She stumbled slightly as she turned away. "Thank you again."

"Any time," Slate said, and this time he was glad she couldn't see his smile. He didn't fully understand it, but her reaction had given him a grain of hope.

THE OUTCROPPING KNOWN as Big Boot was gone. It looked as if the top of the ravine had been smashed and hollowed out by a giant fist. Easing to the edge, Cassidy looked down to the pass below. She saw with a sense of wonder that it was a miracle she and her horse were alive. And Slate, too.

The ground was littered with stones of all shapes and sizes, and a layer of dust hung over the bottom.

"The timing on this is more than a little suspicious," Slate said from ten feet behind her.

The picture of his broad chest, bared in the sunlight, was in the back of her mind. She forced it away as she turned to face the man who had no idea how intimately she'd once known every plane and angle of his body. Or how much pleasure she'd taken in holding and touching him. In so many ways, it was as if he'd never been away. Certainly not in prison. Whether he had his memory or not, he'd kept his dry wit. And the green sparkle that occasionally flashed in his eyes was something from her past—and her fantasies. Even as she met his gaze, the feel of his face lingered on her fingertips.

"You don't think the rock slide was an accident?" It had never crossed her mind that it could be anything else. The outcropping had hung out there so precariously—the slide *seemed* almost inevitable. Except that Big Boot had hung there for decades. And it was odd that the disaster should happen just at the moment they were in the path of it. Ranching was a practical life, and *coincidence* wasn't a word you'd hear on the lips of a man or woman who worked livestock. Slate was right, they should check it out.

Slate called her attention to the remaining face of the rock. His own hand, large and calloused, moved over the concave surface. "It's possible that it was a natural accident, but I want to look around." He began sifting through the rubble.

"What are you looking for?" she asked.

"If it wasn't an accident, there should be a blasting cap or some remaining evidence."

His words were so matter-of-fact, they were even more horrible. Cassidy couldn't help but wonder if prison had hardened him so. The very idea that someone had set a charge—had intended to…kill her—sent shivers down her spine.

She found that he was staring at her, and she couldn't hide her fear. "Who would do such a thing?" she asked. "And why?"

"I can't answer that." He pointed to tracks. "But someone has been up here on a horse shod with heel caulks. Are you running any horses out here shod like that?"

She shook her head. "If the horses are in pasture, they're unshod. I don't like to leave them out with shoes on." She hesitated. "But there are several at the barn with heel caulks."

He stooped over the tracks and brushed at them lightly. "They're fresh." He moved suddenly forward and picked up a long pole. Gazing at it with a speculative look, he looked into the distance again. "You said Cole Benson was after the stallion." It was as much a question as a statement.

"Yes."

"Let me take a look at something." He hurried down to the bottom of the overhang, sliding in his haste. When he reached the ground, he began searching the sides, ignoring the dust that lingered.

"What?" Cassidy called down.

"You'd better come down here," he said, standing up.

He held something in his hand. Cassidy skittered down the rock. The way he stood made her anxious. "What?"

He held out the filament. "It was a booby trap. Set to go off when horses, or something big enough to trip it, went through the ravine. Whoever did it used that pole up there as a fulcrum to loosen the rock formation. This thin wire went across the path and then up to the fulcrum. The rock was precariously balanced. It didn't take much to set the chain reaction in progress. I must have set it off and you got caught in the rock slide." There was cold anger in his voice as he looked up. "Some bastard meant to kill those wild horses."

Her intake of breath was both horror and anger. "This is my ranch, and no one has a right to come here and set traps of any kind for any reason."

"Whoever did this is very foolhardy," Slate said. His green eyes were narrow and hard. "And very calculating."

"Cole wants Joker dead, but I can't believe he would be this stupid." Cassidy really didn't believe her neighbor would do such a thing. "Lindsey could have been riding back here. Or any of the hands."

Slate was watching her, and his stare made her feel uncomfortable. All hint of tenderness was gone. His face might as well have been carved from the very stone that surrounded them. "Slate?" She spoke his name without thinking.

"The idea that someone would be stupid or careless enough to set up something like this—" He broke off. It was clearly with an effort of will that he tamped his anger down. "If you'll get the horses, I want to take another look up top."

"Okay." But it wasn't. Slate's anger, on top of the rock slide, made her feel as if she were walking a tightrope without a net. She heard his boots in the loose rocks as he went up the steep incline. When she looked up, his silhouette was a shadow in the sun. Once again she was flooded with poignancy. She had seen him so often—building a fence or gentling a horse—as just a silhouette against the setting sun. And prison had not changed him. Not physically. But what had it done to him inside? Now the smallest display of anger, even when justified, frightened her. Perhaps it would be better if she didn't hire him to help with the horses and to catch Joker.

As she started toward Cutter and Lightning, she knew she didn't have a choice there. She'd been trying for better than a year to catch the elusive stallion and hadn't gotten within half a mile. Now, the first time Slate walked on the property, the big bay had been within touching distance—twice.

If she were going to have one shot in a million at catching Joker, it would be with Slate. And she needed that one shot, with Cole determined to rid the rangeland of the stallion.

She gathered up Cutter's reins and reached for Lightning.

With both horses obediently following her, she started back to the ravine.

Lightning balked, and she stopped to soothe the mare's fears. Even with patience and a steady hand, it took her ten minutes to get the mare to reenter the narrow pass. By the time she walked out the other side, Slate was waiting for her, his face not exactly grim, but certainly not happy. And her mind was made up. Slate was hired, and he would live in the bunkhouse. Once Joker was captured, she could reevaluate her plan. Until then, she could only pray that Slate didn't recover his memory—or ignite too many of hers.

THE GUN WAS JUST AS Rusty Jones had described it, a beautiful weapon that balanced in Slate's hand. As he tightened his grip around the handle, he saw the young deputy's gaze flick nervously.

Slate tucked the gun back into the holster he'd recently bought. "Thanks," he said.

Sheriff Noll Owens walked up to the counter with a slow, steady pace. "If it were up to me, I wouldn't let you have the gun, Slate. State law doesn't allow a felon to have a gun. But Rusty said it was a valuable collector's piece and that you were putting it somewhere for safekeeping. He said to let you have it." Owens adjusted his black leather belt. "Like I said, if it was up to me, you wouldn't get it."

"But it isn't up to you," Slate responded.

"No, but I don't like the idea of it. And I don't like the way you're looking at it and holding it."

"That's not up to you, either," Slate said.

The sheriff blew air. "Don't be a fool, Slate. That's all I'm going to say to you. Hook'em said you were living out on his ranch. Stay out there for a month or two, work the cows, get back in the routine of being a free man. Don't start any trouble."

"Thanks for the advice," Slate said as he turned and

walked out of the sheriff's office, the gun firmly in his hand.

The town of Boerne, the Kendall County seat, bustled around him, and he stopped to remember the days of his trial. It all seemed like a bad dream now. Every day, he'd walked into the courtroom and seen people who looked at him with sorrow and disbelief. With anger and disappointment. People who'd known him all his life, people he'd worked beside and laughed with. People he no longer recognized. And Cassidy O'Neal had been one of those people. She was there every day, sitting just behind him, so close that he was always aware of her. And yet separated by a distance that was much more than the wooden rail that divided the spectators from the participants in the trial.

There had been hope in her eyes. He recognized the emotion now. But he didn't have a clue what she hoped for—his innocence, his punishment, what?

A horn sounded, and he looked up into the steady brown gaze of a dark-haired man driving a red-and-silver dual pickup.

"Slate!" the man called. He whipped the big truck into an impossibly small parking space and jumped out. He was standing beside Slate in a flash. "I heard you were back. It's good to see you. I'm delighted to hear you're staying in Kendall County."

"Thanks." Slate was adrift.

"Cole Benson," the man said, slapping his arm good-naturedly. "I heard you never regained your memory. And after all the times those broncs kicked you in the head and you never even blacked out."

"Yeah," Slate said. So this was the bronc rider who was trying to capture wild horses—and possibly setting dangerous traps on Cassidy's land. "Speaking of broncs, someone set a trap for that wild stallion. Cassidy was almost killed."

"That's too bad. I told Cassidy that horse was going to get someone killed."

Slate clenched his fist. Cole wasn't admitting or denying anything. But he wasn't suitably sorry. "Well, the next trap set on Double O land is going to cause trouble. Big trouble."

Cole's gaze fell on the gun in Slate's hand. "Is that a good idea?"

Slate blinked as the meaning of Cole's words registered. He was a felon. He couldn't own a gun. He shrugged. "I'm selling it. It's a collector's item, and I need the cash."

"Your father's gun, wasn't it?" Cole asked. "I'll loan you some money and hold the gun for collateral."

Slate hesitated. Cole Benson was acting as if they were friends, just as the newspaper clippings had said. "No, thanks, Cole. I want to keep my personal life and my business transactions separate. There's a dealer in Houston who'll pay top dollar."

"Suit yourself," Cole said. "It's good to see you back on the streets. I'll see you at the barbecue tomorrow night, right?"

"Sure," Slate answered. He knew Hook'em was cooking and that the barbecue was a big deal to his friend. So he would be there. He had most of his gear already packed in his truck for the move to the Double O, but he had to get Stargazer. He wondered again at Hook'em's reaction when he'd told the old cowboy he was taking a job as horse trainer at the Double O. *Delight* was the only word that described Hook'em's expression, though he'd turned gruff and ornery as quickly as possible.

Slate sighed and walked on. Figuring folks out wasn't his forte. If he had any talent at figuring anything out, it was horses. And that's where he intended to focus his energies.

DUST SWIRLED AROUND the legs of the gray gelding that trotted in the round pen, and Slate pulled the truck over so that he could watch as Cassidy worked the two-year-old. He couldn't decide whether to watch the horse or the woman, and he finally settled on Cassidy. She kept her body turned squarely to the young horse, pushing her out to the boundary of the pen.

He noticed that she used the same training techniques that he favored. It was odd—as far as he could remember, he'd never seen anyone else use them. He'd begun to believe he was the only person who understood that a horse could be trained without violence.

He was so impressed, he forgot his things and went to the rail and took a seat. Across the ring, several other hands had stopped to watch Cassidy work.

"That filly makes a fine pet dog, but what are you going to do when you have to put a bridle and saddle on her?" one of the ranch hands asked.

"She won't get upset," Cassidy assured them. "Once she trusts me, she'll do anything I ask, *willingly*. Pay attention, because this is the way I want all of my animals handled. There's no need for harsh treatment."

The man laughed, and Cassidy shot him a look that shut him up.

Slate found that he was smiling. When she finished working the mare, he slid down from the rail and walked into the center of the arena. The gray gave him a wary glance and then stepped closer.

"That was some fine work," Slate said. "I was hoping we weren't going to butt heads on training techniques, but we do it exactly the same way."

Cassidy laughed, and he was startled to see her blue eyes were sparkling with happy memories. "You taught me,

Slate," she said. "I know you don't remember, but I was your first convert."

"You were?" Slate felt a jolt of joy that was as thrilling as it was unexpected. They had known each other, and they had been friends. She'd once respected him.

Cassidy had turned away from him and was signaling the ranch hands for quiet. "This is Slate Walker, the new horse trainer at the Double O." She pointed around the group, introducing the men. She stopped at a tall blonde who stood with a boot hooked on the fence and his eye on Cassidy. Slate recognized him as the cowboy who'd spoken out.

"This is Lucky Hill, our foreman," Cassidy said.

Slate could feel the antagonism coming from the man. He smiled. "Pleased to meet you all."

"I'm not so sure I want to work and live around a bank robber," Lucky said.

Cassidy tensed for a split second before she turned to face him. "I'm sorry you feel that way, Lucky. You're a good foreman, and I'd hate to see you move on. But if you can't get along with the horse trainer, you'll have to go."

She spoke so softly that Slate was impressed with the authority of her voice.

"You're saying you'd let me go to keep him?" Lucky was angry and disbelieving.

"You're a good man. But Slate is the best horse trainer there is. It won't be long before he has his own place and we'll be competing against him. Until then, if I can get him to work for me, he will." She walked over to Lucky and drew him aside.

Slate watched as she talked to him, her voice so soft he couldn't hear what she had to say. He felt awkward, until he saw the flying blond braids of the little girl headed right at him.

"Mr. Walker!" she yelled. "Mommy says you're going to catch the stallion."

Slate laughed. "Maybe."

Lindsey stopped and looked up at him. "You'd better! Mama needs Joker bad."

The men broke up and moved along to finish out the day's work. Slate caught the young gray mare and started toward the barn with her, Lindsey at his side. She was talking nonstop about her kitten and the baby horses.

Slate turned the corner and almost collided with Lucky. The tall foreman didn't step aside.

"Take my advice and move on," he said. "The Double O has enough problems without you here."

"If I were you, I'd move out of the way," Slate said.

"If you were me, you wouldn't have a criminal record. Now, Cassidy has enough on her plate without you making trouble for her." His fingers brushed the handle of a gun he wore in a holster on his hip. "Things have been good for the past two years. But they can turn bad mighty quick for her."

"I'll keep that in mind," Slate said, fighting to keep his temper in check. He felt Lindsey pressing against his leg, and the fact that Lucky was frightening her made him even angrier.

"You won't last a week," Lucky said as he roughly stepped past Slate, knocking his shoulder as he went.

Lindsey stepped away from Slate and looked at Lucky as he strode past her. She eased over to Slate. "I don't like him."

"It could be that he's just overly protective of your mother and the ranch." Slate didn't believe it for a second, but there was no point in upsetting Lindsey more than she already was. Her breathing was short and shallow, and her gaze lingered after Lucky.

She reached up and took Slate's hand. "Sometimes Mr. Lucky stands outside the house, watching Mama. I don't like him."

Chapter Four

Cassidy wasn't surprised when she heard Slate still moving around in the barn. He'd entertained Lindsey for a good twenty minutes, and Cassidy had worked hard to persuade the child to go inside with Nita for her bath. Now, as she approached the barn door, Cassidy wondered if Slate was getting to know the horses...or waiting on her. The rush of anticipation was so strong that she had to take a steadying breath before she walked in. He stood in the center aisle, brushing Cutter. His hands worked over the gelding's burnished coat with an assurance that was a pleasure to watch.

"Did you find a bunk okay?" she asked.

"Everything's fine." He met her gaze and his hands stilled for a split second. Then he went back to work, his attention on the horse. "I checked Lightning over again, and she's fine." He hesitated. "And I want to thank you for the job."

"Was Hook'em upset that I stole you?" she asked with a smile.

"No, he seemed pleased with the turn of events." Slate's face held some confusion. "I don't know if that's a good sign or a bad one. Maybe I'm not a good employee. I don't remember."

Cassidy laughed. She remembered too well that Slate worked harder than any man she'd ever known. Hook'em

Billings was pleased because the old coot thought he was some kind of matchmaker. During the years that Slate was in prison, Hook'em had fanned the flame of her love for Slate. He was still at it.

"What's so funny?" Slate asked. His own smile showed that he was pleased with her laughter, even though he didn't understand it.

"Hook'em is one of a kind."

"Cass—Mrs. O'Neal," Slate stumbled, finally resting his hand on Cutter's back.

"Call me Cassidy. All the men do."

"I need to ask a favor of you. And I want to be up front."

She didn't like the sound of this. "What is it?"

"I got my father's gun today. As a convicted felon, I'm not allowed to carry it. I was wondering if you could put it someplace for safekeeping. I thought of the bank, but then that didn't seem like such a good idea, walking in there...with a gun." His smile was wry.

Cassidy shook her head. "Very funny. This time you might lose more than your memory. As far as the gun—" she had misgivings, but none too strong to heed "—I'll lock it in the house. We keep payroll sometimes, and there's a strong safe. When you leave you can have it back. But this is a good time for me to be honest with you. I'd prefer it if you didn't carry a weapon. For the sake of the men. I don't want any excuse for trouble."

He nodded, and she couldn't read his expression.

"Slate, I know this must be hard for you. I can't begin to imagine how hard. But it's tough for a lot of people." Her throat tightened, and she fought sudden tears. She *knew* how hard it was for her, him standing in front of her without the first memory that they had been engaged, that they'd planned a life together.

"In a way, not remembering may make it easier on me."

He rested his arm on Cutter's rump. "I won't ever know how many people I disappointed, and that may be a blessing."

"Can you put the past behind you?" There was no good answer, at least not for her.

"I hope so. If not, I'll have to move on. But there're some things here that aren't settled. At least not in my mind."

Apprehension whispered at the back of Cassidy's neck. For Slate, and for herself. "Be careful, Slate."

He unhooked Cutter from the cross ties and returned him to his stall. "Tell me about Joker. If you're planning on breeding your stock to him, you must know more about him."

This was a topic that Cassidy could warm to without reservation. "He's a grandson of Mr. Jett."

Slate's eyebrows shot up. "Really. Can you prove it?"

"I'm pretty sure. Once we get him, we'll pull some blood and have the DNA tested. I've been over this and checked as thoroughly as I could, but I believe Joker's mother was stolen by a range stallion several years back from a ranch about eighty miles west of here. The mare, The Queen of Hearts, had been bred to a son of Mr. Jett. There was a big hunt for her, but she was never found. The assumption was that she'd been killed while running with the herd." Cassidy could hear the excitement in her own voice.

"So you believe she delivered the foal."

"I do." She believed it with her entire heart.

"And no one else has figured this out?"

Cassidy leaned against the barn wall. "If they have, they don't care. Wild horses have grown to be more and more of a nuisance as the range is becoming divided into smaller parcels. It used to be that folks ignored the wild herds. It was more of a 'live and let live' attitude. But we're all getting squeezed together. Folks are so used to viewing the wild horses as a problem, they don't stop to think of the possibilities.''

Slate nodded. ''What if he isn't a grandson of Mr. Jett? What will you do with him?''

Cassidy had given this some thought. ''He'll have to be contained. The simplest thing would be to geld him and just let him run as free as he can be on the Double O.'' She bit her lip. ''I hate to do that, but I don't know what else. If he stays out there, Cole or someone else is going to kill him or capture him and sell him to the rodeo.''

''That would be a shame. He's quite a horse.''

''Even if I can't trace his bloodlines, he throws some mighty fine foals. I've been toying with the idea of breeding some nonregistered stock. Performance horses.''

Slate's face showed his agreement and enthusiasm. ''Is there a market?''

''I believe there is. Of course, some folks would say that I'm nuts.''

''I like the way you're crazy,'' Slate said. ''I've always believed that the worth of a horse is in how he performs, not in who his daddy was.''

''There are people who understand that. I believe I could make it work.'' She brushed her hair away from the side of her face. ''I know I can.''

''He's a magnificent animal,'' Slate said. ''And a tough problem. But the first thing is to get him. And if you're agreeable, we'll start tomorrow.''

She pushed away from the wall with eagerness. ''I was hoping you'd say that. I'll get Kip to pack some food. How many of the hands do you want to take?''

Slate's hand moved out to her arm, his fingers almost touching her sleeve. But he stopped.

She didn't need psychic abilities to read his thoughts. He was not a man who could reach out and touch a woman.

He was an ex-con, and even if he could forget that in a moment of enthusiasm, he was afraid that she could not.

The past rose up, a barrier between them that Cassidy knew neither could speak about.

"I want to go alone," he continued, dropping both hands to his sides.

"Alone?" She frowned.

"I wouldn't mind if you came along with me, but, basically, I can accomplish more without a lot of interference."

"How can you catch that rascal alone? It's going to take—"

"I know my prison record doesn't make this easy, but you're going to have to trust me. I know what I'm doing."

It was the one request she couldn't deny. Whatever had been between them in the past, whatever he'd done in that bank, he deserved another chance. "Okay," she said. "You're the horse trainer, we'll do it your way." At the relief on his face, she felt her own tension ease. "I want to come with you, though." At the wariness that sprang into his eyes, she reached out and touched his arm in a gesture so deliberate she knew he had to understand. "Not because I don't trust you or your technique, but because I want to learn."

His smile warmed the green depths of his eyes. "Thanks." He cleared his throat. "May I ask you another question, and this time I may be overstepping my bounds?"

"Go ahead. I'll tell you if you are."

"Lindsey's father? How was he killed?"

Cassidy started to speak, then stopped. The lie that had tasted so bitter when first spoken was now about to poison her. She found she couldn't continue. "Lindsey's father isn't dead. I told her that to spare her the truth. It's better for her and everyone else if she accepts that her father is no longer living."

"Was he that bad?" Slate answered his own question. "He must have been, to willingly leave a child like Lindsey behind."

This was the moment she'd dreaded. "He didn't leave because he wanted to, but he knew it would be best for his daughter, and for me, if he didn't force his way into our lives." Cassidy felt the tears building, and she knew that if she'd ever need to exert self-control, now was the time. "I have to put Lindsey to bed. I'll see you in the morning." She walked away as she spoke, hoping he'd get the idea the subject was closed.

"I'll be ready at six," Slate called after her.

IT WAS A PERFECT SUMMER morning, cool and dry with a gentle breeze, and, sitting in the saddle, Slate felt more at home than he had in five years. He was still riding Cutter, but he was heading out to Hook'em's later in the day to help with the barbecue and to pick up Stargazer.

He glanced at the woman who rode beside him. Her attention was on something in the distance. He guessed her age between thirty and thirty-five, and he wondered again at her single status. What he'd wanted to say the night before, but had not had the right to, was that a man would be crazy to abandon a child *and* a woman like Lindsey and Cassidy. But that was none of his business, and with his past, it never would be.

He'd been troubled by her reference to a man who left her because her life was better without him. He could easily be that man. The timing was right, and she'd tried to see him in prison. But there had been no indication from Cassidy that there had ever been anything between them, and he assumed she'd been trying to give him news of his mother's illness. It was fantasy on his part to even think that a woman like her would give him a second glance.

And Lindsey bore no trace of his dark looks—she was a child of sunlight, like her mother.

Cassidy looked over at him and smiled, and he thought he detected a lingering wisp of sadness in her eyes. She looked at his saddle. "No rope?"

"We're going to watch him today. And tomorrow. And see what happens."

"Okay."

Slate felt overwhelming relief. He knew Cassidy was worried about time, and yet she was trusting his judgment, completely. No questions asked.

"I guess he headed north after yesterday," Slate said. "It's been dry, and if I remember correctly, the creek curves in that direction and there used to be a small valley with elms that would give good cover."

"It's still there."

He smiled at her questioning look. "Little bits and pieces of things come back to me when I least expect it. It gives me hope that one day, I'll get all of my memory back. Right now, it seems that the land is what speaks to me. It's the strangest feeling, like…"

"Coming home?" she asked.

"Exactly."

"You grew up on this land. Your mother sold me a portion of the Three Sisters Ranch before she died. I bought as much as I could. Cole got the rest."

"I'm glad you got it," he said, and meant it. A blind steer could see how she loved the land.

"Your mother was a remarkable woman." She pointed to the west. "Just beyond that knoll there's a ridge. Her grave is there. It's on the Double O property, and I take care of it. It was where she asked to be buried."

"Hook'em told me," Slate said, and found that he missed a mother he didn't remember. He missed her because Cassidy so obviously did.

"If you ever want to visit, I'll be glad to show you. Mary was a good friend to me. And to Lindsey," she added. "I was born around here, but after my folks died, I lived in Houston with my aunt. I came back here to train horses and met your mother. I know you don't remember, but she loved you. You were the sun in her day."

"I'll bet," he said, surprised at the bitterness. "I can see where she'd be real proud of her son, in prison."

Cassidy swung around in the saddle and stopped Lightning's gentle walk. "She wouldn't be proud of *that*." She lifted her chin, her cheeks red with emotion. "She never, not one single day, believed you tried to rob that bank. Surely you know that."

"This isn't something I want to talk about." He nudged Cutter into a faster walk.

He saw that she was perfectly willing to let it drop, and they rode in silence for an hour. As they crested another of the hills, they saw the small band of horses. Slate stopped and got off Cutter.

"What?" Cassidy asked.

"Just let them see us. Wherever they go, we'll follow."

"But they're headed off my land and onto Cole's."

"It's okay. Just follow." He mounted up as Joker began to circle the mares, pushing them north. He seemed in no hurry, moving away from Slate at the same leisurely pace that Slate pursued him.

"What will this accomplish?" Cassidy asked. There was more curiosity than censure in her voice.

"It's an old Indian trick. We follow them, and then they follow us. It works."

"It's worth a try," Cassidy agreed, setting Lightning's stride to stay even with Cutter.

They followed the herd until lunchtime, when Slate dropped back. "They know we're with them," he told Cassidy as he helped her take the saddlebags down. "It's the idea that we're following. I want them to get used to us."

"What if they get used to the wrong people?" she asked.

"We can't let that happen." He unbridled the horses and set them to grazing beside a small stream. Taking a seat in the shade, he motioned Cassidy to sit beside him. "And we won't."

Slate watched as she unpacked the sandwiches and the canteen of tea that Kip had made for them. Her movements were sure and graceful, and he was struck again by her beauty. She was a woman any man would want, and he was no exception. He was also surprised at the ease he felt around her. If she held his prison record against him, she worked overtime not to show it.

He took the roast beef sandwich she handed him and bit into it, relishing the food as he hadn't in years. "Does Kip cook for the hands?" he asked.

Cassidy grinned. "He does. And if you get on his bad side, you'll see it reflected in your plate."

"I'll remember that," Slate promised. "Kip is one person I want on *my* side." He considered talking to her about Lucky, but he hesitated. Maybe there was something between the two of them that Lindsey didn't understand and he would be putting his big foot into Cassidy's private business. No, it would be better to hold off and watch. If he had something solid, then he'd speak.

They finished their lunch and leaned against a tree for a moment's rest from the saddle. Slate heard the hoofbeats first, and when he sat up, Cassidy heard them, too. She got to her feet, and he rose to stand beside her.

The lone rider came across the rocky terrain at too fast a clip. One wrong step and his horse could snap a leg. Slate stepped slightly in front of Cassidy. He recognized the rider as Cole Benson and felt Cassidy tense.

"I was hoping I'd find you." Cole's glance took in the remains of the lunch. "I need a word with you, Cassidy."

Slate was on the verge of stepping between them when Cassidy walked forward. "What brings you in such a hurry that you'd risk a broken leg, or neck?"

"The men are back at the ranch, waiting for you. The fence repair crew. Remember?"

Cassidy put the palm of her hand against her forehead. "I'm sorry, I simply forgot." She picked up her bridle and started toward Lightning. "Cole is loaning me some men to repair a pasture fence," she explained to Slate. "I'll ride back with him. You can finish checking the north pasture fencing on your own, can't you?"

"Sure," Slate said. He realized she didn't want Cole to know the real reason they were out together. He wondered if Joker was the *only* reason, though. There had been a proprietary note in Cole's voice as he spoke to Cassidy, and a gleam of jealousy in his eyes. Was there something between them? He bent to gather up the picnic things. "I'll take care of everything out this way," he assured Cassidy.

She had her mare bridled and swung into the saddle. "I am sorry, Cole. I didn't know you were coming with the men."

"Since we're going to the barbecue together, I thought I'd take a shower and clean up over at your place. Save me a drive home."

Slate wasn't certain he heard hesitation in Cassidy's voice, but he heard her answer loud and clear. "Sure, that's a good idea," she said as she rode off with the rancher.

Even as he bridled Cutter and repacked the remains of the lunch, he kept an eye on Cassidy. Not a single time did she turn around and look at him.

THE FIDDLER SAWED the strings, and the couple on the dance floor swung into a two-step. There was laughter from the dance floor and the tables, where clusters of people finished their barbecue dinners or simply sat back and talked.

Slate stood in the shadows. No one had treated him poorly, but he didn't want to give them a chance. He'd been part of this community once, but now he knew he didn't fit in; he didn't have to be told. He kept his distance from everyone.

He'd been troubled all afternoon by the fact that Cassidy was attending the barbecue with Cole, but as he watched the two of them sweep by doing the two-step, he was glad. Cassidy's face was bright with pleasure, and she and Cole cut a figure as they moved in and out of the dancers. It looked as if they'd been dancing together for years. Was it possible they intended to marry? The idea made him grit his teeth. He was man enough to admit Cassidy would not have had such a good time if she'd been his date. If he'd ever known how to dance, he didn't remember now. But thinking of her and Cole together...

Slate started looking for Hook'em, to thank him for the evening and his help. He was ready to load Stargazer into the trailer and head for the Double O. He'd had about as much of this good time as he could stand.

Across the dance floor he saw a face he recognized. His heart pounded as he remembered the woman from his trial. She'd been the bank teller. The one who'd been terrified of him.

He started toward her, noticing that she was alone for a few moments. He didn't want to upset her, but he had to ask some questions. He couldn't exactly go in the bank and talk to her.

He approached from her right, and he positioned himself in the light so she could clearly see his face. "Excuse me, Miss Best, may I speak with you?"

Her mouth opened as she recognized him, and her eyes

widened. "What do you want?" she asked in a breathless rush.

"I don't want to upset you. In no way am I upset with you or your testimony. I'm not angry at anyone except myself," he said, squatting on his heels so they were at eye level.

"What do you want?" she asked again, this time with less fear.

"I know what you testified to at the trial, and I'm not doubting what you said or trying to make trouble for anyone. I'm just trying to figure some things out."

"What things?" She looked past him into the crowd.

"When I walked into the bank, did I have the gun in my hand?"

"I said you had one, didn't I?" She shifted in her chair. "My husband will be back in a minute. He went to get me a soft drink."

"You testified that I didn't go up to the window. I told you I wanted the money from the middle of the room. Was the gun in my hand then?"

"I don't remember." She took two deep breaths. "I've tried to put that behind me. I was terrified. I don't want to think about it ever again." She looked to the left and right.

"Ma'am, I'm not trying to upset you. I need to know."

"I can't talk about this." She pushed back her chair clumsily and started to stand. "I'm pregnant, and the doctor said I shouldn't get upset. I could miscarry."

She stumbled, and Slate caught her arm and eased her back into the chair. He took a step back. "I'm sorry. I won't trouble you." He saw that his words had a calming effect instantly.

"Don't try to talk to me again," she said. "I can't handle this now. Any stress and I could lose this baby." Her expression brightened as she looked to her right. "Dray!"

Slate saw the man hurrying toward them, a scowl on his face as he recognized Slate.

"Honey, are you okay?" He put the cola down on the table and put his hand on her shoulder. "Is he bothering you?"

"I didn't mean to upset her. I wanted to ask a few questions," Slate said.

"We answered every question we intend to answer during the trial. Come around her again and I'll have you arrested. We did our duty as citizens, and we want to be left alone. I don't think I can make it any clearer than that."

Slate saw the fear in their faces. Were they so afraid of him? "I hear you," he said. He felt the gaze of all the people around them focused on him. "I understand."

"Stay away from us," Dray repeated.

Slate walked away. There was nothing else he could do. For the moment.

IT WAS NOT YET DAWN as Cassidy picked up the packed saddlebags and headed out the door. She'd seen a few lights on in the barn, and she knew it was Slate. The sky outside was dark, but brightening to the east. It was Sunday. Most of the ranch hands took the day off, but she'd known that Slate would go back out after Joker. And she intended to be with him.

She'd seen him at the barbecue the night before—and she'd heard that he'd confronted Amanda Tyree and frightened her. Then she'd lost sight of him. Hook'em had told her he'd left early.

Cassidy frowned as she grabbed a canteen of sweet tea and hurried out the door. Amanda had never been easily unsettled, but pregnancy did strange things to women. She knew that for a fact.

"Slate!" she called softly as she ran to the barn. "I'm going with you."

Slate stopped as he was leading Stargazer out of his stall. "I thought you'd be too tired to ride today. You were out late."

The gruffness in his voice sent a thrill through Cassidy. He was jealous! She knew it. He'd stayed up and waited for her to come in. She wanted to laugh. If only he knew how eager she'd been to get home. She'd even faked a headache to get away by midnight. Cole would have stayed until the wee hours of the morning.

"I'm never too tired to ride after Joker," she said. She grabbed a grooming kit and approached Lightning. "That's a nice gelding," she remarked, indicating Stargazer. "I remember when you rode him in the cutting horse competition and took everything from here to the Dakotas."

"Thanks for letting me keep him here."

He was overly busy tacking up, and Cassidy smiled to herself. "What's one more horse on a horse ranch? He's welcome to be here." She tightened her own cinch. "Did you enjoy the barbecue?"

"It was fine."

With her face hidden by the horse, Cassidy grinned big. He was as sore as a cornered boar. "I didn't see you dancing."

"I wasn't in the mood."

"It occurred to me that maybe you'd forgotten how." She couldn't resist telling him the truth. "There was constant competition between you and Cole, for riding and dancing. I just thought I'd tell you that you won—at both."

Slate came to stand where he could see her. "Who was the judge?" he asked.

Cassidy found that she was snared in her own trap. She met his gaze and swallowed. "I was," she said softly.

Slate's smile was brief, but it was still there when he turned back and began to lead his horse out of the barn. "We'd better hit the trail. I don't think Cole liked the idea that we were out riding together yesterday, and I don't believe he bought that line about repairing a north fence.''

Cassidy followed him out into the pinkening sky and swung up into her saddle. ''I'm afraid you're right. But he had to go to Fort Worth today. He's working with Ramsur Rodeo and provides their bulls and broncs. He said he had to get his contract straight for the fall. So we have a few days, at least.''

''We'll need every minute of it.'' Slate nudged his heels into Stargazer's sides and started off at an easy lope.

Cassidy fell in behind, not pushing Lightning up beside Slate. She watched his back, the way his hips rolled in the saddle and his shoulders remained loose and easy. Her body tingled with forbidden memories. Everything he did was accomplished with such grace, but most especially on a horse. Even loping along, he was something to watch.

They picked up the herds' trail where Slate had left them the evening before. Cassidy put her worries aside and enjoyed the sun and the horse beneath her. It had been a long time since she'd ambled over the ranch she worked so hard to keep. She wanted to tell Slate that Mary Walker had given her two hundred acres free and clear, and she'd bought another two hundred. The rest of Three Sisters had gone to Cole, more than four hundred acres. Mary would have given Cassidy more, but it had to be sold to settle the doctor and hospital bills that she'd accumulated. It had nearly broken Cassidy's heart.

''Are you involved with Cole?''

Slate's question came so suddenly that Cassidy laughed out loud.

''I wasn't trying to be funny,'' he said.

''You get your fur up fast, don't you?'' she asked, still chuckling. ''I'm laughing because the idea is so ridiculous. I've known Cole since we were in grammar school.''

"You may not be interested in him, but he's interested in you."

She lifted her eyebrows. "I suspect he's interested in this land."

Slate stopped his horse and waited for her to draw level. "It's more than that."

"That's not the way I see it." She could feel her pulse accelerating, and she realized that this was one conversation she needed to stop. If Slate was going to stay on the Double O and work, she was going to have to draw a line that he couldn't cross. A line she'd also have to obey. "Even if there's more there, I can't see where it's a concern of yours," she said.

Except for the look in his eyes, he didn't react. "I guess you've got a point there," he said. "I'll keep that in mind." He signaled the gelding, and Stargazer shot forward. She was left staring at his dust.

"Damn, damn and double damn," she whispered under her breath. He was sore. She hadn't meant to cut him to the bone. She knew it was pointless to try to talk to him now, so she picked up a lope and followed fifty yards behind him.

They stayed a good distance behind the herd, and Joker seemed to accept their presence, though he kept moving away. By the time they crossed the trickle of a stream that was Raging Creek during a rainstorm, Slate had recovered his composure, and they rode side by side in an easy silence. The wild herd stopped in a lush meadow and began to graze.

"I'll go out toward them," he said. "Remember that dry gulch near the western boundary?"

"Yes." Another geographic detail had surfaced in his memory. By some measures it was slow progress, but she felt excited.

"I blocked one end of it yesterday."

She understood his plan—to *lead* the horses into it rather than attempt to drive them.

"Once we're in there, you block the entrance," Slate said.

"Okay," she agreed, following him down to the herd. The horses lifted their heads and watched with wariness, but Joker gave no warning and Cassidy watched with amazement as Slate dismounted and turned his back on the stallion.

Cautiously, Joker began to approach. She was only a few feet from Slate, and she held her breath as the big stallion drew close. He was even more magnificent than she'd imagined. His wide-set eyes flicked from Slate to her, and he nosed out, his muzzle quivering as he sniffed Slate.

"Go on and head toward the gulch," Slate said easily. "Get out of sight and don't move. We'll be right behind you."

"I'll be there." She was turning her horse when the shot cracked loud in her ear.

Stargazer bolted, nearly jumping on top of Slate. Lightning reared, and as she fought to control her horse, Cassidy saw Joker stumble to his knees.

"He's hit!" she called to Slate, but she was too late. He'd already seen the stallion going down, and he ran to him as the second shot rang out.

Chapter Five

Cassidy jumped from the rearing horse. She hit the ground hard and rolled, coming to her feet beside Slate. He was already kneeling by the stallion, who was struggling on his side.

Cassidy had the presence of mind to hang on to Lightning's reins, and once she pulled her lariat and rifle free of the saddle, she sent the mare running to safety with the herd. One quick glance told her that both Slate and Joker were covered in blood. Her heart hammered painfully, but there wasn't time to investigate the extent of their injuries. Dropping to her knee, she lifted the rifle to her shoulder and began scanning the horizon for signs of the shooter.

The shots could have come from anywhere—there were boulders, weeds and the ever-present scrub cedars, which provided low, thick cover. To the far right, sunlight glinted off metal behind a cluster of cedars. Cassidy pumped three shots there and the glint disappeared.

"What was that?" Slate asked as he worked to calm the stallion. Cassidy felt relief so intense her legs trembled as she realized Slate was not seriously injured. Joker was sitting up, front legs extended, seemingly stunned.

"Gun barrel," Cassidy answered tightly. "Is he hit bad?" She was afraid to hear the answer.

"It's a head wound, but I think he can live with a piece of his ear missing."

Cassidy had to fight the urge to turn around and see if Slate was lying. "His ear?"

"You may have to change his name to Notch. But I think he's okay."

"But he went down—" Cassidy didn't understand. "An ear wound wouldn't drop a stallion."

"The bullet clipped his poll and then the side of his ear." As Slate spoke, the stallion gained his feet, shaking himself as if waking from a bad dream.

Cassidy saw that he was standing fine, and she refocused on the distance. Ever since she'd fired at the shooter, there had been no other sign of him. She stood up slowly, the rifle still sighted on the cedars. "I think he's gone."

A loud, shrill whistle from Slate brought Stargazer and a trailing Lightning. "You mount up and ride on. We'll do this just like we planned," Slate said. "There's a vantage point there where I can keep an eye out."

Cassidy started to argue. It would be better if they went straight back to the Double O barn, where Joker could get medical attention—and a safe place to stay. She examined the horizon again. They'd crossed the boundary onto Cole Benson's property, which was a precarious position to be in, especially since they had the stallion. "Wouldn't it be better if we went to the barn?"

"Joker has accepted our help, but that doesn't mean he'll docilely walk into a barn, or anywhere else that looks like a trap."

"The gulch is on my land." She wanted to be on Double O property. "I'll meet you there."

"Go easy," Slate said. "And stay alert. The shooter may be gone, or he may be there waiting for a clear shot."

"You're the one with the stallion," Cassidy pointed out.

"I'm not certain he was aiming at the horse," Slate said,

his mouth a grim line. "I think he may have been trying to hit one of us."

CASSIDY RAN THE COOL water over Lightning's legs and gradually moved up to hose off the mare's sweat-and-dust-covered body. After the terror of the shooting, the rest of the day had seemed like a breeze. Slate, with a little assistance from her, had managed to get Joker and the mares into the gulch. They'd pulled dead trees and debris to close off the opening, and Slate had sent her back to the ranch for supplies. She'd dispatched one of the hands with food, medicine and a sleeping bag—Slate insisted on staying with the stallion.

For her part, she'd combed the area where she'd seen the glint of sunlight on a barrel, and all she'd found were two shell casings from a .22 rifle. Someone had been there, but he hadn't left a clue to his identity. The tracks led back toward the Double O, but she'd lost them in a weed-choked field. Slate's words echoed in her memory—someone might have been trying to shoot her. Or him. Was it possible? Had the rock slide, which had been deliberately tripped, been meant to kill her or Slate?

She couldn't imagine who would want to hurt her. She had enemies and competitors, as almost everyone did, but she wasn't a big-enough threat to anyone to warrant such an extreme solution.

And Slate. He'd come out of prison to what was left of his life. She'd never known him to provoke enemies, or to pick a fight. But she had no way of knowing what he'd become embroiled in during his prison term. What if it was someone trying to settle a prison score? Was it right for her to expose Lindsey to this danger?

Her thoughts whirled as she finished with Lightning and then hosed off Stargazer. When both horses were cool and clean, she turned them loose in a paddock and started toward the house. The sight of a small red convertible pulling into the drive made her stop with one foot on the back step. She was surprised to see Amanda Tyree behind the wheel.

"Amanda!" She smiled wide as she went to greet her old friend. "I can't believe my eyes." She didn't hold a grudge against Amanda for her testimony at the trial. Amanda hadn't had a choice. But the trial had been traumatic, and their friendship had suffered. In the past five years, they'd hardly seen each other.

Amanda pulled her sunglasses down to reveal eyes that were bordered by dark smudges. "I meant to come before now. It's just that when I was working and first married, there was no time to do anything." She shrugged her thin shoulders. Her dark hair sparkled in the sun, but her brown eyes were large and serious. "The truth is, this isn't a social visit. I really want to talk to you. I tried to convince myself that this was none of my business, but I can't let it alone."

"I'm dying for some coffee." Cassidy suddenly was in no hurry to hear her friend's concerns. She already knew where the conversation would go.

"I don't have time. Dray's coming home soon, and I promised I'd have pot roast." She rolled her eyes. "I don't know what's more work, the bank or Dray."

Cassidy chuckled appreciatively and waited. "At least come up to the porch and sit in the shade. It's too hot in the car." She noticed that Amanda moved slowly and carefully and recalled that Amanda had suffered several miscarriages. Obviously, she was protecting this pregnancy. Cassidy felt a pang of concern.

"I'm here about Slate," Amanda said, without bothering to sugarcoat her reason. She sat back in the wicker rocker and faced Cassidy. "I'm worried about you. Have you lost your mind, letting him work for you and live on the Double O? You know he went to prison trying to keep this ranch in his family. How's he going to feel when you tell him that you *bought* part of his birthright?"

"I've already told him." Cassidy's cool voice made Amanda stop with her mouth open.

"You've told him? And he didn't get furious?"

"He was glad I got it. Remember, his memory is gone. He doesn't remember owning it, so he isn't defensive about it. He said he was glad I got it because he could see that I loved it."

Amanda leaned forward in her chair. "You took my breath," she said softly, then she inhaled shakily and gave a half laugh. "You always were the one with the surprises." Amanda quit rocking. "Are you going to tell him about Lindsey?"

Cassidy didn't answer immediately. Her feelings for Slate were very confused. There were moments when she knew that she loved him as deeply—maybe even more— than she ever had. And there were times when she convinced herself that she was too smart to let her heart rule her life. That Lindsey was her top priority now. "I don't know," she said.

"You can't do that, Cassidy. You can't!" Amanda struggled out of the chair. "It isn't fair to Lindsey."

Cassidy motioned her to sit back down. "Not telling her may be what's unfair. You should see them together, Amanda." Cassidy inched her chair closer. "They're *drawn* to each other. It's an attraction that exists—that's so strong it frightens me as much as it amazes me." She saw the concern in Amanda's eyes.

"Lindsey is fond of every ranch hand here, and she worships Hook'em. That doesn't mean she needs to think any of them are her daddy."

"That's not fair," Cassidy protested. "None of them are her father, and this...bond between her and Slate is different. You'd have to see it to believe it."

Amanda looked out toward the barns. "You've done a good job here. I never dreamed you'd be able to make a go of it. When you borrowed the money from the bank, I was afraid you'd lose everything. I almost went to Mr. Barlow and urged him not to make the loan." She pressed her lips together. "I was wrong about that, but I'm afraid I'm not wrong about Slate. Please, Cassidy, I'm begging you to fire him and encourage him to move on. He deserves to find a new life, and so do you. This only keeps the past alive, and we both know there's no way to get it back."

Cassidy felt her heart pounding. Amanda's words brought pain, but also a truth she couldn't deny. There was no going back. And Lindsey was her first priority. Before she did anything that would damage her daughter, she would walk on hot coals. But the rub was that she didn't know what was best for Lindsey. Or Slate. Or even herself.

She settled on stating the obvious. "Right now, Slate needs a job and I need him. He has the right to a second chance." That's all she was giving him. A chance to prove himself.

"There are other horse trainers," Amanda pointed out.

"Not like Slate. He's the best trainer around." Cassidy held her ground. "And you know it." Cassidy knew it, too. There were no other *men* like Slate.

"He's a good trainer, but is it worth the price?"

"I don't know what the price is yet," Cassidy said slowly.

"You don't want to find out. Listen to me, Cassidy, don't let this happen to you. He's been gone for five years, and you were finally getting over him. Whenever you walked into the bank, I could see a difference in you. It's been a hard time for you, raising Lindsey on your own and running the ranch, but you've done it. Don't throw it away."

"Why did you come out here, Amanda?" Cassidy had watched the play of emotions on her friend's face. She was extremely upset. It showed in the tremble of her hand and the way her voice shook.

"What do you mean?" Amanda's face pulled into a frown. "Are you implying that I have some ulterior motive? I came here to warn you. To be a friend."

"I've been out here for three years and you've never once come out to visit." Even as Cassidy laid down the obvious, she saw that Amanda was not well. The trip to the Double O was exacting a toll on her.

"I care about you, Cassidy. I care what happens, even if I haven't been the best of friends lately." Tears sprang to Amanda's eyes. She dashed them with the back of her hand. "I'm all emotional with this pregnancy, but even so, your implication hurts. You sound like you think I'm not a true friend."

Cassidy felt bad about the tears, but she couldn't help herself. "It seems to me that our friendship cooled when Slate was tried for bank robbery. It's a little odd that his return would spark a renewal."

Amanda struggled to her feet. "You're right. I felt like a creep for testifying against the man who was the father of the child you carried. It's called guilt, Cassidy, and I had a lot of it. That's why I quit visiting. I was ashamed."

Cassidy reached out and caught Amanda's hand. "As far as the trial goes, you did what you had to do. You told the truth, and that's all anyone can do."

"It doesn't make me feel less guilty." Amanda turned away. "I have to get home." She glanced nervously down and then back up. "Slate tried to talk to me at the dance. Dray was furious. If he tries it again, there's going to be trouble."

"Do you want me to convey that to Slate?" Cassidy was shocked by the anger she felt. Amanda had come to deliver a warning, but it had nothing to do with Cassidy's welfare. It was meant for Slate—leave me alone, or else. It appeared that Amanda's newfound concern for her was just a pretext. "I'll make sure he gets the message."

Amanda grasped the handrail as she went down the steps. At the bottom, she turned back to face Cassidy. "I was hoping we could be friends again, the way we used to be. I've quit the bank and I'm going to be home, now that I'm pregnant. I thought maybe we could…" She stared at Cassidy and then turned back to her car. She drove away with dust jetting from the tires.

SLATE WATCHED THE RED Mercedes pull away from the house before he stepped out into the twilight. He'd heard the last of the conversation—enough to know that Cassidy had been put in a position to defend him. He didn't like that she was having to choose between him and her friendships.

"Slate!" Cassidy saw him and spoke his name on a rush of air.

He realized he'd startled her, stepping out of the semidarkness.

"I came for some alfalfa," he said softly. "I realized when Danny got out to the herd that we'd forgotten feed. I don't think it would be smart to put those wild horses on grain, but a little alfalfa would win their hearts."

"Good idea."

Slate smiled. She knew he hadn't come back to the ranch for horse provisions. He could easily have sent Danny. "I also wanted to be sure you were okay. We had a rough day. Getting shot at tends to have an aftereffect."

He took three steps closer and could feel the tension in her.

"I'm fine," she said, but her voice was breathless.

He stepped closer. "Are you?"

"I am." She sighed, turning so that he could see only

her profile, her eyes downcast. "I found the shell casings. A .22, just as you said."

"And the tracks led back to the ranch?"

She shook her head. "They weren't clear."

"I've been giving it some thought. The rock slide couldn't have been directed at either of us. There was no way anyone could have predicted that we would be going through that pass. I think someone was after Joker and the herd."

"And the gunshots?"

"That's different. Someone followed us. Now, whether they followed us because of the horse, I can't say." Her eyes lifted to his, and for a split second, Slate thought he saw unlimited possibility. The idea, as foolish as it was, that she might care for him, was staggering.

Her gaze locked with his. Slate put his hand on a post to steady himself. He wanted to kiss her, to hold her in his arms and feel her body against his. It seemed as if she were a part of him, severed by some cruel event. The sense of her as a missing part of him was acute, painful.

"Slate?" There was apprehension in her voice, but her gaze held.

His hand lifted to touch her face, the skin soft and barely warm beneath his fingers. He traced her jaw with a gentle touch and then let his fingertips drift slowly across her lips. They parted slightly, and he felt her breath. He closed his eyes and had the strangest sensation that her face was as well known to him as the land on which they stood. She caught his hand and held it against her lips. He felt the softest kiss.

Though he had nothing to offer her, and he knew it, he could not stop himself. His arms moved around her and he held her, at first marveling at the known quality that made her so unique and special. It was as if her body evoked a thousand memories that served to anchor him, to give him a connection that he so desperately needed.

His hands moved over her back, familiar with the angle of her shoulder blades, with the narrowing of her ribs down to the waistband of her jeans. He knew the swell of her buttocks as his caresses grew more intense.

Her touch, too, was electric. The way her hands coursed up his chest and moved around his neck, the fingers tangling in hair that he'd considered too long, the gentle tightening of those fingers as he pulled her up against him—it was as if he'd traveled this path before, and relished every step of the way.

He felt her face lift, and he bent to kiss her. He caught the clean scent of shampoo and the rich smell of leather cleaner. He kissed her lightly, too aware of the fullness of her lips, her breasts pressing into his chest. Her mouth parted beneath his, and Slate knew that he was lost. He could no longer dance around the edges of control. His arms tightened around her and he kissed her with a need and urgency that blotted out all past, and all present. There was no room for thought or reason, he simply felt. And what he felt was a longing and desire for the woman in his arms, so intense that he accepted the possibility that it could be fatal. Nothing had ever seemed more important.

CASSIDY CURLED HER fingers in his hair and had the hopeless sensation that she could save herself by holding on. But even as she opened her mouth to his kiss, she knew she was lost. Slate's hands moved over her with a fluid grace that seemed to set her skin ablaze. This was a familiar dance.

She closed her eyes and the past five years evaporated. It was 1993, a hot summer evening before the big rodeo. The Double O vanished, and instead they were down by the small creek, the cottonwoods rustling in a summer breeze. They had known each other so well, and yet each time they made love it was like the most wonderful present. Each touch was new, each glance a pleasure undiminished by familiarity.

She felt Slate's fingers tugging her blouse free of her jeans, and she knew exactly the way he would slip his hands so gently on the bare skin of her back. He would leave them there, the thumbs circling her waist, and with the most teasing pressure make certain that she accepted his touch.

Perhaps it was that he took nothing for granted. No touch was ever by rote. He always asked—in the most persuasive way.

His kiss deepened and caught her by surprise. Her desire for him was suddenly overwhelming, and she felt her legs tremble. He felt it, too, and his support tightened. Her hands went to his jaw, feeling the strength there, the lean muscle so much more clearly defined in the last few years.

She had dreamed of him, of touching him and being held in his arms. She had longed for him in a way that went beyond sexual or even physical. And when she had given birth to his daughter, while he was in prison, she had mourned for him, that he had missed one of the most important moments in his life.

But she had never thought it possible that she would again feel his hands at the buttons of her blouse, feel the cool teasing of a summer breeze on skin that he laid bare, feel the warmth of his mouth travel down her neck, moving slowly to the top of her breast, which was now covered only by the sheer lace of her bra.

She was aware that dusk had fallen around them. There was the sound of the men bringing in the show horses and taking care of the barns. They were distant and posed no threat. Lindsey had finished her supper and was reading stories with Nita.

The moment opened to her, and she knew she would not pass it up. Whatever the future cost, she had longed for Slate too long, too hard, to pass up a chance to be with him. It was foolish and foolhardy, but she didn't care.

Her arms circled his neck, and she felt his arms tighten even more, compressing her body fully against his so that she had no doubt that he wanted her.

"Slate," she said softly. He eased the pressure, and she slipped her arms down him until she grasped his hand. "Come with me."

Her bedroom was on the far end of the house with a private patio. She had designed it so that she could get up in the morning and watch the sun rise, or sit in the old rocker she'd placed beneath the shady live oak and read on those rare days when she had a moment to sit still. Now the private entrance afforded another reward, and she felt her heart race at the idea of what lay before her.

In the darkness, she led Slate to the small gate. The ivy she'd planted had flourished, and she found that the handle was hidden in the green leaves. Breathless with anticipation, she fumbled and heard Slate's soft chuckle behind her.

His hand slipped past her in the vines, and she heard the latch finally yield to his greater strength. Before she could step through, his hands caught her shoulder. She felt herself being turned, and then his lips were on hers. Her body eased back into the cushion of ivy on the wall.

Slate transferred his weight to his hands, easing slightly away from her. "Are you sure?" he asked.

"I'm sure." Cassidy felt no qualms.

"And Lindsey?"

"She's with Nita. She'll be fine until I tuck her in." She saw the expression of concern on his face, and for one heart-stopping second, she thought he would leave her there. "What?"

"I don't want to involve you in something bad. I'm a convicted bank robber."

"I never believed you did it." She put her hands on his shoulders. "It doesn't matter now, Slate. Give me this one night. I won't hold you to anything else." She had known all along that he would more than likely leave Comfort. And she would not try to stop him. Not even if it broke her heart—again. But this was one night she wanted, devil pay the price for it.

She felt his arm slide under her knees, and he was holding her. He ducked under the thick curtain of ivy and stepped into the adobe-walled garden. The scent of summer roses was so strong that he halted.

"I know this smell," he said, filling his lungs.

Head on his shoulder, Cassidy smiled. "They were your mother's favorite flowers. I dug them up from the old ranch and moved them here."

Slate looked down at her, at the moonlight on her fair skin and the silvery shimmer of her blond hair. The weight of her in his arms, the smell of the roses after a long day in the saddle. He could not begin to talk about what he felt, but it amounted to the awareness that he had somehow arrived home.

Chapter Six

Cassidy felt the cool sheets against her bare back, and the shock of losing Slate's body against hers registered as he laid her on the bed and sat down beside her. Moonlight laced through the live oak in the garden and fell through the window and across Cassidy's skin in intricate patterns. Slate gently traced one hand across her stomach, his finger slowly moving lower.

Her body trembled.

He eased beside her on the bed and kissed her, his hand moving slowly over her flushed skin.

At first, Cassidy thought the gentle tap on the door was her heart pounding against her ribs. Slate froze, and before she could answer he was out of bed.

"What is it?" Cassidy called.

"Mr. Lucky is here to see you. He says it's very important," Nita said, her voice heavy with worry. "Are you sick?"

"No, I'm fine." Cassidy held calm in her voice. "Tell him I'll be right there." She got up and fumbled in the darkness for her clothes. Slate was almost dressed.

"You sound strange," Nita said, still at the door.

"I'm fine," Cassidy said, and this time it sounded as if she meant it. "Where's Lindsey?"

"Watching one of her movies."

Cassidy buttoned her shirt. "Tell Lucky I'll be there in a minute." She turned to Slate in the darkness and found that he was standing in the patio doorway, poised to leave.

"Should I see what's wrong?" he asked.

Cassidy shook her head. "No, I'm sure it's something that could have waited until morning." His gaze made her self-conscious. "I feel like a teenager caught by my parents," she said, trying to interject a bit of humor. "This is crazy."

Slate was only a darker shadow in the moonlight. "Maybe you wouldn't feel so guilty if you didn't think it was wrong," he said slowly.

The words were like a blade. She felt the cut. "It isn't that." But there was no power in her voice. Her protests sounded feeble even to herself. "Slate, we have to talk."

"Later," he said. "I should have been back with Joker long ago. When you're talking with Lucky, you might ask him where he was about ten o'clock this morning."

Cassidy made the connection perfectly. "You think he's the person who shot at us?"

"If it was someone on your payroll, he's my pick of the litter." Slate put his hat on, a tall, lean silhouette in the moonlight. He disappeared through the doorway. There was the crunch of his boots on the gravel path, and then the reluctant working of the gate latch. Then nothing.

CASSIDY TOOK IN THE SCENE of Lucky sitting on the floor with Lindsey as the little girl pointed to the television, where the Scarecrow danced over the yellow brick road.

"He's a good scarecrow," Lindsey told Lucky, but her face failed to show the animation she normally had for her favorite movie, *The Wizard of Oz*. "He's going to help Dorothy."

"There's a witch in this story, isn't there?" Lucky asked.

Instead of looking at Lindsey, he was glancing around the room.

"She's *very* mean," Lindsey said, nodding. "*And* she's green."

For some reason, the scene struck Cassidy as inappropriate. She walked in. Nita was sitting in her favorite corner under a bright lamp, working on the needlepoint that she insisted soothed her nerves. "What's going on, Lucky?" Cassidy asked.

His smile was slow, and he seemed to look her up and down, as if he somehow knew what she'd been doing. But of course that was ridiculous. She sat down on the arm of the sofa. "Well? What was so urgent?"

"I just got back from that gulch where the wild horses are."

Cassidy felt her temper ignite. Lucky had no business anywhere near the wild horses. Nor should he have known about them. But she held her tongue and waited for him to finish.

"When Danny left here with the truck and provisions, he told me what was going on. I decided I'd check and see if Slate needed any help."

"And did he?" she prodded.

"Naw, it seems that everything's under control. But we've got a problem."

"What might that be?" Her gaze never left his, and she wondered if Slate could be right. Was Lucky setting up an alibi for being out around the wild horses when the shots were fired—in case someone had spotted him?

"That dun mare, you remember her?"

Cassidy nodded. There had been an exceptional buckskin mare in Joker's herd.

"That's Cole Benson's prize filly. He bought her two weeks ago, and I daresay he's going to be pretty upset when he finds out she's hemmed up in a makeshift corral with that range stud.''

"We'll cut her out tomorrow and take her back to him." Cassidy was troubled by the information, but it wasn't what she considered urgent. Certainly not urgent enough to interrupt what had been going on between her and Slate. "Is that it?"

"I went down to look at that stallion, and he tried to kill me. He came at me with front hooves and teeth. I had to beat him back with a cedar limb." Lucky rose to his feet. "I think the best thing we could do would be to put a bullet between his eyes and be done with it. I know you got your heart set on taming him, but I think it's foolish."

Cassidy rose slowly to her feet, too angry to speak. It was only the worried look on Lindsey's face that held her in check. Lindsey was only four, but she was smart enough to follow this conversation, and her heart and imagination were heavily invested in the wild stallion.

"Come on out on the porch," she said to Lucky, the softness of her voice completely hiding her fury.

She didn't give him a chance to reply. She went outside and closed the door after him. In the darkness she rounded on him. "You listen up and you listen good, Lucky. You have no business with that stallion. None. Slate is the horse trainer. I don't want you within a mile of him. Your job is to keep the hands working and to make sure my livestock is well cared for. If that arrangement isn't to your liking, pack your things and come by in the morning for a check. And if you ever lift a club to Joker or any other animal on this place, you'll be out of here so fast..." She took a breath to calm herself. If she fired him, she wouldn't have any way to keep track of him. Keeping him employed was the smartest move she could make, for the moment. "You've been a good foreman, Lucky, but you don't know beans about my training methods for horses. You stay away from that gulch.''

She went into the house and closed the door behind her. When it was firmly locked, she leaned back against it and gave her legs a minute to steady.

It had been one helluva day. She'd been shot at, frightened nearly to death, worried sick, taken to the edge of insanity by desire, startled into guilt, and now infuriated to the point that she was afraid a blood vessel was going to burst in her brain.

"Mama?" Lindsey's voice came from the hall.

"Yes, sweetie?"

"Mr. Lucky's not going to hurt Joker, is he?"

"No, he isn't." She went to her little girl and gathered her in her arms. Lindsey smelled of vanilla wafers and baby shampoo, and she kissed her neck and made the little girl giggle.

"Mama, is Mr. Lucky mean like the witch?"

Lindsey's question startled her. "Why do you ask that?"

"He wants to hurt Joker. He said Joker tried to hurt him, but that's not right." Her blue eyes caught Cassidy's and held them with an understanding of right and wrong that was so simple, and so sincere, that Cassidy only nodded.

"Mr. Lucky was wrong. But doing something wrong doesn't make a person mean. Not all the time. That's the hardest thing about growing up, Lindsey, deciding when something is wrong and when it's mean. It's sometimes hard to tell the difference."

"But you won't let him hurt Joker, will you?"

Cassidy gave her daughter her bravest smile. "Of course not. Now, if I decide to ride out and check on the horses, will you be okay with Nita?"

Lindsey's face pulled into a frown. "Couldn't I go?"

Had it not been for someone shooting at them, Cassidy would have bundled her into a truck and taken her. The sight of the wild horses in the gulch was a vanishing part of the West. She wanted Lindsey to have a knowledge of the past. "Not tonight, darling. How about tomorrow?"

"Promise?"

"If you mind Nita and go to bed without a fuss."

"First thing in the morning?"

"We'll take Slate some breakfast."

"Okay." Lindsey threw her arms around Cassidy's neck and hugged with all of her strength. "I love you, Mama."

"I love you, too." Cassidy felt the pressure of unexpected tears, but she quickly blinked them back. "See you in the morning." She tweaked Lindsey's nose and hurried to the back door. This trip, she'd take the Chevy instead of a horse.

She was surprised at the chill in the air, and when she looked up, she saw the sky was streaked with silver-gray clouds. Even as she watched, one drifted across the moon. There would likely be rain the next day, and Cassidy knew they needed it. But it would make camping a little unpleasant. She threw a tarp in the bed of the truck and headed out toward the gulch.

The four hundred acres that she'd managed to buy had small meadows nestled among the hills, and even though there were no roads, as such, she knew she could make it to the gulch without any difficulty.

She drove slowly, her headlights picking out the fleeing shapes of deer and the stolid cows that lifted their heads at her approach. She didn't raise beef, but there were cattle grazing on the Double O. She needed a few head to practice cutting, and she enjoyed the idea of them grazing. There were also coyotes, foxes, bobcats and mountain lions, but they kept their distance from man as much as possible.

More deadly than the predators were the snakes. If the saying that everything was bigger in Texas had any truth, she was certain it had been first applied to rattlers. She'd seen snakes as thick as her arm sliding off into the rocks, their tails giving the warning that they did not like being interrupted.

In the truck, she was safe, but she'd heard too many campfire tales of men who curled up in their bedrolls only to awaken with a rattler cozied up to them for warmth. It was a picture that made her flinch.

She thought of anything to keep her mind off the coming discussion with Slate, and the grim suspicions she had of Lucky.

When she finally saw the gulch in the beams of her lights, she didn't know whether to be relieved or more anxious. Since the other ranch truck was gone, she determined that Slate had sent Danny back to the bunkhouse. She got out of the truck, gathered the tarp and walked to the high point where she knew he would be waiting.

The moon broke through the clouds, and she saw him leaning against a rock, a rifle across his knees.

"Have you seen anyone else?" she asked.

"Just me and the horses." Even as he spoke there was an alert snort from the gulch. Joker was keeping watch over his herd.

"Did Danny tell you about Lucky?"

Slate hesitated, then patted the ground beside him. "Sit down and I'll share my rock." When she was beside him, he said, "Lucky provoked the horse. Danny saw it. Joker was acting like a range stallion, that's all. Lucky was out there trying to get a rope on the buckskin." Slate's voice was tense. "I'm telling you now, if he comes back up here and messes with these horses, I'm going to make him wish he'd never been born."

Cassidy knew he meant it. "He won't be back. But consider something, Slate. You're just out of prison. You don't need Lucky going into town and showing everyone that you beat him up."

"I don't need a lot of things, but if he pushes it in my face, he's going to get the beating of his life. If that bothers you, then you'd better fire me now."

Cassidy smiled to herself. "I was mad enough to clobber him myself."

Slate's chuckle was easy, surprised. "I'll bet you were."

"About earlier this evening..." Cassidy didn't know how to begin, but she knew she had to. "I wasn't feeling guilty for being with you. It's just that—" she felt the blush creep up her face "—it's been a long time. I'm so used to being the ranch owner and Lindsey's mom and the boss that it was uncomfortable being...you know what I'm trying to say. It didn't have anything to do with you or the fact that you've been in prison."

"Are you sure?"

Cassidy gave it some thought before she answered. "I meant it when I said I always believed you were innocent. I still do."

"You were at the trial every day."

It was a statement, not a question, so she didn't respond.

"Why were you there?" he pressed.

"I tried to see you in prison and you would never even talk to me. Why wouldn't you talk to me?" she countered.

Slate picked up a piece of rock and flung it into the night. "You first."

"There were a lot of people interested in the trial," Cassidy said, keeping her gaze on the distant stars.

Slate gave her a long stare. "That's not exactly an answer. That's an evasion."

Cassidy felt like the cow cut from the herd. Slate had sighted her, and he was maneuvering her right to where he wanted her. If he gave it a little thought, he'd be able to figure out why she'd been at the trial.

He reached out and put his hand on her cheek, turning

her face to his. "I knew you before the bank robbery, didn't I?"

"Yes." She didn't have the heart to fake or dodge. So, he'd come to the truth. Along with the worry came an unexpected relief. "We were lovers."

Her answer seemed to stun him. Then she felt his arm move around her shoulders and he pulled her gently into an embrace. "That's why you were in the courtroom, why you tried to see me?"

"Yes."

"I think at some level I must have known." He hesitated. "I wouldn't see you because I was…afraid. That you would tell me something like this. That you would make me remember what I was leaving behind. And I guess I didn't want to know, because I couldn't have stood it. Maybe the reason my memory didn't come back while I was in prison was because I didn't want it to."

"Maybe so," Cassidy agreed. At the time of the trial, Slate had lost his bride-to-be, his unborn child and his dying mother. While he was locked away for a crime he had no memory of committing, he'd lost everything. Amnesia would have been preferable.

His arm tightened around her. "I don't know what to say," he answered. "I don't know what to ask."

Cassidy hesitated. "I don't, either. Maybe you should just leave it alone and see how it feels." Her heart pounded. Now was the time to tell him the truth about Lindsey. But she couldn't. There was simply too much at risk. She wouldn't put her daughter on the line.

A low whinny came from the herd, and Slate instantly tensed. "That's the lead mare, I recognize her voice."

She was answered by Joker's deep, throaty challenge. There was the sound of hooves running in the dry bed of the gulch, and Slate rose slowly to his feet. "I'd better check on them."

"Do you think someone is out here?" Cassidy tuned her hearing to listen for the sound of someone approaching.

"I think they're not used to being confined. I'll take a look." He shook out the blanket and covered her legs. "I'll be back in a few minutes."

The horses had already settled down, but she realized Slate needed some time to think. She couldn't imagine what it would be like to forget who she was—and then constantly have people toss her tidbits of her past. But there had been no point denying that they knew each other. Their bodies had betrayed them with the first touch, the first kiss.

She caught Slate's voice, soft and soothing, as he talked to the horses, and she smiled. He had a way with them. And with her. She felt sleep tugging at her eyelids, and she pulled the blanket higher. Slate would wake her when he came back.

He walked the confines of the gulch and made sure that everything was in order. Joker followed him, about ten paces behind, looking over his shoulder at everything he did. The stallion amused him. Joker had spent his life as a wild creature, but he was more than intrigued by humans. It was the first ingredient for a truly magnificent horse, from a cowboy's point of view. He didn't know if the rest of the world was interested in performance horses, but Slate had learned long ago that bloodlines meant nothing on the range. Performance was everything. And he knew that Cassidy was right about Joker—he would throw some fine babies.

When his thoughts shifted to Cassidy, he didn't know what to think, or feel. He'd known that somewhere in his past they'd been intimately involved. He knew her too well. She evoked too much intense emotion in him. In some ways, he had come to regard her as the key to his past. And perhaps his future.

And Lindsey! She had to be his. He'd been afraid to ask Cassidy immediately—the idea was wonderful and terrifying at the same time. He wouldn't pressure her for answers. Cassidy would tell him when she was ready.

He walked up the steep incline to the hilltop, where he caught sight of her, fast asleep, against the rock.

He settled down beside her and eased her body onto his shoulder. With a sigh, he closed his eyes and let his body relax.

The events of the night played themselves out in his mind, and he felt his desire for Cassidy anew as he remembered her touch, her lips. But the time for passion was past. He needed to be sure of what he wanted. He'd made enough mistakes. He didn't have time for any more.

He heard the low snorts of Joker as the stallion tended his herd, and he fell asleep with a smile on his face.

AT FIRST, CASSIDY DIDN'T know where she was. The night air was cool and crisp, and the rock poking into her back was sharper than a stick. She rolled slightly and felt Slate's warm side against her. She quit trying to think and let her own body curve around his. Even on the hard ground, it was wonderful to be beside Slate.

She was about to drift off again when she felt him stir. The hand she was holding tightened into a fist.

"The money," he said clearly into the night. "In the bag?"

It was a question, and Cassidy hardly dared to breathe for fear of interrupting whatever he was saying in his sleep.

"The bank is empty, and Mr. Barlow is busy." Slate was narrating his dream as if it were happening all over again. "Amanda watching…" There was a pause. "Getting married. Money…for Mother…doctors." Slate struggled, as if he were fighting someone.

Cassidy considered waking him, but she decided against

it. "Slate, what happened in the bank?" she asked softly. If he could hear her, he might answer. Or he might wake up.

"Money for the doctors." Slate sounded more anxious. "Mr. Barlow is busy...waiting." He swallowed. "Father's gun." He lifted a hand as if the gun were in it. "The gun." His voice grew angry. "Gone!"

Cassidy shook his shoulder. "Slate, wake up." She shook him harder. "Slate?"

He lifted his eyebrows and then his eyes opened. "Cass? What is it?" he asked lazily.

She was startled by his use of her pet name. "You were talking in your sleep."

"Sorry," he said, still on the verge of sleep. "Johnny Vance used to complain about it all the time. Since a prisoner who talked in his sleep was a lot less dangerous than one who might try to kill him, he didn't bother trying to find a less talkative cell mate."

CASSIDY AND SLATE were up at first light. They stood for a moment, her back against him as he circled his arms around her, and watched the herd below them greet the new day.

"We need to get that buckskin to Cole," she reminded him.

"Will do. Send Danny back out if you can spare him. He's got a nice way with the animals."

"I promised Lindsey I'd bring her out for breakfast."

Slate's chuckle was right at her neck. Her body reacted with a surge of desire for him.

"She loves Joker, doesn't she?" he asked.

"All of the hands have made up stories and told her about him. I hope she won't be disappointed to discover that he's simply a flesh-and-blood horse."

"She won't be disappointed," Slate assured her.

Cassidy turned her head and lightly kissed his cheek. It was so natural, so easy. Sleeping beside him, she'd had her own share of sweet memories return. "I'll be back," she promised.

He released her. "We'll try to return the mares where they belong, and if you don't mind, I'll bring one or two of yours out here to keep him company."

"Good idea." Cassidy reluctantly walked to the truck. She had a plan—one she didn't want to share with Slate. It was a long shot and probably an action that wasn't hers to take. But during the night she'd hit upon an idea that would involve going into a part of Slate's life where he might not welcome her intrusion. She wanted to follow through before she lost her nerve—right after she brought Lindsey out for breakfast with the wild horses, and Slate.

THE TEXAS HILL COUNTRY was in her rearview mirror, and the flatter vistas of the Lone Star State spread in front of her as Cassidy headed east toward Huntsville Prison.

What had seemed like a flash of brilliance in the night now seemed ridiculous. Slate's cell mate, Johnny Vance, would surely have told someone if Slate had given out clues to his past. Wouldn't he?

Since she couldn't give a definitive answer to that question, she pressed harder on the gas. She could hardly afford missing a day at the ranch. She was already behind schedule with the three-year-old filly she was training for western pleasure. And Slate was using Danny with Joker. That put her two hands short for the day.

Even though she drove as fast as legally possible, she was still startled when she found the exit ramp and the signs directing her to the prison. Cassidy put herself on automatic and managed to get into the assistant warden's office with her request.

An hour later, after stating her undertaking at least a

dozen times, she was sitting in a visitor's room waiting for Johnny Vance to speak with her—if he chose to.

The man who walked through the door was not what she expected. He was in his fifties and lean, a man who'd once spent hours in the sun. His sandy hair was threaded with gray, and Cassidy liked his smile.

"I hear you're interested in Slate," he said as he sat down at the glass partition and picked up the telephone receiver that was their only means of communication.

"I'm an old friend of his."

"Slate always had a streak of luck, though he didn't believe it. Did his memory ever come back?"

Cassidy shook her head. "No. That's what I'm here about. Slate talks in his sleep, and he mentioned that you'd complained to him about it."

"For a man who didn't say two words all day long unless it was absolutely necessary, he ran off at the mouth all night. I could have written a book."

Cassidy felt her pulse—and her hopes—take a sudden leap. "Do you remember any of the things he said?"

"Hell, he talked about horses and that little hick town where he was so determined to save the ranch. He should have sold out instead of trying to take a bank." Johnny shook his head in disbelief. "Convenience stores are hard enough, but banks are completely out of his league." He made a sound of disgust. "Slate never woulda made it as a robber. He didn't have it in him."

Cassidy clenched the Formica ledge of the booth and pressed the phone harder into her ear. "Did Slate ever say anything that might be a clue to who really tried to rob the bank?"

"Hell, he never said *anything*. Except clean that stall or saddle that horse," Johnny grumbled. But the light blue eyes held a gleam. "Slate made it easier for me here. I miss him."

Cassidy had not expected to feel pity for Johnny Vance, but she did. On several levels. She knew what it was like to lose Slate. "He's doing okay," she offered. "He's working as a horse trainer."

"He was good at that," Johnny conceded. "He taught me a lot when we worked the prison rodeo. First time in my life I ever felt like I was really good at something."

"I'm trying to help him. I know Slate talks...in his sleep. He remembers things that he can't when he's awake."

Johnny cocked his head, the wrinkles on his forehead deepening. "He did talk a lot, but it was mostly ramblin' stuff. He talked about the robbery, but it was all jumbled up. I can say that if he did rob that bank, he didn't go in with the intention of doing it."

"What makes you say that?" Cassidy asked.

"The thing that hung him up was his daddy's gun. He tossed and turned over that more than anything. I mean, some nights he worried that gun, thrashing around and mumbling. But I was able to piece some of it together. It seems that him and another boy took that gun and went shooting at some cans in a lake or something. Anyway, they were about to get caught, so they tossed the gun in the water."

Cassidy leaned so close to the glass that her forehead was almost touching it. "Do you know where this lake was?"

"Nope." He shook his head slowly. "He was runnin' on about this and that, and I'm not even certain that's what really happened. But he dreamed a lot about diving down in the water and huntin' the gun. It troubled him. It was a special gun, something that his father treasured."

"There was a gun exactly like that," Cassidy said. "And it turned up at the trial."

"That's what he said. And because he couldn't remember, I guess he was willing to believe he had the gun all the time. But I told him, it seemed that gun put in a mighty convenient appearance. It showed up in a courtroom right when it was needed to put the blame on him. A real coincidence.''

Cassidy put her hand against the glass. ''Thank you, Johnny. When I get up the nerve to tell Slate I've been poking into his business, I'll tell him you were doing okay.''

''Tell him not to forget his friends in here.'' Johnny's eyes were sad, though he held on to his smile. ''He does have that memory problem, you know.''

''I'll remind him, and when you get out, if you need a job, come over to the Double O Ranch in Kendall County. Anyone can give you directions.''

''You didn't even ask what I was in here for,'' Johnny pointed out.

''You want to tell me?''

''I like things up front. Before you offer a job, you should know why I'm doin' time. Manslaughter.''

Cassidy forced herself to show no reaction, though she was shocked. He seemed like such a nice man.

Johnny's face had gone hard. ''The man I killed gave my nephew drugs. The boy died. When I found out there wasn't a way to prosecute the man, I took matters into my own hands.'' He was staring at her hard.

''I'm sorry,'' Cassidy said softly.

''I am, too. But it had to be done.'' He waited for her to respond.

''I can't imagine what I would do in your circumstances,'' she said. ''But I'm glad you told me. And the job offer stands.''

She started to hang up the phone, but Johnny waved at her to wait a minute. When she pressed the receiver to her ear, he had one last tidbit to tell her.

"There's an old tractor wherever the gun is. At the bottom of the water."

"How do you know?" she asked.

"When Slate dreamed about diving for the gun, he was worried that he'd hit the old tractor. He mentioned it more than once."

"Thanks," Cassidy said as she replaced the phone. She gave Johnny a wave and headed out of the visiting area. Johnny Vance had given her a lot to think about, and a thin shred of hope.

Chapter Seven

Joker was not happy as Danny led the buckskin mare out of the enclosure, but Slate soon had his attention again. The other mares had also been rounded up and replaced with several of Cassidy's mares. Soon they would all be home where they belonged.

Slate turned his attention to Joker. It was a slow dance of advance and retreat, advance and retreat. Slate wanted the stallion to come to him willingly.

When he was at last able to stroke the stud's neck, he knew he'd cleared a big hurdle. Joker was intelligent, and though that made for the best horse, it made establishing trust all the more difficult.

He tried not to think about Cassidy. She'd left after breakfast and he hadn't seen her since. His amnesia was a solid stone wall that he kept hitting whenever he thought back to the night just past. He knew her. He knew the feel of her, the way she responded, the things she liked. And she knew him.

He'd loved her before the robbery. He knew that much. But he wanted the texture and details. What had they truly been to each other?

Cassidy presented one big puzzle, and he was no closer to finding out the truth about the bank robbery. Her faith in him was balm on a raw wound, but it didn't provide the answers he so desperately needed.

He gave the stallion's neck one last pat. "Later, old man," he promised as he left the gulch. Danny stood waiting outside the enclosure with the mare on a lead.

"You want me to take her back to Mr. Benson's?" he asked.

Slate almost agreed, but changed his mind. "No, Danny. Stay here with the herd. I'll take her." If Benson decided to act like an ass about the mare, Slate wanted to handle it himself. And he wanted to deliver the message, loud and clear, that Joker was no longer a problem.

Slate also wanted the opportunity to decide if Cole Benson was responsible for the rifle shots the day before. In prison, he'd learned that the best way to find answers was to look for them.

He took the reins of the gelding that Danny offered and swung into the saddle. The buckskin mare gave one look back at Joker, but obediently followed along behind Slate as he headed for the land that had once been part of the Three Sisters Ranch.

As they jogged through meadows that tickled Slate's memory, he found that he did not have the same attitude toward Cole's ownership of the land as he did Cassidy's. Somehow, it seemed right that Cassidy lived by Raging Creek and nurtured his mother's roses in her patio. Cole Benson was another matter.

His thoughts were deep inside when he heard his name called from a ridge above him. He looked up and recognized the paint horse that Benson had been riding on Saturday when he'd appeared to take Cassidy to the dance.

"That's my mare," Cole called out as he put the horse down the treacherous incline. The paint's hooves scrabbled for purchase in the rough shale, but Benson gave her no quarter. He pushed her down at a fast pace.

Slate sat still in the saddle as he waited for the other man to reach him. "I'm bringing her home," he said slowly.

"That's what you say," Cole answered, his face inscrutable, but there was none of the friendliness he'd shown in town.

"What are you driving at?" Slate felt his temper rising.

"You've got a reputation for trying to steal other people's things," Cole said. "Maybe you were headed to Blue Vista, or maybe you were headed somewhere else."

"I guess you'll have to take my word that I was bringing her home." He kept his tone level. He'd learned—the hard way—the difference between acting with intelligence and acting with emotion.

"Where's Cassidy?" Cole asked.

"At the Double O, as far as I know." He glanced beyond Cole and back up the ridge. A small noise had drawn his attention, and his suspicions.

Cole's voice was angry. "Let's get one thing clear. Cassidy is off limits to you. I saw the way you were watching her at the dance. Whatever thoughts you have along those lines, get them right out of your head. The one thing she and her little girl don't need is to be mixed up with you." Cole waited for the effect of his words.

Slate shrugged, his gaze focused on the rifle Cole had hanging from his scabbard. It was a high-powered hunting rifle, not a .22. "Cassidy's a grown woman. I think she can make up her own mind."

"What happened to you in prison, Slate? Did you lose your nerve? There was a time when you wouldn't have let another man talk to you like you were a mangy dog. But then I guess that was before you became a felon."

Slate's hand tightened on his saddle horn. He could feel the need to bury his fist in Cole's taunting face. "Prison was a real education, Cole. I learned a lot about human nature. And I learned that the worst thing a man can do is react when he's being deliberately provoked. So why don't you call your men down from the ridge? I'll turn your mare over to you now, and then I'll head back to my job at the Double O."

Cole's look of surprise was the gratification Slate needed. He knew his hunch was right. Cole had been friendly to him in town, on the streets where everyone could see, with the intention of setting him up out on the range where there were no witnesses—except his paid hands.

"Hey, boys," Slate called out. "Your cover's blown."

In a moment, two horsemen appeared on the top of the ridge. Both carried rifles, but Slate couldn't make out the caliber. He nudged his mount forward and tossed the buckskin's lead line to Cole. "She's a fine mare. I hope you treat her with more respect than you do your other animals."

"You tell Cassidy I'm coming after that stallion. Returning Fleetwood doesn't settle the score. That stallion's a danger."

It was the moment Slate had waited for. "No need to trouble yourself. Joker's been caught. He won't be bothering your herd anymore." He watched Cole's expression closely. Irritation was evident in his dark eyes.

"You've got him now, but that doesn't mean he won't get free again. And if he does and comes onto Blue Vista, you can call the dog-food company, because he's going to end up dead."

"I'll tell Cassidy you asked about her," Slate said, nudging his horse back toward the Double O.

"You stay away from her," Cole yelled at his back.

Slate didn't answer. He was too busy trying to figure out Cole's reaction. Was the stallion's capture a shock to Cole? It was food for thought.

Slate's stomach, more than his watch, told him that it was midafternoon, and he headed to the Double O to pick up provisions for the night—and to check on Cassidy. He hadn't seen her since she and Lindsey had brought out hot biscuits and sausage for him.

Lindsey. Could she be his daughter? No, he couldn't be that lucky. He smiled at the memory of her. She was smart as a whip, and precocious. And probably spoiled rotten, but it hadn't tarnished her sweet disposition. She was going to break a lot of hearts when she got older.

Slate couldn't help but wonder if her mother had broken his.

He rode into the barn at the Double O and caught the glances of curiosity from two of the hands as they loaded hay in the loft for the coming winter. They'd been bantering back and forth, but as soon as they saw him, their conversation stopped.

Slate felt the sting of being talked about, but he nodded at them and took care of his horse. When he was finished, he walked past them. He was at the barn door when one of them called out to him.

"Mr. Barlow's up at the house. He was asking for you."

Slate stopped but didn't turn around. "Thanks," he called back as he continued on.

He saw the banker on the front porch, a glass of iced tea in one hand and a cigarette in the other. Clyde Barlow had aged in the past five years. But so had everyone.

"Slate." The banker stood as Slate approached.

"I didn't expect to see you here," Slate said easily. He hadn't expected to see the banker at all. A faint sheen of perspiration wet the older man's fleshy jowls.

"Since you came back to town I've had trouble sleeping."

"I'm sorry to hear that," Slate said, wondering if Barlow was worried that his bank was about to be robbed again.

"Mary, your mother, was a dear friend of my wife's. It

nearly broke my heart to sell the Three Sisters Ranch after all Mary went through to hang on to it.''

"One good thing about amnesia is that you don't have a lot of painful memories," Slate said. He had no idea where Clyde was going with the conversation.

"I always felt bad that you were away when Mary died." He cleared his throat. "And when Cassidy came by the bank the other day, it set me to thinking."

Slate waited. The fact of Cassidy's visit was news to him, but he had no intention of showing that.

"I thought maybe if you had a grubstake, you could get started somewhere. I mean, land prices were depressed when the bank had to put the ranch on the market. If I'd been able to wait even a few months, I could have gotten a better price. There would have been some money left for you to start over."

"I don't blame you for the economy," Slate answered. He watched a tiny drop of sweat roll down Clyde's face and into his starched collar.

"I did the best I could at the time, but it's been troubling me. Hindsight is always twenty-twenty, but maybe I should have handled things differently." Clyde drew out his hand-kerchief and mopped his face. "It's hot out here. Where's Cassidy?"

"In town, I suppose," Slate answered. Whatever Cassidy had said to Barlow, it had had a very unusual effect on the banker.

"I have a business proposition," Clyde said. "Part of it is the fact that I feel bad about what happened to Three Sisters, and part of it is concern for Cassidy."

"Concern that I'm working for her?" Slate asked pointedly.

"Concerned that she doesn't become a victim of the past," Clyde answered. "She's worked hard for this ranch,

Slate. Harder than you can imagine. And she's earned the right to stability and peace. For herself and that little girl.''

Slate's eyes narrowed. Everyone he ran into seemed overly concerned for Cassidy and Lindsey. It was beginning to sound more than a little suspicious.

Clyde came to the edge of the porch and leaned on the railing so that he could lower his voice. "I'd like to give you a small amount of money. It would be enough to get you started somewhere else, someplace where you can start clean and not have to drag all of this behind you."

Slate found it difficult to believe the words he was hearing. Clyde Barlow was offering him money to get out of town. It was almost too corny to be taken seriously—except the banker was very serious.

"It isn't a great amount of money. But ten thousand should get you started somewhere," Clyde said.

"I owe Hook'em ten thousand for saving my horse and truck," Slate answered, wondering how far Clyde would take it.

Clyde's eyes shifted and his mouth pursed. "I might be able to come up with fifteen, but that's as much as I can pull together. You're a talented man. There's work to be had for someone with your skills."

Slate pushed his hand back on his forehead. "Let me get this straight. You want to give me fifteen thousand dollars to start over. A gift. Not a loan."

Clyde swallowed. "You make it sound so...sinister. As I told you, I've been feeling badly about how you ended up with nothing."

"Mr. Barlow, I was convicted of trying to rob your bank. I wouldn't think you'd waste a lot of sympathy on me."

The banker stepped back. "You're angry." He was surprised. "I thought you'd be happy that someone wanted to help you." He took another step away from Slate's cutting gaze. "I was only trying to help you, Slate. Why are you so mad?"

"You're trying to pay me to leave town, Clyde. You'll give me fifteen thousand dollars to leave Comfort. Now, the question I have to ask is what secret is worth fifteen thousand?"

Clyde mopped his brow again. "There's no secret." He looked longingly at his car. "There's absolutely no secret. I was just trying to help, to be kind to Mary's son." He started across the porch and down the steps, moving fast in the heat. "I'm sorry you took this the wrong way, Slate. I really am. I was only trying to help you." He opened the car door and sat heavily in the seat. In a moment he was gone.

CASSIDY GRABBED an armload of supplies from the back of the truck and headed toward the kitchen door with them. She was in such a hurry that a bag burst and cans of food rolled across the porch.

"Double damn," she said as she nudged one away with her foot and tried to manage the bags and get the door open.

"Cassidy!" Nita pushed the door open and took one of the bags from her arms. "Lindsey has been looking for you. Mr. Barlow from the bank came by. Lucky is looking for you, and Cole has called here four times. He sounded angry."

Cassidy took a deep breath and decided that there was no response that would cover all of that information. "Where's Lindsey?"

"She's in the kitchen. We've been baking cookies."

Cassidy finally noticed that the wonderful smell wafting through the house came from the kitchen. "What kind?" she asked.

"Your favorite. Chocolate chip."

"Now, that's the first truly wonderful thing I've heard

today," Cassidy said with a smile. "Has Slate been up to the house?"

Nita's eyebrows lifted slightly. "Everyone but him. He did talk with Mr. Barlow, but he didn't come in."

"He didn't leave a message?" Cassidy tried to keep the question casual, but Nita's knowing look stopped her in her tracks. "He has Joker. I thought maybe he'd left some word of the horse's progress."

"I'm sure the horse was at the top of your concerns where Slate Walker is involved."

Nita's arch tone made Cassidy laugh. Who was she kidding? Her thoughts about Slate were not at all employer-employee, and she was insane if she thought she could hide her feelings from a ranch full of people who watched every move she made. She rushed into the kitchen and gave Lindsey a kiss on the cheek. "Hello, sweetheart. Chocolate chip, yum." She took the cookie dough Lindsey offered on her finger. "Delicious. Okay, Nita, did Slate leave a message about anything?"

Nita shook her head.

"What did Barlow want?" she asked, stealing another swipe of cookie dough and making her daughter laugh.

"I don't know," Nita answered. "I should have listened at the window. All I could see was Mr. Walker's face, and he didn't look very happy."

Concern stopped Cassidy as she was putting the groceries away. "Where is Slate?"

"He went back to the wild horses."

All the way back from the prison, Cassidy had thought about what Johnny Vance told her. Her thoughts circled back to the sunken tractor. There were several ponds on the Three Sisters. If Slate and Rusty had taken the gun from Slate's father, then it made sense they were on the Three Sisters Ranch when the gun was thrown into the water.

It shouldn't be that hard to find out if a tractor had ever

been lost in one of the ponds. Even if Slate didn't remember, there were some older residents in the Comfort area who would surely have a recollection of such a tale. The loss of a tractor would have been big talk for months.

She had to see Slate. They could hire divers to search for the gun. If it was there, it would vindicate Slate—and prove that someone who had an intimate knowledge of his background had set him up by substituting a replica of Slate's father's gun at the scene of the crime.

That was the ugly side of Slate's innocence. Someone else had to be guilty. And chances were it was someone Slate had trusted.

She went over the testimony that had sent Slate to prison. Amanda and Dray Tyree had been the witnesses in the bank. Their testimony and the gun had given the prosecution a tight case.

Clyde Barlow had been in the bank, but he'd seen nothing. His testimony had neither helped nor hurt Slate. But the bank had handled the sale of the Three Sisters Ranch when Mary died. And there had been gossip, which Cassidy had refused to believe, that Clyde Barlow had skimmed money off the top of the deal.

Now the bank president had appeared at the Double O on personal business with Slate. It didn't seem right.

Cassidy helped Lindsey take the first three batches of cookies from the oven and then signaled Nita that she was going up to the wild horses.

"I want to take Slate some dinner, and some flashlights and things I got in town," she said, whispering so that Lindsey would not hear her. Her pale skin flushed slightly. "I may be late getting back."

Nita gave her a knowing look. "Be back before breakfast. I don't want your daughter to see you coming in with the rooster." She smiled, but her eyes were tinged with sadness. "Be careful, Cassidy. This man may not be the man you knew five years ago. People change."

Of all the warnings, Nita's struck Cassidy where she lived. The middle-aged woman had been with her since Lindsey's birth, and she was like a mother to Cassidy.

"Do you think I'm making a mistake?" Cassidy asked.

Nita hesitated. "I can't answer that. No one can know that but you, and perhaps you won't know it until it's too late." She lightly grasped Cassidy's shoulders. "What I do know is that five years have passed since he went to prison. In that time I've not seen your face flush with such anticipation or your eyes so alive with desire. The biggest mistake may be not taking the risk."

Cassidy bent and kissed Nita's cheek. "Thank you," she said, "for reminding me what I've always believed in."

"Hurry," Nita said. "Night is falling and I want to know that you're not driving around this ranch in the dark."

"Lindsey—"

"Will be fine. She doesn't understand what's going on, but there's something about Slate that fascinates her. In a strange sort of way, she wants you to be with him."

Cassidy felt her heart pounding. "Does she know?"

Nita shook her head slowly. "Not as a fact, but in her heart I believe she does. And whatever anyone else tells you, Cassidy, the truth is always the best thing for a child."

Cassidy closed her eyes for a moment, visualizing Slate and Lindsey together. The image warmed her, yet it also terrified her. "I'm not sure I agree with you there, Nita, but we'll see what happens."

SLATE CHECKED the coffeepot, leaning into the small campfire to smell the aroma. He'd forgotten how wonderful it was to be free. A small thing like a starry night, a pot of coffee on a fire and the sounds of horses nearby were so incredibly wonderful.

During the years he'd been in prison, working with the inmate rodeo was the only thing that had kept him sane. He knew in the very core of his being that whatever else happened in his life, he would never go behind bars again.

He heard the sound of the truck motor long before he saw the headlights bumping over a rise, and he wondered if it was trouble or pleasure.

That one word was the sum total of Cassidy. *Pleasure.* He delighted in looking at her. Touching her was as close to heaven as he'd ever been.

But what would leaving her be like?

That question brought him down to earth fast.

Clyde Barlow had insulted him, and angered him. But after several hours of sitting alone, Slate had to admit that perhaps Clyde was in the right and he was in the wrong. The entire town loved Cassidy. He could see that plain as day.

And everyone had tried to get him to leave her alone. Maybe they were all right.

Yet she'd been willing to go to bed with him.

He watched the headlights draw closer, and he knew it was Cassidy. Pleasure *and* trouble. He would not be able to resist her if she showed the first sign that she wanted him.

Even if it was only for a night.

He heard the truck door slam and the long steps she took as she came toward him. In the moonlight, she was a slender figure, almost a shadow. As she drew near, he saw the anticipation in her eyes, the smile on her lips.

He was the luckiest man alive. He stood and walked toward her. Her pace increased, and he walked faster, until they were running toward each other. He caught her in his arms, and the most incredible feeling of peace and contentment, mingled with sharp desire, washed over him.

"Slate," she said softly.

"Cass," he answered, burying his face in her silken hair. "My God, Cass."

Against his closed eyelids, he saw another scene. It was summer, and Cassidy wore a red-checked sleeveless blouse tucked neatly into shorts. She was in the creek, knee deep, splashing water at him.

"Maybe I won't marry you," she had teased when he splashed back, soaking her blouse so that it clung to her body. He felt the hot surge of desire, the longing that was so much more intense than he'd ever thought possible.

He had caught her in his arms and held her tightly. "You'll marry me," he said, lowering them both into the cold water. He felt her gasp, and then he kissed her.

"Slate?" Cassidy asked.

Against the night sky of stars, she was staring at him with slight worry.

"Are you okay?"

He took a sudden breath. "I remembered something."

"What?" The line of worry increased.

"We were going to be married, weren't we? In the summer."

Cassidy pressed her lips together. "Yes," she answered. "We were."

Her eyes were like spangled blue crystals. "What happened?" he pressed.

Cassidy held his gaze and spoke in a voice so low and soft he had to bend to hear her. "You were arrested for the bank robbery and went to prison."

"That's why you kept trying to visit me. Even when I was at Huntsville."

Cassidy seemed to struggle for breath, but she answered, gaze unflinching, "That's right."

"And after a while, you quit coming."

"There didn't seem to be a point."

For the first time, her gaze broke away. Slate wondered

how badly he'd hurt her. Yet she was with him again. She was willing to give him a second chance. If he could only give himself that luxury.

He smiled a tiny smile. "You're the first memory I've had. The first real taste of the past." He knew his voice was shaky. "I think if I'd been in prison and had to think about you I would have gone insane." He touched her face lightly. "I felt such intense love for you. Such powerful love. Was it really like that?"

Cassidy blinked. "It was, for both of us."

There was a question Slate wanted to ask. He wanted to know if she thought it could ever be that way again. But he couldn't ask it. Not until he knew the truth about the bank robbery. Until then, he would not play fast and loose with Cassidy's heart. He'd already hurt her once. He wasn't going to do it again.

"I think you should go home," he said softly, his fingers still caressing her cheek.

"I don't want to go home," Cassidy answered.

Slate kissed her forehead. "I don't know what's going to happen to me. Clyde Barlow offered me fifteen thousand dollars to leave town today." He saw the surprise in her eyes.

"You didn't take it." It was a statement.

"I didn't. But I have to ask myself why everyone except you thinks I should leave. Maybe it would be the best thing for you, and in the long run, for me."

"Without ever learning the truth about the bank robbery?"

He saw something in her eyes, something akin to teasing, but not quite that. "Most folks think the truth came out at the trial."

Cassidy shifted her hands to his shoulders. Her fingers pressed into the muscles that defined his arms. "Think about this, Slate. Think about you and Rusty Jones stealing your father's special pistol and going out to shoot cans. Think about throwing the cans into the water—a pond or cattle tank or something. Think about the cans bobbing and the two of you shooting at them and laughing. But your father comes up, and he's angry. The two of you panic, and Rusty throws the gun into the water.''

He felt her intense gaze on him. Everything she said seemed familiar. It was as if he'd seen the movie or read the book but couldn't remember what happened next until she told him.

"Feel it, Slate. Close your eyes and feel it. Watch his arm as the gun arcs high, spinning in the sunlight over and over before it splashes into the water. See it. Falling through the water, falling deeper, falling to land beside—"

"The old tractor." Slate opened his eyes with a smile.

"You remember," Cassidy said, not daring to believe it was really true.

"I remember," he answered, leaning down to kiss her. He wanted to consume her, to inhale her so that they became one. When he drew back and took a breath, he whispered in her ear. "I remember, Cass."

Chapter Eight

Cassidy pulled the quilt up around her neck and settled on Slate's arm to gaze up at the stars. Beneath the soft cotton of the quilt Nita had stitched, she and Slate were naked. She rested her hand on his chest and felt the steady rise and fall that told her he had, at last, surrendered to sleep.

Although Slate's breathing was soothing and more comforting than any sound she'd heard in a long while, Cassidy could not sleep. Their lovemaking had stirred too many emotions, and she veered from feeling utopian to panicked.

Whatever else Slate had forgotten when he struck his head in the bank, he remembered how to please her. The passion between them had been so intense that it had left them both spent and breathless, only to discover that the lightest touch, a whisper of breath, could reignite it.

There had been moments when she wondered if she were hallucinating—dreaming the past.

She shifted so that she could see his profile in the moonlight. How many nights had she lain awake, thinking of him? Remembering. Knowing that he could not even miss her because he had no memory of what they'd shared. It had been hard. And she had been tempted to try to forget him.

Almost everyone she knew had encouraged her to do that—to forget. But she hadn't been able to. Slate was woven into the fabric of her being. He was part of her. And Lindsey. No matter what advice everyone gave her.

Her thoughts drifted to the people she knew.

Cole Benson had made it clear that he was interested in her, and she'd honestly tried to care for him.

Cole was like Slate in many ways—they were both physical men with great intelligence and the energy to make their dreams reality. They were both handsome men, though different in appearance. Slate's profile was strong, the jaw square and unflinching, the nose straight. It was the profile of a conqueror. It was only in his green eyes that the true spirit of the man could be found. He was, essentially, kind. And those green eyes were often lit with humor.

Cole did not have that compassion. That he could be generous was not in doubt. He'd often shown her great generosity. But there was a difference. Slate was kind to all living creatures, Cole only to the chosen.

Her hand drifted across Slate's chest, and she felt the steady thud of his heart. He was the sort of man who laid a permanent foundation in life. From the first day she'd met him, when she'd gone to Three Sisters Ranch to try to get a job working for Mary Walker, she'd recognized Slate as a man who built. Brick by brick, lesson by lesson, he moved through life creating a world of integrity.

Slate didn't know that—didn't remember—but it would come back to him, and then she'd have to make a choice. He stirred beside her and she knew he was also awake.

"What are you thinking?" he asked, capturing her hand and holding it tightly.

"About the past," she answered, truthfully.

Slate rolled to his side, pulling her against him, and she was caught by surprise at the sudden surge of desire the simple brushing of his thighs against hers could bring. "Do you regret making love with me?" he asked.

"Then or now?" Her smile was touched with sadness as she thought of the nights of pleasure Slate could no longer remember.

"Either or both."

"Then…" She thought about regret, honestly confronted it, because Slate deserved as much honesty as she could give him. "When you went to prison, I thought I'd die. It was as if someone had cut off a part of me." She was glad for the warmth of him against her. Even though she knew how fleeting such security could be, he made her feel safe. "I thought I might grow to hate you, but I never did."

"I'm sorry," he said, stroking her hair.

"I knew you hadn't tried to rob the bank. I never believed that you did, but I was helpless to stop what was happening to you. To us." She heard the tremor in her voice. This was the time to tell him about Lindsey. It had only been the knowledge that the baby was growing inside her that had kept her from losing her mind. "I felt powerless."

"I should have seen you in prison. I should have talked to you. But I didn't know how I'd hurt you and I didn't want to find out. I thought it would be better, for both of us."

"I thought for a long time it would have been easier for me if you'd at least talked with me. But thinking about it, I can't say that for sure. You didn't know who I was. You didn't remember me. That might have been the cruelest part of the whole thing." Cassidy snuggled closer to him.

"Are you sorry for what we shared back then?"

Her smile this time was wide and sure. "Not at all." She thought of their little daughter. "You gave me so much, Slate." More than he could know. She wanted to tell him, but she couldn't. What if he decided to move on? What would the knowledge do to him and Lindsey? She had to wait to see what his future would be.

"And now?" he asked. "Will you regret tonight?"

"I can't predict the future," she said, "but I can't see how."

Slated sat up, drawing the quilt over her shoulders. "I think about the future, and I get a sense of panic. I have nothing to offer you," he said. "I'm in debt to Hook'em. Your hands aren't exactly thrilled to have me around. The only person who seems glad to see me is that pretty little girl of yours."

"And Joker," Cassidy added with a smile.

"He's going to make a fine horse," Slate said. "To-morrow—"

He broke off at the sound of a shrill whinny coming from the makeshift corral. Hooves echoed against rock as the herd began to run.

"I'll find out what's going on," he said, pulling on his pants and boots.

The hoarse cry of the stallion rang out in the night, clear and furious.

Cassidy dressed, her heart thumping in her chest. "Mountain lion?" she asked, though it would be odd for one of the predators to take on a herd with humans so close. "There's a rifle in the truck, and a pistol under the seat."

Slate ran to the truck. When he came back, he offered the handgun to her. "Stay here, by the fire."

"Slate, I—"

"By the fire. I have to know where you are, in case I have to shoot. I won't risk hitting you."

She took the gun he offered. "Okay," she said, her fear growing as the sound of panic in the gulch increased. Several of the mares cried out in fear.

Slate snatched up his shirt and hurried down the steep incline toward the edge of the bluff. As he disappeared, Cassidy forced her own fear down. This was the time for careful thought, for control and reason. She dressed hurriedly. If it was a mountain lion, Slate would handle it. He'd grown up ranching.

And if it was something else?

"Stop!" Slate's voice rose over the confusion of the horses. "Stop!"

A shot rang out on the velvety night air.

Cassidy finished buttoning her blouse. She knew what she needed to do. She killed the campfire, then ran to the truck. Without giving herself time to reconsider, she turned on the ignition and drove back the way she'd come, finally circling so that her headlights illuminated the opening of the gulch.

She heard her sharp intake of breath as her mind registered what her eyes saw. The trees and limbs that she and Slate had dragged to seal off the opening had been moved aside. In the glare of the headlights, she watched the panicked horses racing around the enclosure. She saw Joker register the route to freedom, and with teeth bared, he pushed the band of mares toward it, driving them past the truck and into the night.

Cassidy made no effort to stop them. It would be futile, and possibly only spook them more. Before the dust had settled, she saw Slate walking toward her.

"Are you okay?" she called out.

Slate nodded. "I saw someone spooking the herd. He was right in the middle of the horses, driving them through the opening. I tried to frighten them back into the enclosure by firing the gun, but it didn't work. The son of a bitch got away."

"Get in!" she said.

He responded to the urgency in her voice. Before he closed the door, she stepped on the gas.

"It's a long shot, but the mares may lead Joker back to the Double O," she said, hoping that the ten mares would remember the barn with the grain and alfalfa. "They were headed in that direction."

"Go!" Slate urged her. "It's worth a shot."

Cassidy needed no more encouragement. She pressed the truck up to fifty and they rocked and careered down the almost nonexistent road toward home.

SLATE HELD THE RIFLE loosely in his grip and wondered at the rage that had threatened to overwhelm him in the small arroyo. Someone had deliberately set the horses free. Someone he should have noticed. The horses were running wild because of his carelessness.

As much as he was troubled by his neglect, it was his rage that concerned him. In prison, he'd been confronted with plenty of situations where he could have let his anger rule him, but he'd never even come close. He was the man who was always in complete control of his emotions. Or so he'd thought.

Had he been able to catch the person responsible for setting Joker free, Slate had the terrible feeling that he might have shot him. And asked questions later.

That he could be provoked to violence left Slate with gnawing self-doubt. During the five long years in prison, he believed in his innocence because he was not a man to commit rash actions. His cool, calm approach to danger was one of the few things he knew about himself, since he couldn't remember his past.

But the events that had just transpired proved that he wasn't nearly as in control as he'd assumed.

Perhaps his mother's illness, her desperation to hold on to the land—all things that Hook'em had told him about—had pushed him over the edge. It was possible that he had gone into Comfort Ranch Bank with the intention of robbing it. Cassidy's voice pulled him out of the slough of painful introspection.

"Did you see the person who let the horses out?" she asked, her words tense and clipped as she concentrated on keeping the truck upright.

"He was gone before I got there." Slate had a few solid ideas, though. He'd go back to the arroyo in the morning and search for the evidence.

Dawn was already breaking as the truck slewed in loose rock and swung east. The sky had lightened, and the first pink tint was teasing the horizon. He and Cassidy had been awake most of the night, he realized, and he was struck with another painful thought. He'd asked her about regrets because he had a few. But those were issues he'd have to confront once Joker was safe.

"Look," he said, pointing ahead.

The truck was on a smooth piece of ground, and Cassidy pressed the accelerator. She, too, saw the faint remnants of dust that indicated the herd had recently gone that way. They were indeed headed for the Double O.

"Where will the mares most likely go?" Slate asked. The layout of the ranch was clear in his mind.

"If we're lucky, they'll go to the barn where the weanlings are," Cassidy said. "They can run straight through and there's good pasture beyond that." She blew out a breath. "Once they're in the pasture, we can easily close the barn doors."

Slate nodded. It was the best possible place, and the most logical. Some of the mares Cassidy had brought for Joker had recently weaned young ones.

The truck topped a small rise, and Slate caught sight of the herd. They were running wide open some six hundred yards ahead. The dark gray mare Slate recognized as the dominant female was in the lead, and Joker was driving the slower horses to keep up. He felt the truck slow and realized that Cassidy, too, was spellbound by the incredible sight of the horses running wild. In the distance, the steel roofs of the Double O glinted in the rising sun.

Cassidy recovered quickly and aimed the truck for the ranch as Slate tried to figure out the possible scenarios they would face in a matter of moments.

The dust was still thick as the truck flew into the driveway of the ranch. The horses were running at full tilt, and Slate began to worry that the fences would not be able to hold them. Serious injuries could occur—to a horse or any luckless human who stepped in the way.

As the truck whizzed past the bunkhouse, Slate saw that the thunder of hooves had alerted the hands. They were pouring out of the bunkhouse as they buttoned shirts and rubbed sleepy eyes. Only one of them, Lucky Hill, was fully dressed and completely alert. Lucky also did not look happy about the turn of events. Slate made a note to remember that. Lucky was racking up a lot of negatives in his book of suspicions.

"They went to the weaning barn," Cassidy said, relief in every word. Even her hands on the truck wheel relaxed slightly as she pulled to the front of the big barn.

Slate was out of the truck before it had come to a halt, and he dashed into the barn. He was just in time to see the horses slide to a stop at the far fence. They milled for a moment, uncertain what to do. Trumpeting a cry, Joker headed back toward the barn at a wide-open gallop.

"Slate!"

He heard Cassidy's warning cry. There was no time to shut the barn doors. He could step aside and let Joker escape, or he could hold his ground.

He had not worked with the stallion long enough to know what the horse would do. Still, there was no other choice. He spread his hands wide and stood tall. "Easy there," he said loudly while keeping his voice friendly. "Easy there, fella."

Joker's legs churned so hard the dust boiled beneath the huge bay horse. His head was up, his ears forward and his nostrils flared so that Slate could see the red lining.

"Hold steady," he said to the charging horse. "Easy, there."

Joker closed the distance to ten yards before he sat back on his haunches and skidded to a halt, his chest only inches from Slate's body.

"Holy Christmas," Cassidy whispered, leaning against the side of the barn as her legs nearly gave out on her. "Slate, you could have been killed!"

The stallion stood trembling before him, sweat and dirt caked on his neck and chest. Slate eased a hand out to pat his shoulder and felt the skin twitch beneath it. "That's a boy," he said softly. "That's a good boy."

Cassidy moved carefully toward the barn doors and pulled them shut.

"What about the fences?" Slate asked loud enough for her to hear.

"They're solid. We redid them last month."

"Water?"

"There're two troughs," Cassidy answered, her voice sounding stronger and firmer.

"Hay?"

"I'll have Danny put four bales of alfalfa in here with them."

"There's plenty of grass, but the alfalfa will help." Slate stepped back from Joker. The horse stared at him as if he meant to read the human's intentions in his eyes. When Joker was satisfied, he snorted and trotted back to the mares, who'd already settled down to grazing.

Slate walked over to Cassidy. "Now that we've got him here at the ranch, work will progress much faster." Beneath the immediate worry of the moment, Slate could see her satisfaction. Joker was home at the Double O.

"You could have given us some warning." Lucky Hill's voice came from the fence beside the barn, and Slate and Cassidy turned to face him.

Slate saw the muscle in Lucky's jaw twitch and his light eyes were cold with anger.

"We didn't bring them in," Cassidy said, her back straightening as she spoke. "Someone set them free."

"That horse is dangerous. He would have killed anyone in his path." Lucky's words were hot.

"But he didn't. He's not your concern, Lucky," Cassidy answered quickly.

"When someone gets hurt, you remember that I tried to warn you." Lucky pushed off the fence and walked away.

CASSIDY PUT THE PLATE of scrambled eggs and toast in front of Lindsey and sat down beside her. "You can't go out until you eat breakfast," she told the little girl.

Lindsey squirmed in her chair. "Joker's here," she said, eyeing her eggs with frustration.

News of the stallion had traveled fast. As Cassidy caught sight of the silver-and-red dual pickup pulling up to the house, she realized how fast.

Nita, purse in hand, entered the kitchen just as Cole's knock came at the back door.

"This looks like the happening place to be," Nita said, stroking Lindsey's head, "but if I don't go into town and buy some groceries, we won't have dinner tonight."

"Kip gave you his list?" Cassidy asked as she rose and went to open the back door.

"I've got the list. Anything you need?"

Cassidy shook her head. "No, thanks. Cole, you want some breakfast?" She motioned him into the kitchen.

Cole Benson stepped inside, took off his hat and ran his hand through light brown hair. "Eggs sound good."

Cassidy went to the stove, casting a questioning eye on

Lindsey. The little girl had turned her gaze on her plate and was suddenly very busy shoveling eggs into her mouth. "Slow down, sweetie."

Cole took a seat at the table where he could watch Cassidy at the stove. "It's a beautiful morning."

"It's going to be hot." She beat the eggs she'd just cracked and poured them into the pan. Moving briskly, she put bread in the toaster.

"I hear you had quite a night."

Cassidy didn't miss a beat, but she felt the heat in her neck and cheeks as Cole's words brought back a vivid tactile memory of her hours with Slate. But, of course, Cole was talking about Joker. "News travels fast around here."

"That stallion has been a thorn in my flesh. I've offered a bounty on him, so there were several folks disappointed that you got him before they did. I'd feel a lot better if he had a bullet between his ears."

Cassidy moved the eggs from the pan to a plate and picked up the toast as it popped up. She put the plate in front of Cole and turned to get a cup of coffee. There was no point in getting into an argument with Cole over the bounty. Joker was safely on her property. Still, the idea irked her, and she did her best to keep her expression pleasant.

"Joker's mine now. He won't be a problem to anyone else."

"I hope you don't have to eat your words," he said carefully.

Lindsey slammed her fork down on the table, blue eyes narrowed with anger. She looked directly at Cole. "You don't like Joker, and I don't like you!" She pushed her plate back, the eggs obediently eaten. "Mama, can I go outside?"

Cassidy was startled at her daughter's outburst. Lindsey was a sunny child. "Lindsey, you can't talk to Cole that way. Apologize, and then you can go outside.'' She kept her voice calm and knelt beside her daughter, putting a hand on her slender back.

''I don't like him.'' Lindsey cast hard blue eyes on the man sitting with his breakfast untouched.

''Apologize.'' Cassidy held her ground. She didn't blame Lindsey, but her daughter had to learn not to yield to outbursts.

''No!''

Lindsey dodged around the table and bolted for the door. It took Cassidy a second to realize that she was running out of the house.

''Lindsey O'Neal!'' Cassidy turned to Cole. ''Please, eat your breakfast. I need to have a talk with my daughter.''

She didn't wait; she was out the door and after the four-year-old, who was running for all her worth toward the weanling barn and the stallion.

Cassidy lengthened her stride, wondering how she should handle the situation. Cole's talk of killing Joker was wrong, but Lindsey had to learn how to temper her own reaction. She didn't blame her daughter for getting mad. Cole's words had angered her. Still, Lindsey had to learn to mind.

Cassidy continued toward the weanling barn, determining which course to take with her daughter. She was going to give her daughter a hug and tell her not to repeat her behavior. That would be the end of it. Cole was just as much at fault as Lindsey.

She entered the barn and halted. She'd expected to see Lindsey at the doors, peeping out at the horses. There was no sign of her little girl. ''Lindsey?''

Her only answer was the neighing of two of the young horses. Out in the pasture, a mare answered, and there was the sound of hooves approaching the barn. The mares with weanlings in the barn would have to be rotated out of

Joker's herd. She made a mental note of it and moved on to hunt for Lindsey.

As she started to leave, she noticed the door to one of the empty stalls was ajar. She walked in, but the stall was empty. A shaft of light showed her that the window had been opened, though. She walked to it, reaching out to catch the shutter and pull it closed. An unexpected movement caught her attention. Lindsey was in the middle of the pasture walking determinedly toward the stallion, who had not yet noticed her.

Cassidy felt as if time froze. She scrabbled up the side of the stall, climbed through the window and dropped down on the other side. Moving slowly, she started across the open field after her daughter. The most important thing, she knew, was not to spook the herd.

"Lindsey," she called softly.

The child turned and faced her mother. "I don't like him and I won't apologize!" She started toward the herd again.

Cassidy felt her heart pounding hard in her chest. Joker had spotted them, and he was watching with interest. Lindsey's outburst, her emotion, had registered with the stallion. It was very likely that he would interpret that emotion as a danger to his herd.

"Lindsey, don't go any closer," Cassidy said, her voice easy and soft. "Stop right there and I'll come and get you."

"You think he'll hurt me, but he won't. I'll show you." Lindsey walked fearlessly toward the stud, who was tossing his head and dividing his attention between the herd and the little girl who approached him.

"Lindsey!" Cassidy couldn't stop the panic in her voice.

Joker's reaction was instant. He whirled and reared, his front legs striking the air. It was the stallion's challenge to danger.

Cassidy ran—she put everything she had into a burst of speed that carried her to her daughter. Scooping the little girl into her arms, she veered right and started back toward the safety of the fence. But even as she ran, she knew it was impossibly far. Beneath her feet the ground shook as Joker charged after her.

Cassidy stumbled, and she felt herself going down. She hit hard, on her side, and then rolled her body over Lindsey's as the shadow of the stallion blotted out the early morning sun. Even as she watched, he rose straight on his hind legs, prepared to come down on top of her.

"Mama!" Lindsey pushed at her. "Mama!" Wiggling with all of her might, she managed to push partially free of Cassidy's body.

"It's okay," she said to Joker. Evading Cassidy's attempts to keep her covered, Lindsey held out a hand to the horse. Joker settled onto all four feet, snorting as he leaned down to examine the hand that Lindsey held out to him.

He took a sniff and then whinnied, turning to run back to the herd of curious mares who'd begun to close in on the two luckless humans huddled in the dirt.

"I told you he was nice," Lindsey said with satisfaction.

"Lindsey O'Neal, if you ever do anything like that again—" Cassidy sat up and gave herself a moment to regain her composure. Her heart was thundering, and her emotions swung from fury at her daughter to wild joy that she was not injured.

"Joker won't hurt me," Lindsey said. "I told you."

Cassidy grasped her daughter's shoulders. "You've been raised around horses, and you know that what you did was wrong and foolish. You could have been killed, and so could I."

She watched the tears well in her daughter's eyes.

"He wouldn't hurt us. I know."

"He could have, Lindsey. He could have so easily killed either of us." She brushed a streak of dirt from Lindsey's face. "He might not have meant to. The mares could have panicked and run over us. You can't take foolish risks. If I can't trust you to obey the rules, then we can't have horses. I mean it, Lindsey. You're more important to me than any horse. If you take foolish risks, then we'll quit this business and move into town.''

Lindsey brushed a tear away. ''I won't do it again. I promise.''

''And I'll tell Cole he's never to speak of killing Joker again in front of you. He was wrong, too.''

Lindsey nodded.

Cassidy gained her feet and only then noticed that several of the hands were on the fence, watching. But they weren't watching her and Lindsey. Their attention was on Slate and Cole, who was sprawled in the dirt beside the fence. Slate towered over the rancher with a gun pointed at his chest.

... promise.

Chapter Nine

Cassidy walked Lindsey through the barn, taking care to
shut the doors firmly. She held her daughter's hand and
bent to give her a kiss. "Lindsey, Kip is making lunch.
Will you help him?"

"Sure." Lindsey kissed her. "I'll be good, I promise."

Cassidy found a smile. "I know you will. I have to talk
with Cole, but then I'll be along in a few minutes." She
had a sudden thought. "Tell Kip to pack us a picnic lunch,
for three."

"A picnic?" Lindsey's eyes widened. "You promise?"

"I do," she said. "Stay with Kip until I come and get
you."

Lindsey raced toward Kip's kitchen, her long braids
bouncing in the sun.

Cassidy straightened and walked into the teeth of the
trouble brewing between Cole and Slate.

"You'd better get that gun off me," Cole said as Cassidy
walked up. He saw her and his face flushed with fury. Other
than that reaction, both men ignored her.

"You've been looking for an excuse to kill that stallion," Slate accused.

"I was trying to save Lindsey, you fool!"

"You were looking for any excuse." Slate lowered the
gun and turned his attention to Cassidy. When she walked

up to him, he handed the revolver to her. "It's his gun. Give it back to him when he's ready to leave the Double O." He cast Cole a contemptuous look and turned to walk away.

"If you were any kind of man, you'd be more concerned about your daughter than a horse."

Cole's words were like a jolt of lightning. Slate froze in midstep. Cassidy saw his back stiffen and felt her own body squeezed free of oxygen. She knew then that she'd made a terrible mistake in not telling Slate the truth about Lindsey. She'd had the perfect opportunity, and her own apprehensions had kept her silent. Now it was too late.

The cowhands had drawn closer, impelled by the drama. Cassidy nodded to them. "Back to work," she said. She didn't wait to see if they obeyed. She gave Cole a furious look and prepared herself for the confrontation with Slate.

When he finally turned to look at her, his face was carefully blank of all emotions, his eyes a glassy green.

"Everyone knew Lindsey was my daughter. Except me," he said, as if there was no one there except the two of them. "Were you ever going to tell me?"

Cassidy's mouth was as dry as the Texas plains. She swallowed. "I wanted to. I meant to."

"When? After you saw how I'd turned out? After you were sure I made the right decisions?" The accusation was loaded with equal amounts of anger and pain.

"I was trying to decide what was best for Lindsey," Cassidy said quickly. "And you."

"You thought it might be best for her if she never had to face the fact that her father was a convicted felon. I suspected she was mine. I convinced myself you would tell me the truth. *Everyone* knew but me."

To deny it would be even stupider than her other actions. To point out that Lindsey's parentage was obvious to everyone who knew her and Slate would be cruel. Cassidy knew that, so she said nothing. Her gaze was locked with Slate's, and she wanted to try to explain her reasoning, but he was in no mood to understand.

"Can you blame her?" Cole had regained his feet, and Cassidy saw the red swelling of his jaw where Slate had obviously hit him. "Cassidy's worked her tail off to make this place a go. She and Lindsey are happy here. They've made it five years while you were behind bars. Why should she suddenly open her doors and let you back into her life after you'd screwed it up so badly?"

She saw Slate's hands tighten and knew if she didn't intervene, the fistfight would continue. "Cole, this is between me and Slate," she said carefully.

"No, it's about me, too. I've waited five years for you to get over the damage he did to you. I've been a good neighbor, and a good friend. And just when you were beginning to see those things about me, he comes back from prison." Cole rounded on Cassidy. "You're so blinded by the past that you can't see the present. I'd make a good father to Lindsey. I'd make you a good husband."

Cassidy felt as if she were being pulled into little pieces. She looked from Cole to Slate and realized that whatever her own bad choices had been, she was furious with both men. Cole had betrayed her, and Slate was angry over something she wasn't sure he had a right to be this upset about. She'd wanted to tell him about Lindsey—and she'd tried, more than once, when Slate was in prison. But he'd refused to see her.

Anger made her head pound. "I want you both off the Double O property. Now." She brushed past Slate and hurried to the house, uncertain whether she wanted to cry or to take the gun she held and start shooting.

SLATE LEANED HIS ARMS on the fence and watched Joker prance around the herd. Behind him, his truck was loaded with all of his belongings, and Stargazer was in the trailer behind the truck. He was ready to leave the Double O, but not before he spoke with Cassidy—and had a chance to see his daughter.

Lindsey *was* his child.

From the first moment he'd seen her, he'd felt something for her. She was a beautiful child, smart for her years. He'd thought he was responding to those traits, but somehow he'd known that she was his.

She was the spitting image of her mother, physically. He wouldn't have had a clue that she was his flesh and blood. Except…he'd felt so close to her. And she'd responded in kind to him. She'd welcomed him. He smiled as he thought how she'd even been the first to realize he was the trainer who should take on Joker.

As if the horse knew Slate was thinking of him, he trotted toward the fence. He stopped a good fifty yards away, and Slate examined him once more. He was a fine horse.

He pushed off the fence and went to his truck. Cassidy could put him off the Double O Ranch, but she couldn't keep him from seeing his daughter. He intended to make that clear before he left. He drove slowly toward the house.

He saw her coming out of the kitchen with a basket in one hand and Lindsey grasping the other. He looked at the child with a sense of awe, noting her perfection. She was an identical, smaller version of her mother, and yet she bore his blood. Both of them turned to look at him, and he was caught between the differing reactions.

Cassidy's face plainly bore worry and determination. But Lindsey—her smile was welcoming and her blue eyes were alight with pleasure.

"Mama, it's Slate!" She tugged at her mother's hand in an effort to make Cassidy move toward him.

"Lindsey!" Cassidy restrained her daughter.

But the little girl was not to be deterred. She slipped free of Cassidy's grasp and darted toward the motionless truck. Slate killed the engine and stepped out. He held open his arms, and she ran into them with a giggle of laughter.

"We're going on a picnic. Come with us," Lindsey suggested.

Slate didn't need to ask Cassidy's opinion on that. Her lips were thin and her eyes angry.

"Slate has other business, Lindsey," Cassidy said quickly. "We wouldn't want to make him late."

For a second he was tempted to dance with the devil and accept Lindsey's invitation, but his common sense prevailed. Lindsey would pick up on the tension. There was no point punishing the child for the sins of her parents.

"I'm leaving," Slate said calmly, though he felt a strong desire never to let Lindsey out of his arms. He put her down beside her mother. "This isn't over, Cassidy. I have legal rights."

She cast a quick glance at the child, who was watching them both with a frown. "This isn't the time," she said brusquely.

"Apparently, if I left it up to you, there might never be a time. But I'll take whatever measures necessary. Understand that."

"I should have listened to my friends," Cassidy said bitterly.

"You should have told me the truth," Slate countered.

"I tried," Cassidy replied icily. "Remember, you were the one who refused to see me. When you go toting up all the wrongs that have been done to you, you can add that in the column of self-inflicted injuries. You turned me away without even giving me a chance." She took Lindsey's hand, and for once the strong-willed child asked no questions but obediently followed her mother toward the farm truck.

CASSIDY PARKED in the shade of a huge cottonwood. As she spread the picnic cloth, she listened to the leaves rustle in the breeze that made even a hot summer day tolerable.

The location she'd chosen for her picnic with Lindsey had been meant to serve two purposes. Even as she gazed at her daughter's happy face as she picked a bouquet of wildflowers, Cassidy's focus shifted to the small pond only a few feet away. The water was dark blue, and she knew it was deep. She also knew that it was on Cole Benson's property, part of the original Three Sisters Ranch.

She'd planned the outing to include Slate. In the back of the pickup were flippers, masks and snorkels. If there was an old tractor in this pond, she'd hoped that Slate could find it.

And now?

She asked herself that question as she watched Lindsey shoo a bee away from a painted daisy. There were times when Lindsey was so clearly Slate's child that any fool could see it. She was as iron-willed and determined as her father had ever hoped to be. She was also kind and loving. Cassidy closed her eyes.

"Mama?"

She opened them to smile at her daughter's frown. "What?"

"Why are you mad at Slate? Did he do something wrong?"

Cassidy reached out and brought Lindsey into her arms. She rolled backward in the grass, tickling the child. After a few moments of play, Cassidy pulled her daughter onto her lap and held her. "Lindsey, you're old enough to know that children have two parents, a mother and a father."

"But my daddy had to go away," Lindsey said, repeating what Cassidy had told her whenever she asked. "He didn't want to, but he had to."

"That's true." Cassidy knew that nothing but the simple truth would work. "Slate is your father."

Lindsey's eyes widened. "He is?"

"Yes, he is." At the wide grin that spread over Lindsey's face, Cassidy couldn't help but smile back.

"That's good." Lindsey nodded wisely.

Cassidy was at a loss. She'd expected questions, at least. Possibly anger. "Is there anything you want to ask?"

Lindsey's forehead furrowed. "Can we eat the picnic now?"

Cassidy's laughter made her daughter smile. She tugged Lindsey's braid and opened the picnic basket. Her daughter so often amazed her. Whenever she dreaded something or thought the worst, Lindsey accepted it with such élan and ease. And the times when she never anticipated trouble, Lindsey obliged with temper or fear.

"What did Kip send?" Lindsey asked, abandoning her flowers on the edge of the checkered cloth Cassidy had spread.

"Well, there's BLT and chicken salad." She cut several wedges of sandwich and an apple and made a plate for Lindsey. She found that she had no appetite. Though Lindsey had accepted the circumstances of her birth, Cassidy was far from over the scene that had played out between her and Slate and Cole. As she thought of Cole, her anger was renewed. He had no right to blurt out Lindsey's lineage.

"Mama, will Sla—Daddy come to live with us?"

Cassidy swallowed back her quick answer. "Things are very complicated, sweetie."

"But aren't daddies supposed to live with their families? Nita said that one day my daddy would come home."

Cassidy framed her answer carefully. "There are things that Slate has to do. And me, too."

"But he'll help with Joker, right?"

Cassidy felt helpless to find the right answer. She didn't want to fib to Lindsey, but she also didn't want to raise her hopes. Slate was angry at her. And she could not make promises regarding what he would or would not do. "Can we wait on answering that for a few days?" she asked, snuggling Lindsey against her. The excitement of the day and the heat were making her little girl's eyelids droop. "Take a nap, and when you wake up, we'll swim in the pond for a while."

"Okay," Lindsey said, asleep almost before she could finish speaking.

Cassidy leaned back against the trunk of the tree and stared into the depths of the pond. It would take only a few minutes to dive down and hunt for the tractor. After the earlier scene, she knew Cole would never allow Slate on the Vista Blue property.

If there was a tractor beneath the water—and possibly the gun that would clear Slate—then it was up to her to find it. She was still angry with Slate, but she also had to admit that he had plenty of reason to be mad at her.

A red-winged blackbird skimmed over the water and landed in the branches of the cottonwood. The bird's shrill cry reminded Cassidy of a hundred summer days when she'd worked on the ranch beside Slate. When she'd begun to fall in love with him.

The blue water looked cool and inviting. She eased Lindsey down to the ground and stood. She could explore the pond while Lindsey slept.

Her mother's instinct warned her not to leave her daughter unattended. Not even for the five minutes it would take to make the dive. She scanned the horizon. The summer flowers rippled in the gentle breeze. The drone of bees made the location hum with a sleepy contentment.

Undecided, Cassidy went to the truck and got the flippers and mask. She slipped into her swimsuit and then hesitated.

Lindsey was a sound sleeper. She was a smart girl; she knew better than to go into the water without an adult.

She was also a little girl. And she had a very strong will. Cassidy edged to the water, testing it with her bare foot. It was cool, but not too cold. She waded in up to her waist and put on the flippers. The incline was gentle, designed for cattle to wade in and drink. She moved out deeper and found the drop-off. It would take one good dive and she'd have the answer to her question.

She glanced at her daughter and saw that she was fast asleep. Adjusting her mask, she took a deep breath and plunged beneath the water.

SLATE DROVE TO HOOK'EM'S but didn't tarry. He unloaded Stargazer, jumped in the truck and headed back to Boerne. He had some scores to settle, and this time he was determined not to come away empty-handed. It was apparent that almost everyone in Kendall County knew he was Lindsey's father, but it had been a great conspiracy. No one had bothered to clue him into the facts. He was angry, and most of all he was mad at Cassidy. Not even during his trial had he felt so betrayed.

She had denied him the most important thing in a man's life—his child.

And he had denied her the support of a husband and father. Caught up in his own feelings, he'd forgotten what Cassidy might have gone through.

He remembered her at the trial, sitting with her hands clasped in her lap. She'd watched him so intently. And she had been so sad. When she'd tried to talk to him, he'd refused her, and she had no way of forcing him to listen, of making him assume the burden of responsibility that came with fatherhood. He'd avoided the truth, because he didn't want to face her.

He pulled his old truck to the side of the road and stopped. Leaning his forehead on the steering wheel, he was overwhelmed by regret. Lindsey did not know he was her father—but that wasn't Cassidy's fault. It was his own.

He glanced in the rearview mirror, saw the road was clear and did a U-turn. Whatever else he'd done to Cassidy and Lindsey, this time he was going to take responsibility for his past actions.

It was not quite noon when he pulled up at the house at the Double O. Nita was on the porch, snapping beans.

"I have to see Cassidy," he said.

She continued rocking, the bean snapping in her fingers and dropping into the metal colander. "She's gone on a picnic with Lindsey. I hear there were some fireworks around this morning."

Slate couldn't tell by her expression what she might feel. "I owe Cassidy an apology."

"I'd say you owed her a lot more than that." Nita put the beans down and stood up. She went to the porch railing, and he saw the crisp snap of anger in her eyes.

"Cassidy nursed your mother when she was dying. She took care of her like she was her own. And Miss Mary loved Cassidy and that little girl. I hear the cat is out of the bag and you know that Lindsey is your child. Well, know this, too. Everyone tried to make Cassidy abandon you. Men courted her. Her female friends talked to her until we were blue in the face. Your own mother urged Cassidy to get on with her life and find a mate. But she wasn't having any part of it. She was waiting for you."

"Where is she?" Slate asked.

"Even without a shred of encouragement from you, she waited. Five years, Slate. I imagine you know how long five years can be. So when you decide to go making accusations and threats, maybe you should think of someone besides yourself."

Slate nodded. "You're right. One hundred percent. I came to that conclusion myself and that's why I'm here. I want to apologize to Cassidy and make it clear that I have no intention of forcing myself on her or Lindsey. Whatever she decides to do is what I'll abide by."

Nita's expression shifted. "Maybe there's more to you than I thought." She sighed. "She's over at Crater Pond. It's up the Creek Road about four miles." She waited. "That's Vista Blue property, so be prepared for Cole if you head up there."

"Did she go with Cole?"

"No, she went alone with Lindsey. But Kip said she packed a lunch for three. Somehow, I got it in my head that she might have been planning on taking you with her. They haven't been gone very long. You could catch up with them if you tried."

"Thanks." Slate meant it, for her faint words of encouragement were more kindness than he deserved.

THE RED-AND-SILVER PICKUP blocked the road, and Slate had no choice but to stop. Cole Benson got out of the cab with his hand resting on the gun beside him on the seat.

Slate stopped and got out. He wasn't afraid of Cole. And he wasn't backing down.

"You're on private property," Cole said, with a mean grin.

Slate had prepared himself for this confrontation. "I don't want any trouble. I'm looking for my daughter."

"If she's on Blue Vista property, you can wait until she leaves." Cole lifted the gun, motioning with it to indicate Slate was to leave.

"I'm not leaving without talking to Cassidy and seeing Lindsey."

"Either you go on your own, or..." He fired one shot

in the air and Slate watched as several men appeared at the top of a small bluff. It was like a Wild West shootout.

"This isn't necessary, Cole. I'm not trying to start trouble, and I don't have a weapon. I only want to talk to Cassidy."

"Then do it on her property."

Slate swallowed his anger. "Look, Cole, whatever happened this morning was unnecessary. We both lost our tempers, and Cassidy was the loser. Let's put this behind us. I understand we used to be friends."

"We were competitors." Cole grinned. "If you had your memory, you'd hate me. I won the purse on Mr. Twist. I got the half million in prize money that allowed me to buy your mother's ranch." His smile widened. "And I'm going to get Cassidy and Lindsey."

His words were almost more than Slate could tolerate, but he held his temper in check. "If Cassidy chooses you, I have no option but to back off. But that's up to Cassidy. I only want to talk to her."

"Not here. Now, get going."

"I can't do that." Slate shook his head. He saw the shadow beside his boot too late. Even as he swung around to see who had crept up behind him, he felt the blow to his head and realized that he was dropping onto his knees. His last sight was of Cole Benson's triumphant grin.

CASSIDY SURFACED and treaded water, pulling air into her deprived lungs. The small pond was deeper than she'd thought, but on the last dive she'd found the tractor. Now she knew exactly where it was. There was no hope she could search the bottom without an oxygen supply, but she was exhilarated at finding the tractor. It proved that Slate's dreams were an accurate reflection of reality.

If only she could find the gun. That evidence would dissolve the link between Slate and the robbery weapon, but more important, it would prove that someone, or several someones, were lying about Slate's involvement in the attempted robbery.

If there ever was an attempt made on the bank.

For Cassidy, the tractor validated so many of the things she'd felt but been unable to prove. Slate was innocent. She had the first bit of solid proof.

She took off her flippers and started up the bank. As soon as Lindsey woke up, they'd take a dip and then head into town. The first person Cassidy wanted to see was Rusty Jones. Rusty had presented the gun as evidence against Slate. But had he considered that someone might have made a duplicate gun?

A chilling thought struck Cassidy. If someone had gone to the trouble to create a replica of Slate's father's gun, then they'd intended all along to frame Slate. He hadn't happened into the bank and unluckily become part of a robbery attempt. Someone had planned to implicate Slate—had planned to send him away to prison.

The crowning glory had been Slate's amnesia.

Suddenly Cassidy realized what a ticking time bomb she'd stumbled onto. If she was correct and Slate had been deliberately framed, then whoever had done it was waiting, anxiously, to see if Slate would recover his memory.

It didn't seem likely after five years in prison, but it was possible that a return to the location where he'd developed amnesia might trigger something from the past. And if it did, whoever had created the frame would be waiting.

"Lindsey!" Cassidy called out as she scrabbled up the side of the pond onto the dry grass.

She looked under the tree and for a moment she felt as if she'd been sun-blinded. The blue-checkered cloth was undisturbed, and the place where she'd left her daughter sleeping was empty.

Chapter Ten

Cassidy stumbled across the grassy field and stopped at the edge of the checkered cloth. There was a slight impression where Lindsey had lain, but the child was gone.

"Lindsey!" she called out, turning in a complete circle as she shouted her daughter's name over and over again.

When it was obvious her daughter wasn't around the pond, Cassidy faced the water. The smooth blue surface was calm. There was no sign that a five-year-old might have slipped beneath the water. Cassidy choked back a sob and grabbed the mask and flippers. She dove again and again, until her lungs burned with a need for oxygen and rest. There was no sign of Lindsey in the murky depths.

Once she forced herself out of the water, Cassidy knew she had to calm down. She had to think—to be clear.

If Lindsey hadn't gone into the pond, then she had to be somewhere around the area. She was a little girl; she couldn't have traveled far. Not alone, and not on foot.

Cassidy snatched on her clothes and jumped into the truck. She decided to drive in ever-widening circles around the pond, until she found her daughter.

The summer sun had reached its zenith, and it burned down with a relentlessness that made Cassidy dizzy. But she left the truck window down, calling and listening for Lindsey. As she topped each small rise, she imagined her beautiful blond daughter there, playing, oblivious to the anxiety she was causing her mother. But at the crest of each gentle slope, she found only empty grassland and clusters of live oaks.

It was a half hour later when she moved into land that had been reclaimed by cedars. The scrub growth was thick and Cassidy felt her hopes plummet. The dense, scrappy trees would provide hiding places for Lindsey and make the search much harder. Still, she pressed on, calling out as she drove and stopped, drove and stopped.

A glint of bright red caught her attention, and she angled toward a thick cluster of cedars that had grown along the edge of a rocky ravine. As she approached what appeared to be an abandoned vehicle, a herd of five deer broke cover and took off, bounding over rocks and scrub, their white tails bouncing. Cassidy drew closer to the parked truck with caution.

She recognized it as Slate's. Hook'em had stored Slate's big red diesel for five years, keeping it in mint condition for Slate when he got out of prison. Now the front fender was mangled and there were scratches along the paint.

Cassidy felt her stomach knot even tighter. The truck looked as if it had been in an accident—and it looked empty. She got out of her vehicle and approached on foot.

"Lindsey!" Cassidy had a terrible thought. Slate had vowed to see Lindsey. What if he'd picked her up at the pond and then had an accident? To hell with caution, she thought as she ran to the truck calling her daughter's name.

"Mama!" Lindsey's face appeared in the truck window.

"Lindsey!" Cassidy felt relief so great her knees actually trembled.

"Mama!" Lindsey burst into tears.

Cassidy sprinted around the truck to her child. She opened the door and held out her arms as her baby girl threw herself into them. As she pressed Lindsey to her chest, she saw Slate slumped over in the seat. Blood caked the side of his head and had dripped onto the truck seat and dried.

For one terrible moment, Cassidy thought he was dead. She held her sobbing daughter and reached across the seat to find a pulse. To her relief, Slate moaned.

When his eyes opened, they were clouded with pain. As his mind cleared, Cassidy saw that he registered her presence, and Lindsey's.

"What happened?" he asked, frowning.

Cassidy was relieved that Lindsey quieted as soon as Slate spoke. The little girl still held tightly to Cassidy's neck, but she turned to look at Slate. "He's hurt," she said, whimpering. "He was bleeding and he wouldn't talk to me."

"It's okay," Cassidy reassured her, though she wasn't certain at all that it was. "Slate? Do you know who we are?"

Slate nodded slowly. "But I don't know how I got here." He looked out the window. "I was…"

Cassidy eased Lindsey to the ground. "Let me look at Slate's head, honey. He may need Doc Jameson to put in a few stitches."

"Like Kip had to have when he cut his hand?" Lindsey's voice was already stronger and calmer.

"Exactly like that," Cassidy said, though she knew that with Slate's history of amnesia, another blow to the head could not bode well. She eased onto the seat and gently touched Slate's scalp. The gash was in his hair, but she could see that it was about two inches. It definitely needed a needle and thread.

"Slate, what were you doing with Lindsey?" She asked calmly enough, but she felt him tense and knew he understood perfectly the underlying focus of her question. She was actually asking what in the hell he was doing on such a godforsaken strip of the Double O with her daughter.

"I assumed you brought Lindsey with you," he said.

Cassidy swallowed. "You don't remember taking her from the pond?"

"I don't remember because I didn't do it."

Cassidy used a clean napkin she'd tucked into her pocket to dab at the wound. "You'll need stitches." He sounded so certain. So positive.

"What I need is some answers." Slate's voice was angry. "Are you telling me that somehow Lindsey ended up in this truck in this—" he looked around "—place? I'm not even sure where we are, much less how I got here."

"What happened to your head?"

Slate hesitated. "I don't know."

Cassidy sighed, suddenly angry at him. "That's a mighty convenient memory you have there, Slate." She eased out of the truck, her hand wrapped tightly around Lindsey's. "You almost frightened me to death. When I came out of the water and Lindsey was gone, I was terrified she'd gone into the pond and drowned. There was no trace of her. Not even a note. You can't imagine how that made me feel." As she talked, her anger grew. "But then I suppose that might have been what you intended."

Slate straightened up and got out of the truck on the driver's side. He walked around the vehicle. "It looks like I hit a tree or a rock or something," he said, calling her attention to the dented front bumper. "Don't you think I'd remember having a wreck?"

"I don't know what you might remember," Cassidy said in a soft voice. "All I know is that one minute Lindsey was there, and the next she was gone. Then I find her with you, at least two miles from the pond where she was sleeping."

Slate's green eyes were wide and clear. He stared at her

for several seconds before he spoke. "Any jury would convict me of abducting my daughter, right?"

Slate's words were calculated to hurt her, and they did. "That's not fair."

"So far, a lot of things in my life haven't been fair. Today is just one in a long list."

Cassidy turned to Lindsey. "What happened?" she asked. "You were asleep under the tree, remember?"

Lindsey frowned. "We ate the sandwiches and I went to sleep." Her small forehead was furrowed. "I heard men talking, but it was a dream, I think. And then I woke up here and Slate was hurt. He was bleeding, and he wouldn't wake up." Tears formed in her eyes and slowly traced down her cheeks. "I thought my daddy was dead."

Lindsey's words melted her as nothing else could. Lindsey had accepted Slate as her father with the open, trusting heart of a child. She only hoped Slate would appreciate—and protect—that trust. "It's okay," Cassidy reassured her. "It's okay, sweetie. We're going home and getting Slate taken care of."

She met Slate's gaze. It was as clear and green as she remembered, and filled with awe. So he was aware of the magnificence of Lindsey's acceptance. She knew instinctively that he would protect their daughter, and then she wondered if she was a fool or just plain stupid, because she was beginning to believe him. Again. "We'll get to the bottom of this. Don't you remember anything?"

Slate's face took on a closed look. "In fact, now that my head is clearing, I do. I remember going after you and Lindsey. I wanted to talk to you and to see her. Cole stopped me on the road." He instinctively felt his head. "While I was talking with Cole, someone slipped up behind me and coldcocked me. That's the last I remember."

Cassidy looked again at the badly dented fender. "You don't remember hitting anything?" She didn't know what to believe. Lindsey hadn't levitated and floated across the ranch to drift into the window of Slate's truck. She glanced down to look for tracks, but the ground was so hard there wasn't a trace of anything.

"Nope." Slate knelt down to examine what was left of some moisture on the ground. He opened the hood. "Looks like I lost the radiator, too."

"Climb into my truck," Cassidy said. Her primary concern was her daughter. "We'll sort things out after you see the doctor and Lindsey has something cold to drink."

SLATE STARED OUT the window. Though he kept his expression blank, his mind raced from one bit of memory to the next. He *did* remember everything up to the point that Cole's man bushwhacked him. He hadn't lost his memory. He was positive about what had happened.

As the cool air conditioner of the truck blasted over him, he was suddenly aware of the little girl who sat between him and Cassidy. His daughter. He looked down at her and felt a sharp sense of wonder. Her wide blue eyes were on him, and the tiniest frown pulled at her high forehead. She picked up Slate's hand and held it in both of her own.

"The stitches won't hurt too much," she said wisely.

Gazing down at her, Slate knew terror. His fear was that he would never remember the important things of his life—and that he might one day lose the memories he had of Lindsey and her mother. That thought was too much to bear.

"Who was with Cole?" Cassidy asked into the silence.

"There were three up on the ridge, but I didn't know them. And then the one who slipped behind the truck and hit me." Slate watched Cassidy's reaction and was rewarded with nothing. She kept her eyes on the road and her hands steady on the wheel. He couldn't tell if she believed him or not.

"What were you doing on Blue Vista land? You should have known Cole wouldn't welcome you."

"I was on the way to the pond. Nita told me where you had gone. I was leaving, but I wanted to see you. To see Lindsey."

Cassidy glanced at him. "That doesn't explain how Lindsey got in your truck."

Slate had thought about that. "There are two possibilities. Cole or some of his men took her and put her in the truck—after they'd wrecked it and put me in it. Or else I was dazed from the blow to the head and I took her." He felt his heart pounding as he waited for her reaction.

"Why would Cole do such a thing?"

He knew Cassidy was carefully choosing the path of the conversation. "Why would Cole tell me about Lindsey?" he countered. "I'm certain you'd made it clear to everyone that you wanted that information kept from me." He saw he'd scored a point. "Look, my truck was close enough to the pond so that you were certain to find me and Lindsey. He knew either I would regain consciousness and return Lindsey, or you would find us." Slate knew it was time to shut up and let Cassidy think.

"And you think Cole did this in an effort to blacken your name."

"More likely, you'd figure I wasn't safe to have around Lindsey. If I was doing things and blacking out, you wouldn't be tempted to view me as a responsible parent."

Cassidy nodded slowly. "I can see that possibility. Cole has always been a man who made things work out to his satisfaction."

Slate took the deepest breath he'd taken since he'd come to. Cassidy was at least considering his interpretation of the facts.

He felt her gaze on him and turned to find her blue eyes strangely curious. "What is it?" He could see that she hesitated, that she wasn't certain whether to broach the subject or not. "Tell me," he pressed.

"I don't know if you're aware of the way you talk in your sleep, but something you said to Johnny Vance led me to believe that your father's gun may be at the bottom of that pond."

Her statement was so unexpected, so startling that Slate was momentarily speechless. "Dad's gun is locked up at your house."

"Maybe, maybe not." Cassidy's smile was tight. "What if someone had a copy of that gun made?"

"Who would…?"

"Exactly," Cassidy said. "Who would do such a thing? When we answer that, if we can, then we'll also know who set you up for the bank robbery."

"You still believe I'm innocent?" Slate asked, hardly daring to wait for her answer.

"More than ever," Cassidy said. "Slate, everyone in town must have known about that gun. It was your father's pride. Mary told me stories, showed me pictures… Anyone could have seen them."

"Sla—Daddy is going to stay at the ranch, isn't he?" Lindsey asked.

"Come hell or high water," Cassidy answered. She looked at Slate for confirmation. "Right?"

"Why are you doing this?" he asked.

"Because it seems to me that both of us are being used. If I'm wrong, then you can pack up and leave. But if I'm right, then we have some scores to settle. We can do this, together."

Slate reached across the seat and touched her face. Her belief in him was such an intense experience that Slate could only stare into her eyes.

It seemed his vision clouded and yet somehow cleared, and he saw something else—Cassidy sitting on the back of a striking paint. Even as it was happening, Slate knew that it was a memory, not a dream. He saw his hand on Cassidy's thigh as she gazed down at him, excitement and challenge in her eyes.

He remembered the moment, the discussion they were having about the horse. Rocketman. The black-and-white horse had been seriously ill, but he and Cassidy had saved him. They had worked night and day. Together.

Slate felt a rush of pure elation as he held on to the memory that Cassidy's words had triggered. He *remembered.*

The memory faded, and Slate refocused back to the present. He found that both Cassidy and Lindsey were staring at him. "Rocketman," he said slowly. "A four-year-old paint. I remember him."

Cassidy slowed the truck and then finally stopped. "Rocketman," she said, shaking her head. "You remember."

Her voice was husky, and Slate thought he saw the glimmer of tears in her eyes.

"The doctors said you might regain your memory. They said it could come back in tiny fragments, or in big chunks." She blinked rapidly a few times to clear her eyes. "We'll settle for fragments. And Rocketman is a good one." Her expression shifted from one of happiness to concern.

"What?" Slate asked, almost afraid of what she might tell him. The treacherous thing about selective memory was that it could lead him directly to knowledge he didn't want to have.

Cassidy squeezed his hand. "The one thing we can't allow anyone to know is that your memory is coming back to you." Her blue eyes darkened with worry. "If you remember what actually happened at the bank, you could be

very dangerous to them. Dangerous enough that they might
try to kill you.''

THEY SAT ON THE PORCH and sipped the cool lemonade that
Nita had made them. Slate had absolutely refused to go to
the doctor, so Kip had closed the wound with a series of
butterfly bandages.

Though Lindsey protested, Nita, looking at Slate and
Cassidy, insisted that the little girl needed a bath and a nap.

''Talk,'' she advised Cassidy in a stage whisper. ''When
the two of you were together, there wasn't anything you
couldn't overcome. Talk,'' she said as she led Lindsey into
the house.

It seemed like the best advice in the world, but as the
silence between them grew, Cassidy didn't know how to
begin. At last she thought of something. ''I have some photos,'' she said. She heard the emotion in her voice and
remembered the day she'd sat for eight hours organizing
the images of her past into an album. It was right before
Lindsey's birth, and she'd wanted to make a record for her
child—a history of the past.

Slate stood up and walked to the end of the porch. Cassidy knew that he could see the weanling barn, and possibly
Joker. She couldn't know what he was thinking, but it occurred to her that he might be viewing all of the things he'd
lost because he couldn't remember. She thought of the
photo album and bit her bottom lip. Perhaps she was pushing him too hard.

''Slate, we don't have to do this,'' she said.

He turned and looked at her. ''Yes, we do. So let's get
on with it.''

Cassidy went inside and returned with the thick album.
She'd begun with their childhood, photos of the two of
them. Mary had given her the pictures of Slate. She'd wondered, as she organized the album, if her child would be a

boy or a girl. If it would look like Slate or her. She'd been relieved when Lindsey was born, so obviously her daughter. It had delayed the time when she would have to answer questions.

She sat beside Slate on the steps as he flipped slowly through the pages, pausing at certain pictures. He touched a photo of his mother when she was a young woman holding an infant in her arms.

"That's you," Cassidy said softly.

Slate nodded and turned the page. He went through childhood without comment. He was about to turn the page when Cassidy stopped him.

"There." She pointed to a picture. Cassidy felt a surge of adrenaline. "Look, Slate. Look what you're holding." She pointed to the pistol. "It's your father's gun."

Slate bent closer to examine the photo. "So it is."

Cassidy took the album from him and opened the sleeve to withdraw the photo. It was dated on the back. "June 1974. You were twelve."

The look he gave her was bleak.

"Keep looking." Cassidy said, returning the album. "I want to get something." She hurried into the house and went to the safe where she'd locked the gun. As she worked the combination, her heartbeat accelerated. If the real gun was at the bottom of the pond, as she suspected, then they might be able to detect a difference between the gun Slate had given her and the one in the photo. She gingerly retrieved the pistol and also a magnifying glass. She looked at the glass and felt a pang of loss. It had been Mary Walker's, one she'd used for reading as her illness had robbed her of her vision. Even if Slate had full use of his memory, he wouldn't recognize it, and this was one fact she would keep to herself. She could spare him that.

When she walked back out to the porch, she found that he was absorbed in a photo of them together. She saw that the picture had been taken at one of the rodeos, and Slate had just won a trophy for bronc riding.

"You were the best," she said as she sat down, the pistol held inconspicuously at her side.

"I didn't realize that Dray Tyree rode."

"He was pretty good, but not as good as you." She bent closer to the picture. "There's Amanda," she said, pointing to a pretty young girl hanging on to a fence in the background. "She was crazy about Dray even then."

Slate glanced down the page but returned to the rodeo picture. "You and Amanda were close, I gather."

Cassidy nodded. "We were."

"And it was my trial that came between you?"

"Not completely." Cassidy tried to sum up the past five years. "I was so busy working here that I didn't have time for friends. And Amanda and Dray married. I guess our lives went in different directions." She thought of Amanda's recent visit. "She felt guilty about the trial, though I told her then that I understood."

"Understood that she had to tell what she saw?"

Cassidy knew where he was going. It was a place she didn't like, but she'd already come to the conclusion that someone in that bank had lied about Slate. The most likely person was Amanda. "I honestly couldn't bring myself to believe that she'd lied," she said softly. She felt Slate shift beside her, and she reached out to put a hand on his knee. "But someone lied. Someone had to have, Slate. And now that you're out and we're together, we can figure out what really happened."

"Even if it means finding out that people you've known most of your life lied?"

"Yes."

"And that they could go to prison?"

Cassidy knew that was true. "You lost five years of your life over something neither of us believe you did. I lost having you as my husband. Lindsey lost her father. Whoever lied did a terrible thing to us. I'm not out for revenge, but if they have to be punished, then so be it.''

Slate's arm slipped around her shoulders, and she yielded to the comfort he offered. "Are you sure you want to pursue this?" he asked.

Cassidy leaned against his strong shoulder. "I thought at first that the best thing would be to forget the last five years. I thought if we could put it behind us, we might have a chance. But not…''

"Now?" Slate pressed.

She knew he would do whatever she asked, and it was that knowledge that gave her the courage. "Now I know we can't simply let it go. You were framed. Someone did this deliberately, and that person can't get away with it.''

"Cassidy, this could be dangerous.''

She'd thought about this, too. "Someone has already shot at us. Someone took Lindsey, and though they didn't hurt her, they could have. Someone has been on my property, meddling in my business. And we haven't done anything except try to mind our own affairs. I think it's time now to pursue this with everything we have in us. Let's put it to rest once and for all.''

Slate reached down to catch her chin. His hands, so gentle and sensitive, tilted her face up so that he could look into her eyes. "I don't believe I could ever have loved you more than I do right at this moment.''

Cassidy slipped an arm around his neck and pulled his head down so that she could kiss him. It was a long kiss, filled with banked passion and more than a little sadness.

When they ended the kiss, she lifted the gun and magnifying glass she'd laid by her thigh. "We have to find out if this is your father's gun or a replica." She reached for the photo album.

With the album nestled on her knees, she examined the photo with the magnifying glass as Slate held the gun.

"I can't tell," she said in exasperation. "The picture is too small."

"We could have it blown up," Slate suggested.

"Your hand is covering most of the handle. I don't think it would make a difference."

He took the magnifying glass from her and looked. "You're right." He hefted the weight of the gun in his hand. "It's been such a long time."

"We don't have a choice," Cassidy said with grim determination. "We're going to have to sneak back onto Blue Vista property and dive into that pond."

"Tonight?" Slate asked.

"The sooner the better. Whoever took Lindsey knows I was diving in that pond. They're bound to wonder why."

"You're right. If the gun is there, it could disappear."

Cassidy sighed. "That's one piece of bad luck we can't afford."

"Tonight, then."

"Tonight," Cassidy said, rising to her feet. "I'll gather the equipment."

Chapter Eleven

Slate shot an arm out and caught Cassidy's elbow as she slipped in the darkness on the loose rocks. They were both overburdened with equipment. He hefted an air tank and gear while Cassidy carried a heavy-duty underwater flashlight and a gun. She had not wanted to bring the gun along, but Slate insisted. He had no intention of leaving her alone on the bank of the pond without some way to protect herself.

They were both panting as they topped the last incline. The small pond glimmered like a large black pearl in the moonlight. Several white-tailed deer, startled as they took a drink, bounded away. The sight made Slate feel better. In the back of his mind had been the terrible suspicion that someone might be waiting in ambush for them at the pond.

Perhaps whoever had taken Lindsey had thought Cassidy was simply taking a swim. Perhaps. But Slate really didn't believe that. Cassidy had her own swimming hole on Raging Creek. There was no good reason for her to be on Blue Vista property.

"Wait," he whispered as Cassidy started forward.

They'd left the truck in the cedar stand. It was the closest cover for the vehicle, and it had been a long walk. If they found the gun, Slate had already determined that he would leave the air tank in the pond.

"It looks okay," Cassidy whispered.

Slate curbed the impulse to reach out and touch her hair, as silvery as spun fairy silk in the moonlight. His heart seemed to twist, and his carefully controlled fear broke free. He could not risk her. He could not. "Cassidy, please go back to the truck," he said. "It's on your property. You'll be safer waiting for me there."

"And you? What if someone comes up on you in the water? They could knock you in the head—again!—and sink you like a rock."

"And if you're there, they'll drown you, too," he noted dryly.

"Or maybe I'll shoot them."

He knew she didn't make the threat lightly. Cassidy would never deliberately hurt anyone. Not even someone who'd hurt her. But she wasn't a pushover. He'd come to appreciate that fact. She would fight—to protect those she loved.

"I hate this. I hate putting you in danger."

"Think about this. If whoever is behind this begins to think that I suspect them, they'll kill me, anyway. This way, at least we're together. We're a united front."

Slate accepted her argument in silence. She was right, but that didn't make it less dangerous.

"Okay," he said, taking the lead. "I'll go down and be back as quickly as I can."

"Just be careful," Cassidy said, as they halted once more on the bank of the pond. The cottonwood tree rustled softly in the summer night breeze, and the whir of the crickets made them seem safe and isolated. "The old tractor is down there, but it's rusty and a real hazard. Luckily the bottom of the pond looks like it's limestone, so there's not a great amount of sediment."

"That's the only lucky break we've had lately," Slate said.

Cassidy put her hand on his shoulder and stood on tiptoe to plant a quick kiss on his cheek. "I wouldn't say that. We're together."

Slate pulled her against him and kissed her once with such need that he felt dizzy after releasing her. "I love you, Cassidy."

She had thought it would be hard to commit to him, to risk her heart again. But in the darkness and danger of the night, she found her love far outweighed her fear. "I love you, Slate." She bent to pick up the tank and hold it for him to slip into the harness. When she handed him his goggles and the flashlight, there was a smile on her face, though Slate could see the worry in her eyes.

"I'll be fine," he promised as he stepped into the water.

He was not wearing a wet suit, and the water was chilly, but his body adjusted quickly and he stepped in deeper, fixed his mask and dove.

At first he could see nothing, so he turned on the flashlight and a narrow arc of brilliance illuminated the depths for several feet in front of him. He kicked rapidly toward the area where Cassidy said the tractor would be. He saw the old tractor, a 1948 model with a bush hog still attached. Slate wondered who had driven it into the middle of a pond and why. Perhaps that was a mystery that would never be solved. He moved forward.

In the murky shadows of the pond, he clearly heard a soft voice. He did not panic, because he knew it was coming from his memory.

"Old man Jarvis got mad at his brother, and in a fit of pique, he drove their very best tractor into the middle of my pond," the voice said, filled with amusement. Slate knew it was his mother's voice, and in the humor and merriment, he suddenly missed her with a terrible aching need. In his mind, he saw her clearly, a woman with sun-wrinkled skin, green eyes and steel gray hair.

Holding fast to the nugget of memory, he swam down to the old tractor. He'd remembered the story of the tractor, and now he knew that his father's gun had been thrown into the pond. It was not a dream, it was a real memory that had been trying to surface for five years. It had taken Cassidy to believe in it.

He would not leave until he found the gun.

THE MOONLIGHT FILTERED through the cottonwood tree and made shifting patterns in the grass where Cassidy sat. Though she tried to force herself to relax, she couldn't. At first she'd followed the trail of Slate's air bubbles, but now she'd simply given herself to waiting. And keeping faith.

The gun was in the pond. She knew it, but she wasn't certain Slate would be able to find it. It had been down there for years. It would be rusted and hard to see, maybe covered by sand and debris. Several clandestine trips might be required—and that was not an idea she relished. But whatever it took, that's what they'd do.

The gun was the proof they had to have—the one thing that would make the authorities listen to them. Even if the metal was rusted, the handle would be intact.

She held the automatic Slate had insisted that she bring. It was nothing like the revolver they sought. It was a very efficient nine millimeter. She knew how to use it, but she desperately hoped she wouldn't have to.

While she waited, she went over the possibilities of who had framed Slate. Amanda had to be involved. As she finally acknowledged that to herself, she felt the pain of betrayal. Her friendship with Amanda had cooled, but at one time they'd been very close. And Amanda's sympathy toward her, the anguish she'd displayed at having to testify against Slate, had seemed so sincere. Cassidy felt a rush of strong anger at her old friend.

Dray was undoubtedly involved, too. Dray was the one

who'd shot Slate. If the bullet had been a fraction to the right, it would have killed him. Even as she sorted the facts, Cassidy found it hard to grasp that two of her friends had framed and almost killed Slate. Why? That was the question.

Amanda had no real reason, as far as she could tell. Dray had been jealous of Slate's rodeo abilities, but that seemed like such a foolish reason to frame a man for bank robbery—to shoot him. Although Dray was an excellent shot and the bullet only nicked Slate.

An excellent shot. The phrase echoed in her mind. Whoever had been shooting at them was either an excellent shot or a bad one. Joker's ear nicked. The near misses. Were they deliberate? She'd never considered that possibility. She'd assumed the shooter had simply missed. But what if he'd *deliberately* missed?

It was an open door that Cassidy wanted to walk through with Slate. She turned back to her list of suspects.

The other people in the bank had been Clyde Barlow and his secretary, Karlie Mason. Neither of them had anything to gain from Slate's imprisonment.

Except that Clyde had been able to take over the Three Sisters property and put it on the market. He'd made money on selling the ranch. A lot of money.

There was also Cole. He and Slate had been keen competitors. The rivalry had been friendly, but never less than serious. At the time of the bank robbery—which had been a week before the major rodeo—Slate had been the favorite in the bronc riding division for the big purse. Cole was second.

When Slate had been locked in jail and out of the picture, Cole had won. The prize money had allowed him to buy the bigger portion of Three Sisters Ranch. If Slate hadn't been in jail, it was almost certain that he would have won.

More troubling was Cole's recent declaration of interest.

Cassidy realized that over the past two years, Cole had begun to show up more and more frequently in her life. It had been gradual—casual invitations to community events, an offer of help, a chance meeting in town that extended into lunch or dinner.

But five years before he hadn't shown any desire for her. She'd been pregnant with another man's child, and not exactly prime romantic material.

She continued down the list, to the man she now suspected as the prime culprit. Rusty Jones. He hadn't been at the bank—as far as she'd been able to tell. But that, in a way, made him seem even more guilty.

Rusty had been with Slate when the gun had been thrown into the pond. And yet he'd never raised a doubt as to the authenticity of the weapon during the trial. They had been childhood friends, and Rusty had never once doubted Slate's guilt.

What Rusty had gained from Slate's conviction was a tremendous amount of publicity, which he'd used as a political base. He was an ambitious man, and his name in print as the prosecutor putting dangerous criminals behind bars was worth a lot of money.

Cassidy watched the moon rippling on the water. Betrayal was a bitter pill to swallow, no matter who it came from. Five years. It was a long time to lose—a heavy price to pay for a pack of lies. It was five years she and Lindsey had lost, too. Five long years without Slate.

A coyote howled in the distance, and though the night was warm, Cassidy felt a chill. The coyote was known as the trickster. He was a powerful symbol to many of the Indian tribes that had once roamed freely throughout Texas, an apt symbol for her thoughts.

Which one of their friends was a trickster? Cassidy almost didn't want to know who it was. She wished she could turn back the clock to that hot summer day when Slate had told her that he was going to the bank for a loan.

Slate had not wanted her to go with him. It went against his pride to ask for money, even a loan. He had not wanted her to witness him begging.

If she had gone with him, the frame could never have happened. But she had been so busy preparing for their wedding. She'd been decorating the porch of Three Sisters Ranch with Slate's mother, getting everything ready for the ceremony planned for Sunday. She and Mary had been so happy, so excited.

It was a memory she seldom allowed herself because of the pain that came with it. She missed Mary Walker, almost as much as if she'd been her own mom. Cassidy's parents had died in a car accident when she was ten, and she'd moved to Houston to live with her aunt. But her heart had always remained in Comfort, with the horses. When she'd come back, Mary Walker had hired her to help on the Three Sisters ranch. And she'd fallen in love with Mary's son....

The coyote howled again, an unending cry that held longing and sadness. Cassidy stood up and walked to the edge of the water. It was time for Slate to surface. He'd been down too long. Surely he'd pop up any moment, a triumphant smile on his face and the gun in his hand.

Cassidy was staring at the water when she heard a horse whinny. The import of the sound didn't register at first. Living on a horse ranch, she was used to the varying sounds of equine language as they communicated with one another. The whinny was not panicked or afraid. It was simply one horse calling to another.

But then she realized that Cole didn't run horses on this portion of Blue Vista during the hot months. This was the land he used as winter rangeland for his herd. She focused all of her energy on listening.

The whinny came again, and it wasn't far away. It sounded as if it came from the west.

Someone was out there, watching the pond. In a panic, Cassidy realized there could be more than one person hiding in the darkness.

Her grip on the gun tightened, and she went back to the cottonwood where she had cover. To the naked eye, she might not be visible. But there were so many nightscopes available now, she knew that it was very likely she was being observed through one. How long had they been watching? Did they know Slate was in the water?

Her heart raced as the adrenaline pumped through her. What would they do? She couldn't even begin to guess. One thing for certain, Slate had to get out of the pond before they rode down on top of them.

She hesitated. If she went into the water to warn Slate, the watcher could be at the pond, waiting for both of them when they surfaced. At least now she had a gun.

Her eyes strained as she tried to penetrate the darkness, but she could see nothing. The watcher was well hidden.

The water slapped gently against the bank, and in the moonlight, Slate's head surfaced.

Cassidy held her breath. She watched as Slate pulled the mask from his face. The moonlight made him a perfect target in the water. She started to call out to him but held back, afraid that to do so would only put him in more danger.

When the rifle shot rang out in the night, she cried out. Slate made a noise, then slowly sank beneath the water.

Cassidy wasn't absolutely certain where the shot had come from, and she didn't have time for hesitation. She aimed to the west, to the small rise they'd come down only half an hour before, and opened fire with the automatic. She fired until the clip was empty. Her lungs were squeezed tight with fear for Slate and fury at her inability to protect him.

In the still night there was no sound, only the echo of her shots.

The surface of the lake was empty. Slate had slipped beneath the water.

Cassidy dropped the gun to the ground and kicked off her boots. There was no time to think of a plan, no time to wonder what was right or wrong, smart or dumb. She dove into the lake and swam with all of her strength to the place she'd last seen Slate. As she plunged beneath the surface, she caught a glimmer of the light he'd been holding. She couldn't be certain if he'd dropped it or if it was still attached to his wrist, but the light was all she had to aim for.

Hampered by lack of a mask, she swam toward the bottom. Just when she thought her lungs would burst, she saw him. He seemed to be suspended in the water, the flashlight bobbing from his wrist.

She could make out little else. She kicked with all of her might and caught him. Locking an arm around his chest, she pulled him with her to the surface.

She knew when she broke through the water into the air that she, too, would be a perfect target. She could only hope that the shooter hadn't anticipated that Slate would have help—wouldn't know that there were only two of them. She could only pray that her volley of returned fire had frightened them off. In the darkness, there was no way to tell how many people might be on either side.

Slate's body was dead weight, and she made for the shore near the cottonwood tree, the place where she'd left the gun. She didn't allow herself to think that Slate might be dead.

As she made the bank, she heard him groan, and it was one of the sweetest sounds she'd ever heard.

Tugging him up in the grass as far as she could, she

reached down and unhooked the flashlight from his wrist. Knowing that the light made them both an easy target, she swept it over his head and torso. She saw the bullet wound instantly. It was a small, neat hole in his right shoulder. Blood trickled from it.

"I'm not dead," he said, so softly she had to lean down to hear.

Cassidy thought she would cry with relief.

"IT'S BETTER IF THEY think I'm dead," Slate whispered to her. "If you've ever considered acting, give it a try now."

To his surprise, Cassidy rocked back on her heels and gave a cry of pain that sounded liked a wounded animal. Against the pain of his shoulder, he found a grin of delight. She was better than anything he'd hoped for. She was one helluva woman—to trust in him to the point that she was willing to make herself a target. Without asking a single question.

"Drag me up to the tree," he whispered.

He wasn't badly injured. The gunshot had shocked him, but he'd deliberately allowed himself to sink in the pond. If the shooter thought he was still alive, chances were he'd come down to the pond to kill him, and that meant that Cassidy would also die. He'd faked his own death in the hopes that the shooter would think he'd accomplished his goal and leave—without hurting Cassidy.

"Can't you give me a little help?" Cassidy panted as she hauled his inert body up the shallow bank.

"Keep dragging," he instructed.

"I hope I'm not playing to an empty theater," she answered, hauling on his uninjured arm.

"This is enough," Slate said when he was out of the water. "A little more theatrics might be a good idea."

Cassidy knelt beside him and began to cry.

"You're good. You're very good," he whispered. "Now go back to the bank and get the gun," he added.

The words had an instant effect. Cassidy leaned over him. "You found it?"

"I did," he answered, "but don't act happy. Remember, I'm supposed to be dead."

"The next time you frighten me almost to death by sinking to the bottom of a pond, you're going to wish you were dead." Cassidy stumbled to the pond and collapsed at the edge of the water and sobbed more.

She was back in several moments, kneeling once more beside him. "I've got it." Her voice was tense with excitement.

"Good. Go get the truck and drive back here." Slate knew they had to get away as fast as possible. He hadn't worked out much more of a plan than that.

"I'm not leaving you alone."

Slate knew that she would be hard to convince, but he also knew he had to succeed. "You have to. And take the gun."

"Absolutely not."

"Do it, Cassidy. They think I'm dead. They won't bother me at all. You're the one in danger now. You have to listen to me."

Although the gunshot wound wasn't fatal, it was beginning to hurt, and Slate found that his energy to argue was limited. "Please," he whispered.

"The last time I did what you asked, you ended up in prison," Cassidy said. "You asked me not to go to the bank with you, remember?"

Clear as a bell, Slate saw an image of Cassidy in a sleeveless red gingham blouse. She wore jeans and boots, and her hair was pulled back with a red ribbon.

"I'll go with you," she offered, putting her hand on his arm.

"No," he said. *"I'd rather do this alone."*

"Are you sure?" she asked, and her hand drifted up to touch his cheek. *"It's okay, Slate. You'll get the loan and you'll win on Mr. Twist."*

He smiled at the memory, at the certainty in her face and voice. "You know, I do remember," he answered. "I remember perfectly." He eased his hand over so that he could touch her leg. "The past is coming back to me in tiny vignettes. I remember talking to you before I went to the bank."

"I should have insisted and gone with you."

He tightened his grip on her leg. "We can argue that later. Just go get the truck. Like you're coming back for a dead body. They won't bother me, so take the gun. I promise, if they do come down here, they'll have a big surprise," he reassured her. "In a way, it would finally be a relief to see my enemy face-to-face, instead of having him hide behind shrubs and ambushing me. Now, go. When you get back, we'll decide how we're going to hold my funeral."

CASSIDY CALCULATED the distance to the truck and figured that if she could jog the entire way, she'd make it in little more than ten minutes. Then it would take only a few more minutes to drive back to get Slate. A total of fifteen.

Fifteen minutes for Slate to be a sitting duck.

She didn't like the numbers at all.

But as she found her boots and slipped them on over her wet jeans, she knew that he was right. She had to leave him. There was no other way. They couldn't wait for daylight—and one of Cole's hands to ride up on them.

She knelt down and placed a hand on Slate's chest. "Are you sure?" she asked.

"There's no other choice."

She could tell that he was in pain, but he did his best to hide it. She stood up slowly. "I'll be back," she promised.

Before she could lose her nerve, she started away from Slate and the pond at a fast jog.

The ground was mostly grass, but there were places where loose rock and shale slipped under her boots. She held the automatic in her right hand, and she tried to listen for the sound of anyone following her. Mostly what she heard was her own ragged breath. Her wet jeans clung to her legs, slowing her to what seemed a crawl.

Still, she struggled on, topping the incline where she'd thought the shooter was hiding. As far as she could tell, the area was empty.

She continued on, forcing her body to move as fast as it could. When she saw the cedars, a darker black on the horizon, she felt as if she'd won a prize. She was on Double O property now, and she felt a small bit safer. She jerked open the truck door and climbed in. The keys were as she'd left them, and she said a small prayer of thankfulness.

The truck roared to life, and Cassidy decided against headlights as she started back to the pond. Images of something terrible happening to Slate kept rising in her mind, and she fought them back, concentrating instead on the rough terrain and her driving.

When at last she topped the rise and saw the lake below her, she took a breath. She couldn't see Slate, but she didn't see anyone else, either.

She drove around the pond, parking under the cottonwood.

"Exactly how are you going to load a dead body?" Slate asked.

Cassidy wanted to laugh with relief. "I've heard stories of women who lifted cars from their children. It's called adrenaline rush, and I think I qualify."

She slid out and went over to him. "I won't complain if the body gives me a little help," she said.

"I think whoever was up there is gone."

"If we're lucky." She hadn't seen anyone, but that didn't mean squat.

"We make our own luck," Slate said, using his legs and good arm to help her half haul, half drag him to the truck. "Put me in the back," he said.

"That won't be good for your shoulder."

"A dead man doesn't feel pain," he insisted.

Cassidy lowered the tailgate and then got him in. "What now?" she asked.

"I could stand a drink and the services of a doctor. One you can trust to keep his mouth shut."

Cassidy knew just the man. "Doc Jameson won't be hard to find," she said. "But I don't think I should take you to the hospital." She had an inspiration. "We'll go back to the Double O. I can sneak you into my room, and then we'll tell everyone that Lindsey is sick. Doc sometimes makes a house call for small children."

"He sounds like a wonderful man."

Slate's voice was growing slurred, and Cassidy felt the panic threaten to return. "Hang on, Slate," she said. She picked up the pistol he'd recovered from the lake. It was rusty, but even in the darkness of the night she could feel the intricate pattern carved into the grip. There was no doubt that this was Slate's father's gun. The weapon locked in her safe was a replica.

She put the old gun in Slate's hand and waited for him to tighten his hold on it. "We'll be back at the Double O in no time," she said, then she closed the tailgate and hurried to the driver's seat.

Chapter Twelve

Doc Jameson patted the tape into place and nodded to Cassidy as he turned a long, hard look into Slate's eyes. "Stay in bed. You're a mighty lucky man. That bullet was millimeters from causing you grave injury."

"I'm fine, and thanks, Doc," Slate said.

Cassidy finally released the breath it seemed she'd been holding for days. Although she'd driven as carefully as she could, the rough ride home in the back of the pickup had taken a toll on Slate. "I'll keep him in bed," she reassured the doctor. She went up and gave the older man a hug. "Thank you for coming out here. And thanks again for keeping this quiet."

Slate started to sit up, but Cassidy gently pushed him back in the bed. "Doctor's orders," she warned.

"You're a little too spry for a man who wants to be dead," the doctor said, snapping his black leather bag shut. "You'd better listen to Cassidy. Whoever shot at you very nearly succeeded in killing you. If you're going to try to pull off a charade involving your death, you'd better behave or it won't be a sham."

Cassidy saw the troubled frown on the doctor's face. By calling on him and trusting him with their secret, they'd pulled him into the web she and Slate were building.

"I'm sorry we had to trick you into coming here," Cassidy said. She didn't like putting her friends in a position of being used. "I didn't know what else to do."

Doc shook his head. "It's no problem. But I'm worried about you, Cassidy. The bottom line is that someone tried to kill Slate. This should be reported to the authorities. A crime was committed, and I have to say I'm not comfortable with the risks the two of you are taking."

Slate spoke up softly. "We can't report it."

Cassidy bit her bottom lip. "I wish we could go to the authorities and expect them to take care of this, but we don't know who we can trust." She thought of Rusty Jones, the man who had the power to press for a conviction— even when he knew the person charged was innocent. "We can't trust anyone yet, but I promise we won't carry this too far. It's only a matter of time. But if we can buy a few hours, it could make a difference."

Doc Jameson looked from Slate to Cassidy and back. "I never believed you were guilty, Slate. Not in my heart. I suppose I let the evidence convince me intellectually. I should have listened to my heart."

Slate smiled. "Thanks."

"I was with your mother a lot before she died. Mary and I were good friends, you know. She never lost faith in you or your innocence. She believed that one day you'd be vindicated." He put his arm around Cassidy's shoulders. "And Mary believed that the two of you were destined to be together." He gave Cassidy a squeeze. "Who am I to go against the beliefs of a woman who was regarded as the smartest rancher in Texas?"

Cassidy put her arms around the doctor and gave him a hug. "We'll keep you out of this, Scout's honor."

"Don't bother. I haven't had a good scrap in a long time. That's what's happening around here, just like everywhere else. Folks are getting afraid to take a stand. You can count me in, for whatever it takes. Now, I've got three patients waiting on me at the hospital, so I'd better go.''

Cassidy walked him to the door and gained the moment of privacy she sought. ''Is he really okay?''

''He has the luck of a dumb mule,'' Doc said, smiling. ''Another fraction of an inch and he would have bled to death.''

''I won't be able to keep him down for long,'' she admitted.

''Do the best you can.'' Doc frowned. ''Be careful, Cassidy.''

''I will,'' she promised.

As she watched him walk out into the dawn, she rubbed her hands up her bare arms. His words had chilled her. So much depended on the next few hours—and the role she'd agreed to play.

She and Slate had decided that the best thing to do was pretend that Slate was dead and that she was hiding that fact. It was a plan of desperation, they both knew that. But it was the only lure they had to try and draw out the culprits behind the frame-up of Slate and the recent attacks.

Cassidy had a pang of conscience. Doc Jameson wasn't the only person they'd have to deceive. They could not even risk letting Lindsey know her father was there. It broke her heart to hide the truth from her small daughter, but Lindsey was talkative, and she scooted around the ranch into everything. As hard as it would be, Cassidy would have to keep Lindsey and Slate apart—at least until they could spring their trap.

Cassidy had already decided to send two ranch hands up to ''dig a hole.'' The obvious grave would be the bait. She and Slate would set the snare around the pretend grave to see who came to check it out.

It was sort of like trying to catch a rabbit with a stick, a string and a cardboard box, but it might work.

It *had* to work, Cassidy thought as she went back to the bedroom. To her relief, Slate was sound asleep. She picked up Slate's boots and felt inside for the rusty gun they'd found in the water. She wanted a good look at it in a lighted room.

She held it in her hand, her thumb moving over the carving that had not been dulled by years underwater. Proof. Evidence. And the more she thought about it, the more it pointed to Rusty Jones as the man who had set Slate up for a prison term.

The thing that troubled her about Rusty was that it seemed his part in Slate's conviction would be more a crime of opportunity. Only someone at the bank could have known when Slate had an appointment. Someone at Comfort Ranch Bank had been involved.

Turning out the light and adjusting the blinds so that the rising morning sun wouldn't disturb him, she hurried to her office. This "evidence" had to be locked up someplace secure. And she wanted to compare it to the duplicate gun that had been offered into evidence against Slate. The fact that they had both guns in their possession made Cassidy's heart race with excitement. It was enough for a retrial, if not a downright reversal.

Her fingers turned the dial, and the tumblers rolled and slid into place as she worked the combination. The door swung open and she reached inside for the gun. When she found only a small cash box and a sheaf of papers, she bent down, thinking she'd slid the gun to the back of the safe.

She didn't allow the panic to set in until she'd gotten a flashlight and thoroughly searched the interior of the safe. The gun was gone. Vanished without a trace.

Cassidy swallowed back the surge of fright as she acknowledged that someone had been in the ranch house, had invaded her home and robbed her. She replaced all of the items in the safe and carefully relocked it. For several moments she studied the dial, but there was no sign that it had been tampered with. Whoever had taken the gun had known how to open it.

To her knowledge, no one knew the combination.

She went over the facts. She'd locked the gun in the safe after she and Slate had tried comparing it to the pictures. She'd had no need to open the safe since then, so she hadn't checked it. Afterward, she'd been out of the house constantly.

Nita and Lindsey were almost always in the house, but Nita ran errands and kept herself busy with Lindsey. And a four-year-old girl was noisy with games and videos and shrieks of laughter. Anyone could easily have slipped in and out at any time of the night or day.

Cassidy's conclusions were more than troubling. They were downright frightening. When she'd told Doc Jameson that she couldn't trust the authorities, she had a firm list of suspects. That list hadn't included someone on the Double O Ranch.

Now she couldn't rule anyone out. It made her heart sink to realize that any one of her employees could be working against her.

She took the rusty gun with her as she left the office. This time there would be no obvious hiding place. There were nooks and crannies in the house that she alone knew. Like the small hidey-hole built into the fireplace. She'd never once mentioned that to anyone. She hadn't even known about it the first year she'd lived in the house.

As she walked into the den, she was aware of the sounds of the ranch waking up. The morning sun filled the big room with warm light, and Cassidy realized it was full daylight. On a horse ranch, especially during the summer, the day started early. It grew so hot by midday that she encouraged the hands to take a long noon break. They preferred to rise early and work late, making use of the coolest parts of the day.

She moved the stone and slipped the gun into the hole. When she replaced the stone, it looked as if it were solid. Satisfied that the gun was as safe as she could make it for the moment, she turned to the kitchen. Even though she'd been up all night, it was time for Lindsey's breakfast.

As she put water on for grits and chopped an onion for an omelette, she heard the slap-slap of her daughter's running footsteps.

"Slow down," Cassidy called out even as the kitchen door burst open and the child rushed into the room.

Cassidy was aware, as always, of how her daughter was synonymous with sunlight. The entire room brightened whenever she entered. "Hello, sweetheart," Cassidy said, bending to kiss Lindsey. "Sleep well?"

"I dreamed you ran away last night. You and Sl—ate."

Cassidy noticed the hesitation in her daughter's voice at Slate's name. The day before, Lindsey had called Slate Daddy. Now she was confused, and Cassidy knew it was time for a talk. She put aside the breakfast things and sat down beside Lindsey. She smiled and reached out to push a silky strand of hair from her daughter's face.

"You like Slate, don't you?"

Lindsey nodded. "He's going to tame Joker."

"I think he might do that," Cassidy agreed, but beneath her smile she struggled for a way to talk about Slate that Lindsey would understand.

"Remember I told you that everyone has a mother and father, but they don't always live together?"

Lindsey nodded. Her wide eyes reflected the seriousness of her mother's tone. "But now he's going to live here?"

"That's what we need to talk about," Cassidy said. "Your father was accused of doing something he didn't do. Slate's been..." There was really no way to soften it, and she trusted Lindsey's understanding. "Slate was accused of trying to rob a bank. Even though he was innocent, he went to jail. That's why he hasn't been here with us."

"But now he's going to stay, right?"

Cassidy smiled. To a child, the past was unimportant. The present was what really mattered.

"He is, in a little while. He had to...go away for a few days," she reassured Lindsey. "But you're a part of all of this, and I want to make sure you understand what's going on. That you're happy about the decisions that get made. You always have a say, Lindsey."

"I want him to stay." Lindsey looked to the stove where the grits were bubbling merrily. "Can he have breakfast with us?"

"Slate's...busy. He'll be around later." How was she going to protect Lindsey from the gossip of the men? It was a new twist in the convolutions of deception. "How about if Nita takes you into San Antonio today. You need some clothes, and maybe you could go to a movie?" It was a ploy, but it would keep her daughter safe for another day.

"Yeah!" Lindsey pointed to the stove. "Can we have breakfast first?"

Laughing, Cassidy went to make the omelette. "Lindsey, you can call Slate by his name, or you can call him Daddy."

Lindsey smiled. "If he's nice, he can be Daddy. But if he fusses at me, he'll be Slate."

"Now, that's a plan," Cassidy said, laughing again.

She flipped the omelette and served the grits onto two plates. In a few moments she had the food on the table.

"This is good," Lindsey said.

Cassidy had to agree. She hadn't realized how hungry she was. When Slate woke up, he'd be ravenous, she knew. The idea of making him breakfast made her smile. It was something she'd done many times before, but now it would be new to him.

Just as Lindsey was finishing her grits, Nita came into the kitchen, stretching. "Good morning. I thought I heard vehicles last night. Is something wrong?"

"We're going to San Antonio," Lindsey declared, sparing Cassidy from having to answer. "Mama said we could go to a movie. You can pick."

"We are?" Nita sat down and accepted the coffee and the plate of eggs and grits Cassidy handed her.

"Lindsey needs some shoes and clothes. I thought it might be fun for the two of you."

Nita cut a bite of omelette before she looked up, a frown on her face. "Are you sure everything's okay? I get the feeling our trip is more than just for fun."

Cassidy put her hand on Nita's shoulder. "Everything is fine," she said. "I have errands to do today, and it's a good time for you to take care of this. Besides, Lindsey adores going to the movies. And I understand you like it, too."

"Sounds like a good plan," Nita said, turning her attention on her breakfast.

Cassidy rinsed her plate and put it in the dishwasher. "I'm way behind on working some of the three-year-olds, so I'm going to hustle down to the barn. You girls got everything you need?"

"Charge everything?" Nita asked, grinning.

"Don't go nuts, but have fun." She dried her hands and hurried out to the barn.

THE NOONDAY SUN WAS HOT and bright as Slate stepped onto the porch of the bank. The front door opened and Hook'em Billings came out. Slate felt pleasure at the sight of his friend, but he noticed that Hook'em looked troubled.

They talked about culling his cowherd and Hook'em walked away. Slate felt a sense of foreboding as he entered the bank. They had denied Hook'em's request for a loan. Would Clyde Barlow give him the money he needed to keep Three Sisters Ranch away from the creditors?

Slate was thinking about the rodeo and the big purse that he had a very good chance of winning in seven days. But he had to have some money immediately. Would Clyde float a loan for a few weeks on the chance that Slate would be able to win on Mr. Twist? That was the question.

He felt the wood of the door give as he pushed it open and stepped into the air-conditioned coolness. The bank was empty, but that wasn't unusual at a few minutes before noon. Folks in Comfort took mealtime seriously. Ranching was hard work, and lunch was a time to rest and prepare for the afternoon.

He saw Amanda Best behind the teller's window. She was one of Cassidy's best friends, and she'd been helping Cassidy plan the wedding. He gave her a smile and a warm greeting.

She stared at him, her hands fluttering as she moved behind the counter to check and see if anyone was in Clyde's outer office. Slate looked too, and, saw Karlie Mason's desk was empty and the door to Clyde's office was shut. The only other office in the small bank belonged to Dray Tyree. That door was open, and Slate caught a fleeting glimpse of the back of someone's head. Dray had someone with him.

Slate glanced down to make sure his boots were shiny, and when he looked up again, Amanda was holding up both hands.

"Don't shoot! Don't shoot!" Her cry echoed in the small bank.

Slate felt confusion. He started to look behind him to see who she was talking to. He found that he turned slowly, suddenly gripped by a force stronger than his own will. He struggled against the power that held him in place, slowed

*each movement to an eternity of struggle. He heard the loud
crack of a gun at the same time that something stung his
head.*

*His body began to fall, and though he did everything in
his power to remain upright, he could not stop it. Slowly,
slowly he went down, the room a kaleidoscope of objects
and colors as he fell into blackness.*

SLATE SAT UP IN THE BED, his breathing shallow and ragged. He remembered the bank! He remembered what had
happened. Though some would classify the experience as
a dream, Slate knew it was memory. He'd remembered the
clothes he wore, the hat he'd left in the truck, the fact that
he'd had no weapon on him.

He'd gone into the bank unarmed! There was no doubt
about it. He'd gone in and someone had shot him and
framed him.

But who?

Amanda Tyree was involved. She was the best place to
start.

He put his feet down on the floor and stood up. He expected some momentary weakness, and he was gratified to
discover that the only thing he felt was serious hunger.

He glanced out the window and determined by the sun
that it was close to noon. As he looked for his clothes,
which were gone, he remembered that he was a prisoner in
the bedroom. He was supposed to be dead. He grinned to
himself at the idea. Someone was in for a very big and very
unpleasant surprise.

He returned to the window and listened to the sounds of
the Double O. In a distant corral, he saw Cassidy working
with a flashy chestnut with white socks. Since he was confined to the room, he pulled up a chair and admired the
way Cassidy worked with the animal. She was one talented
horsewoman. And the best friend anyone could ever have.

For all the unfair things that had happened to him, he had Cassidy on the positive side. The scales tipped heavily in her direction.

He wondered about the risk of going into the kitchen and looking for something to eat, but decided that to do so would be a foolish risk. He wouldn't die, no matter how much his stomach grumbled.

Cassidy worked the horse in intricate patterns at the trot and lope, and then slowed to a walk to cool the animal. Slate was impressed. With a little more work, the horse would be ready for the show ring. As the possibility of his future expanded in front of him, he felt a sense of happiness that he hadn't known in a long time.

His memory was coming back. It was slow, and frustrating, but he believed, in time, he would recover everything he'd lost—except the five years in prison.

For that, someone was going to pay a hefty price.

Tired of inactivity, he flexed his shoulder and felt only a minor twinge. He was ready to get busy. Time was wasting.

He looked out to find that Cassidy was walking toward the house. He couldn't help but admire her walk, so confident and yet feminine. The desire he felt for her was instantaneous, but it was entwined with other feelings, much deeper feelings that came with such intensity he had to take a deep breath.

He considered getting back into bed and pretending to be the good patient when he saw her stop and whirl around. He heard it then, the sound of a horse, furious and frightened. Curious, he leaned closer to the window for a broader view that took in the training corral beside the weanling barn. At the sight of Lucky Hill on Joker, Slate's mouth went dry.

Fury was his first reaction, and then concern for the horse. Lucky had saddled the stallion and somehow managed to climb aboard. And Joker was fighting with everything in his being to get rid of the cowboy.

Joker executed a series of turns, jumps, twists and lunges that Slate had never seen in world class bronc riding. The only way Lucky Hill was able to hang on was by using the deep, heavy saddle he'd placed on Joker.

As Slate watched helplessly, he saw the cowboy gouge the stallion with spurs. "Damn him," Slate whispered. A horse like Joker might never recover from such brutal treatment. He wanted to rush out the window and beat the life out of Lucky Hill.

He saw that Cassidy had the same impulse. She was running toward the corral, and the anger in her voice was a whip.

"Hill, you're fired!"

The battle had drawn some of the ranch hands, who were running to the fence to watch.

Helpless to intervene, Slate stood at the window, wishing a thousand mishaps on Lucky Hill. Before he could finish his thought, the cowboy rose high in the air and came down in the dirt.

Slate was beginning to grin when he saw the stallion whirl. Joker rushed the cowboy, who was scrabbling out of the corral as fast as he could.

But not fast enough.

Joker went up on his hind legs, his front feet striking the air as he shrilled a cry of rage and terror.

Unable to look away, Slate saw the stallion coming down on the cowboy. "No!" Slate said aloud. "No, Joker!"

It was too late. The stallion came down on top of Lucky. There was a cry from the men who'd gathered at the fence, and three of them jumped the rail and rushed into the corral. One went to work driving Joker away while the other dragged Lucky out of danger.

Slate knew the cowboy was dead. A man didn't survive

a deliberate stomping by a twelve-hundred-pound animal. Lucky's stupidity had cost him his life, but few people would see it that way. Joker would be labeled a killer, a rogue.

Slate looked at Cassidy, who had rushed to the cowboy lying prone in the dirt. He saw her kneel down, and to his surprise, she drew back and slapped the man across the face.

Slate was still in shock from that action when he saw the other hands haul Lucky to his feet. After a moment, Lucky stood without help.

"Get off this ranch," Cassidy said. Her fear and worry had turned to anger. "Don't wait for your check. I'll mail it to you."

"That horse is a menace. Too bad the rock slide didn't kill him." Lucky didn't seem to realize that Cassidy hadn't talked to the hands about the slide.

"Go!" Cassidy brushed past him as she started to the corral. She whirled back. "You have no idea how much damage you've done." She stepped closer. "Get off this ranch. I'll have your stuff packed and sent to you." She looked at the two hands who stood with their fingers tucked in their jeans pockets. "On second thought, take him to Kip's kitchen and keep him there. I have some questions for Mr. Hill that I want answered."

The men were still gawking as Cassidy walked away from the cluster of men and headed into the corral with Joker.

"Miss Cassidy! Miss Cassidy!" One of the hands ran after her. "Don't go in there. That horse is a killer. He tried to stomp Lucky. You saw it with your own two eyes."

"Joker *could* have killed him," Cassidy snapped. "The idiot fainted. There isn't a mark on him. Joker never touched him and he won't hurt me." Cassidy shut the corral gate and stepped toward the stallion.

Slate found that he watched the unfolding scene with pride in Cassidy and a tearing need to rush out and protect her. Not even in prison had he felt so helpless. He forced himself to remain in the room. Though his impulse was to protect her, he realized that Cassidy was fully able to take care of herself.

She was every bit the horseman he was, and now she was about to prove it to herself and everyone else.

Chapter Thirteen

As Cassidy turned to face the stallion, she knew she had to let all of her anger at Lucky go. Joker stood snorting and shaking his head, occasionally snapping back to bite at the saddle he'd been unable to shake loose. "Damn that idiot," she said, thinking of Lucky. He'd probably set Joker back six months. Maybe a year.

"You should have stomped him," she said to the horse as she relaxed her shoulders, put a caress in her voice and stepped forward. Joker had to be caught, the saddle had to be removed, and then she had to spend some time soothing him in whatever way he'd allow. She had her voice, her hands, and if nothing else, simply her presence.

"Come on, fella," she said, turning so that she didn't confront him directly. Slate had taught her not to go face-to-face with a wild animal. She didn't want Joker to fight or flee; she had to win his confidence. "Take your time," she said softly.

For a split second, she felt as if Slate were beside her, and she glanced at the ranch. She had the distinct impression that he was watching, sending her encouragement and support. The thought steadied her.

When Joker's snorting subsided and he seemed willing to trust her a little, she inched closer. He was a smart animal. He knew the difference between her and Lucky.

It was slow work, and twenty minutes later she'd finally managed to stand beside him and get her hands on the saddle flap. She mentally cursed Lucky when she saw that he'd managed to pull the girth so tight it was going to take a lot of careful effort to unknot it. "Easy, easy," she whispered as her fingers worked at the girth strap.

Releasing the saddle would be tricky, but pulling it off the horse's back would be even trickier. But Joker seemed to be holding steady. She worked the leathers free, then reached up for the horn.

Joker saw her movement and flinched, but held his ground. Working quickly but with fluid movements, she pulled the saddle toward her, surprised when he didn't bolt away. She eased the saddle to the ground and then removed the halter. There were several places where the skin was rubbed raw. Cassidy gritted her teeth in anger at Lucky. She bent to examine Joker's legs and saw the raw wounds below his fetlocks. Lucky must have snubbed the horse up short to a post and then put ropes on a front and back leg, stretching him out and pulling him off balance. If Joker had fought, he would have fallen over. It was a cruel act of dominance and taught a horse nothing except to fear his captor.

"That little son of a bitch," she whispered softly. When she got to the kitchen, she'd take Kip's chili paddle and beat the hell out of Lucky Hill. She wondered how he'd like being on the receiving end of abuse.

Joker snorted, making her aware that he read her every emotion.

"Easy, fella," she said, daring to touch his shoulder. "Lucky won't get away with this. I promise you." She ran a hand down his sleek shoulder and stepped away. She needed medicine.

"Clay!" she called to one of the hands who still hung

on the fence, watching. "Bring me some Furox, and make it fast."

He was back in three minutes and waited respectfully at the fence, unwilling to go into the corral with the horse. "He doesn't seem so bad with you," he said as she walked over to get the antibiotic ointment. "He sure wanted to kill Lucky."

"*I* want to kill Lucky, and when I get my hands on him he's going to wish he were dead. I can tell you one thing, if Joker had meant to hurt him, he'd be pounded into hamburger meat."

"I've never seen a horse that could buck like him," Clay said with admiration. "Mr. Twist is the only horse who even comes close, and he was world champion. Joker makes him look like a kid's pony. Maybe you should sell Joker to the rodeo."

Cassidy shook her head. "Not in this lifetime. Now, I think you should get to work. I want you to find Randy and go up to the small cemetery on Sycamore Ridge. I need a hole dug there. Make it six feet long and six feet deep." She allowed her eyes to fill with tears and her voice to tremble.

At her evident emotion, Clay cleared his throat. "You mean a grave?" His doubts were obvious in his tone.

"Look, don't tell anyone about this." Cassidy dabbed at her eye. "I'm relying on you to keep quiet."

"Yes, ma'am," Clay said, casting a long look back at her as he left to get busy.

Cassidy found the stallion to be amazingly gentle as she doctored his wounds and talked to him. Whatever damage Lucky had done, it wasn't half as bad as she'd thought it would be.

Still fuming at the former foreman, she put the medicine away and headed to the kitchen. When she got there, a sheepish Kit rubbed his jaw and shrugged. "He came up from behind and socked me. He was out the door before I could get any help."

Cassidy hid her disappointment and frustration. She'd wanted to search Lucky's truck before he left. It had occurred to her that he might have taken the gun from the safe.

"Are you okay?" she asked the burly cook.

Kip rubbed his jaw. "My pride's hurt a lot worse than my jaw. I can't believe that little snake caught me from behind. When I run into him, and I'll make it a point to do so, he'll learn that skullduggery has a price."

"Give him a punch for Joker," Cassidy said ruefully.

"That's one bucking devil," Kip said, his eyes lighting. "I've never seen better. You could—"

"He's not going to the rodeo," Cassidy said, not unkindly. "He's got a lot more potential as a performance horse."

Kip nodded. "You know your horses, Miss Cassidy." He shrugged his shoulders. "Where'd Clay and Randy get off to? They were acting strange."

Cassidy wanted to smile but didn't dare. She had a role to play. "I sent them to do a chore."

"You seem upset. Is something wrong?" Kip asked.

"I'm okay," she said as she made for the door. Word would soon be traveling back to the people she wanted to hear it. Her only regret was that Lucky had gotten away before she could figure out a way to tail him. But he wouldn't go far, not with all of his belongings still in her possession.

She made a stop in the bunkhouse, and while everyone was gone, she went through Lucky's things without any success. She'd hoped to find the missing gun, but she hadn't actually expected it to be there. If Lucky had it, he'd managed to get off the Double O property with it.

It was well past noon, and Cassidy headed to the house.

Slate would be up—and hungry as a bear. She needed to tell him about the disappearance of the gun and to lay the plans for the rest of the trap.

At the guest room door she tapped lightly and then opened it. At first glance, the room looked empty, and she felt a split second of concern before Slate's arms swept her into an embrace.

"Has anyone ever told you you have a way with wild horses?" he asked as he kissed her neck.

"You were watching?" She'd strongly felt him with her, and it was gratifying to know she'd been right.

"I saw every move you made. You don't need me. Joker was eating out of your hand."

"He's smart," she agreed, slipping from his embrace.

"Is everything okay?" Slate asked. "I've been like a caged animal. I never realized playing dead was so...exhausting."

"Lucky's gone and the plan is in motion." Cassidy reported the good news, then hesitated. "I'm certain Lucky had something to do with the rock slide. And someone managed to open my safe and steal the replica gun."

Her words were a blow to Slate, she could tell by his reaction. Typical to his nature, he moved right on to the important issue.

"How did they open the safe?" he asked.

"That's a good question. It had to be someone on the ranch, and the more I think about it, the more I believe it had to be Lucky. He had plenty of reasons to be in my office for payroll sheets and things, and I opened it a few times to get things for him while he was in the room. No one would think much about him going in and out."

Slate walked to the window. "It's a troubling turn of events."

It was, but there was also a bright side. "We have the

real gun that was your father's. We don't need the replica anymore,'' Cassidy pointed out.

Slate faced her. "You're right. It just bothers me. There's something about it…" He let the sentence drift unfinished.

"It bothers me, too," Cassidy admitted. "But on the positive side, if that gun disappears completely, it won't be like we can't get witnesses to its existence. You had to get it from the sheriff's office, for heaven's sake. They can't pretend they never had it. And Rusty gave you the authority to have it. The gun is documented."

Pacing the room, Slate sighed. "You're right."

Cassidy saw that he was still troubled, but there was nothing he could do. He couldn't go and hunt for the gun, or take on Lucky. They had set their trap so that Slate was a dead man.

In an ironic twist, he was also a victim of the trap they'd set.

Taking pity on his forced inactivity, Cassidy thought of something. "Clay and Randy should be finished with the grave by three. The ground is rocky, and they're having to dig by hand. But once the grave is dug, we need to fill it in."

"I'll slip up there and do it," Slate said.

"Your shoulder?" It was an objection she knew he'd ignore.

"If I stay in this room any longer, I'll have an ulcer from worrying myself to death."

"Okay," Cassidy reluctantly agreed. "I can load Cutter in the horse trailer and say I'm going over to the covered arena for some practice. I'll drop him and you off. You can hide in the trailer with him," she said, smiling.

"Lucky me," Slate responded, but he caught her hand and brought it to his lips. "Some folks might think I've had an unlucky life, but I want you to know that the time I've had with you makes up for everything I lost in prison.

I consider myself the luckiest man in the world to have you and Lindsey.''

Cassidy felt the tears in her eyes, and this time they weren't pretend. Her feelings for Slate were so deep, so strong that she knew words would never express them. She went to him and offered her lips.

THE ARROYO WAS a starburst of terra cotta, orange and gold, and Slate gently slowed Cutter from a trot to a slow walk as he examined the bluffs that closed around the dry creek bed. The layers of the earth were clearly visible and vibrantly colored. On a whim he nudged the horse forward, following the creek that would swell with water during the spring rains.

He liked the small arroyo. It reminded him of a time long past, when Texas was wide-open range. Even better than recalling old history, he remembered the place from his childhood.

Slate felt elation as his memory sharpened and focused. This was not one isolated memory, it was a consistent string. As he rode into the gulch, he allowed the memories to come.

He remembered coming to the gulch with his father to find the clay that Lucas Walker used to make pots. Slate grinned to himself—his father had been an amateur potter. Molding and spinning the beautiful hues of the earth had given Lucas peace and contentment. As Slate remembered excavating the clay from the small arroyo with his father, his senses came alive to the past. He could feel the clay, smell it. He heard his father's laugh and the happiness it gave him was like a warm blessing.

The memories whipped through his mind, a dizzying whirl of emotion-laden images. He watched his father spin the pots, hands shaping the wet clay; his mother packing a picnic lunch for them; his first pony named Adam; his mother's laughter; his father's work-calloused hands patting him on the back for a job well done.

Slate rode into the arroyo, but he was not alone. The ghosts of his childhood were waiting for him. He stared at the dazzling colors and saw images that had been locked away from him for five long years.

After such a long time of wanting his memory, Slate didn't fight it. He accepted the pain as he remembered his father's sudden heart attack, and the terrible sorrow of his mother's decline. Sitting on Cutter, he let the memories whip through him until once again he was alone with the horse and the vivid-hued walls of the gulch.

"Be careful what you ask for," he said to the horse as he prepared to leave. "You might get it." But though the onslaught of memories had been painful, they had also held moments of joy and love, and he didn't regret the return of that small portion of memory. And he knew not to push too hard. The rest would come, in its own time.

He rode to the rear of the arroyo, hoping to cut through and continue on to Sycamore Ridge, but a rock slide blocked the far end of the gulch. Slate turned back the way he'd entered. He checked his watch and saw that it was nearly three. Clay and Randy would probably be gone. It was time for him to get hopping.

He loped toward the place where his mother's grave was, and where his own had been dug. There were harder memories to face, but Slate knew he would meet them head-on. He didn't have a choice.

As he neared the grave site, he heard the clang of metal on rock and stopped. Sliding off Cutter and tying him to a scrub cedar, he inched forward in time to see the two cowhands up to their shoulders in the hole and still digging.

"If this isn't a grave, my name's not Randy Patrick," Randy said, wiping the sweat from his eyes with his shirtsleeve.

"I wonder who died?" Clay asked as he threw the last shovelful of dirt out and jumped up on the side of the grave.

"Don't you think it's a little suspicious that *we're* digging the grave instead of the undertaker?" Randy asked.

"More than a little," Clay agreed, nodding his head. "Having us dig the grave makes it look like…Miss Cassidy wouldn't bury just anyone up here by Mrs. Walker. The only person would be Slate." His eyes widened. "Maybe we should—"

Slate watched as the two cowhands came to the conclusion that he and Cassidy had hoped for.

"Maybe we should get in that truck and get back to the ranch. This is none of our business. Miss Cassidy's been good to us. We can't get in trouble for what we don't know, and right now, I don't know anything!" Randy said, putting action to his words as he dropped his shovel and headed for the truck. "You can come or you can wait here and see what happens next."

Clay jumped to his feet. "You're not leaving me here. You forgot your shovel."

"I didn't forget it. She may need it. I'll come back up here tomorrow and pick it up."

"And see if the grave's still empty!" Clay taunted.

"Let's go," Randy said, getting behind the wheel and starting the truck with a roar.

Slate waited until they were gone, then he retrieved Cutter and walked up to the empty grave. His focus was on the solitary headstone that marked his mother's grave.

He read the inscription. "Mary Elizabeth Walker, wife of Lucas and mother of Slate." It listed the dates of her birth and death, and a short epitaph. "A woman of Texas, a woman of the land." He knew that Cassidy had ordered the stone.

Slate placed a hand on the cool marble and knelt on one knee. "I remember," he said. "I'll get Three Sisters back, and I'll see to it that Dad's grave is moved out here with you.''

He started to rise when the memory of the bank seemed to spring up around him. Once again he was standing in the lobby, empty except for Amanda Best. The details were exquisitely sharp. He could feel his cotton shirt, hot from the summer sun, across his shoulders. The cool air-conditioning of the bank was a sweet relief, and he flexed his hands to make sure they were dry before he had to shake with Clyde Barlow. He saw Clyde's office door ajar, Karlie's empty desk, and he turned to Dray's office.

Slate was fully aware that he was remembering. His right hand still touched his mother's gravestone, yet he was back in the bank five years before—empty-handed and staring at the back of a man's head while Dray Tyree cast him a furtive glance.

Slate held the memory. He tried to seize more detail about the man in Dray's office, but there was only the brief glimpse. The broad shoulders and the hat pulled so low that not even hair color was distinguishable. And then the memory was gone and Slate was back on Sycamore Ridge, a hawk crying shrill and daring as it glided high above him.

He stood up and went to the pile of dirt and rock that Clay and Randy had so laboriously dug. Stretching his shoulder once, Slate picked up the shovel and set to work. As he fell into a steady rhythm, he allowed the memories to wash over him again. This time he thought of Cassidy and felt anew the wonder of their first love.

CASSIDY KILLED THE ENGINE and got out of the truck at Blue Vista. Although two Australian shepherds came up to greet her, there was no sign of Cole or any of his hands. He'd told her he was going to Fort Worth to meet with Ramsur Rodeo about supplying stock, and that was probably where he was.

Cassidy had felt certain Lucky Hill would slink over to the Blue Vista seeking employment. Her goal was to find him and ultimately to tell Cole why she'd fired him. Cassidy tried not to micro-manage the ranch and had given Lucky a free hand. He had betrayed her. Lucky was not to be trusted as a foreman—not even as an hourly hand. He had a real mean streak.

"Cole!" she called out as she walked around her truck and went up to the front door. She gave the old wood a good solid knock and waited. She didn't like to visit Blue Vista. It held too many memories of Slate and Mary Walker. As she stood on the front porch, she remembered the day before her wedding. She and Mary had laced garlands of wildflowers along the porch railing and up the posts. They'd created a bower for her and Slate to stand under right in the very spot where she was standing now.

She shook off the memory and banged the door again. "Cole, are you there?"

She gave it another two minutes and turned to leave. She had plenty to do at the Double O, but she was struck by another thought. Amanda Best Tyree. Now was the perfect opportunity to question Amanda. Dray would be at the bank, and Amanda would be alone.

And this time Cassidy intended to tape whatever Amanda confessed to, and confess she would.

She started to leave Cole a note but thought better of it. The one thing she didn't want was him rushing over to the Double O as soon as he got back. She wasn't certain what role, if any, Cole had played in past events. She was taking no unnecessary risks.

On the way to Amanda's she stopped and bought a microcassette tape recorder. Whatever she gathered wouldn't be admissible in court, she knew, but she wasn't worried about legalities. She also wasn't concerned about unfair tactics. She was determined to do whatever it took to get Amanda to confess to her part in Slate's frame-up.

She pulled into the drive of the new two-story home that Amanda and Dray had built. Looking up at the imposing house, Cassidy was reminded of Amanda's love of shopping. She would take pleasure in filling every inch of space in the house.

She knew Amanda was home because she saw her peeping out of an upstairs window, and when she wouldn't come to the door, Cassidy used her booted foot to get across the point that she intended to be let in. It took three solid kicks before Amanda made it to the door.

"Just a minute, Cassidy!" Amanda huffed as she fumbled with the locks. "What are the neighbors going to think with you trying to kick the door down?"

"They're going to think I really want in," Cassidy said as she barged past her old friend and stopped in the black-and-white-tiled foyer. Despite herself, Cassidy was impressed with the formality of the house.

"Is something wrong?" Amanda asked.

Cassidy noticed that there were dark circles beneath her old friend's eyes, and Amanda's skin was sallow. "Yes, there's something wrong. It looks like you're sick."

Amanda shrugged. "I'm tired. I was sleeping. That's why I didn't—"

"Don't bother lying, Amanda. I saw you at the window. You weren't going to let me in because you don't want to talk to me." Cassidy squared her shoulders. This was harder than she thought it was going to be. Amanda did look sick and pathetic, and it went against her nature to jump on someone who was sick. She reminded herself that sick or well, Amanda had cost Slate five years of his life.

"You've got a lot to account for, and I'm here to find out the truth." Her words were more effective than a slap.

"I don't know what you're talking about, and I don't feel up to this. I'm afraid you're going to have to leave."

Cassidy shook her head. "Not this time, Amanda. I don't want to do anything to jeopardize your health, but I'm going to learn the truth. Today. Right this minute."

Amanda cast a furtive look up the stairs, as if she hoped that help would arrive from that quarter. "You sound as crazy as Slate. Both of you think you can rewrite history because you don't like the way it happened. Slate came into that bank and tried to rob it. Dray had to shoot him. That's the truth, Cassidy, like it or not."

Cassidy unobtrusively reached into her purse and clicked on the tape recorder. "I don't like that version, Amanda, because I know it's a lie. Now you can tell me the truth and I'll do as much as I can for you, or you can keep on lying. If you choose the latter, I swear to you that I'll make the worst enemy you ever dreamed of having. I will hound you to your grave." The harshness of her words had the intended effect. Amanda blanched and grasped the stair railing.

"Cassidy, I can't believe what you're doing." Amanda put her hand on her stomach. "You could make me lose the baby."

"I hardly think a good dose of the truth will hurt you," Cassidy said coldly. "If you're in danger from anything, it's a guilty conscience. I don't know how you sleep at night after what you did to Slate."

The first tears welled in Amanda's dark eyes. She didn't bother to wipe them away as they traced slowly down her cheek. "You're right," she said in a whisper. "I don't sleep at night. Neither does Dray. We thought the house and the baby would make things better, but they haven't." The tears dripped down her face. "They've only made things worse, but I can't tell you anything, Cassidy. I can't.

If I do—'' She put her hands over her face and began to sob.

As hard as she'd fought to toughen her resolve, Cassidy felt her own eyes begin to fill. It was terrible to watch someone so obviously in anguish. "Tell me the truth, Amanda," she said. "It can only make things better."

"I doubt it," Amanda managed to say.

"It will." Cassidy took her arm and led her through the house, finally finding the kitchen that was filled with gleaming appliances and the latest of gadgets. She pulled out a chair at the big kitchen table and put a kettle of water on the stove for tea. She gave Amanda privacy for the time it took to make two cups of tea. When she placed them on the table, Cassidy saw that the brunette had gotten a grip on her emotions.

Cassidy slid into a seat. "Tell me," she said, her gaze unflinching.

"You have every right to hate me," Amanda said. This time she held on to her composure. "Everything I said at the trial was a lie."

Even though Cassidy knew it to be true, she still felt as if she'd been hit in the head with a block of wood. "All a lie?" she repeated.

Amanda nodded. "Everything. Slate didn't have a gun. He wasn't trying to rob the bank. None of it was true."

"And you let him go to prison for five years?" Cassidy asked the question softly, but she saw Amanda recoil at the harsh truth of what her actions had cost.

"I didn't have a choice," Amanda said. "Dray and I had to do it. We had to."

"No one has to lie and put an innocent man in prison," Cassidy responded. Her tone was still soft, but all compassion for Amanda was gone. She felt completely devoid of any emotion except an anger that was so hot it made her cold. "Why?"

Amanda looked down into her cup of tea and found the courage to meet Cassidy's gaze once again. "I'd embezzled funds at the bank. I'd stolen thousands of dollars."

"You intended to rob the bank to cover the money you'd embezzled?" Cassidy was astounded.

Amanda shook her head. "No. It was just that if I didn't go along with the plan to frame Slate, then I was going to be turned in. Dray had…" She looked beyond Cassidy, and her eyes filled with tears again. "Dear God, you can't begin to know the hell Dray and I have lived in."

"My sympathy is limited," Cassidy warned her. "Who put you up to framing Slate?"

Amanda gripped the table. "I'll tell you everything but that. Everything. I can't tell you who it is. He'll kill Dray. My husband disappeared from the bank today at lunch." The tears were rolling down her face again. "Dray would never do that, just disappear from work and not go back. I'm sure someone has him. Someone who intends to make him keep quiet." Amanda collapsed on the table and began to sob. "He said he would kill both of us if we ever talked. He paid the bank back all of the money I'd embezzled, and he forced us to tell those lies about Slate, but he said he would kill us if we ever revealed what we'd done. He said he'd kill us one at a time, and that he'd make us suffer."

Chapter Fourteen

Cassidy pressed hard on the gas as she drove back to the Double O. Nothing she'd threatened Amanda with had been more terrifying than her fear that Dray would die if she spoke the name of the man who'd masterminded framing Slate. Cassidy had left Amanda's house still not knowing the true face of her enemy, but she had on tape Amanda's confession that Slate had been framed.

Cassidy desperately wanted to go to the sheriff, but she didn't trust the law officers, and she certainly didn't trust Rusty Jones. The way things were shaping up, Rusty seemed the most obvious culprit. Right or wrong, he had power over the local law enforcement.

Her only hope was to get back to the ranch and to get Slate. If they could find Dray and produce him safely, Amanda had agreed to tell the complete truth—in front of everyone.

The Hill Country flashed by her window, and she looked out on the pastures that rolled to the rugged outcroppings of rock that defined the horizon. The land had a harsh beauty that she'd always loved. It was so much like Slate, she realized. So much like herself. Like the land, they had endured. They had not given up, and ultimately, they would prevail. She had to believe that.

Misgivings about leaving Amanda gnawed at her. Her

only consolation was that Amanda was so truly frightened for Dray's life that she would remain at home and cooperate on the hope that Slate could find her husband and bring him back alive. Slate could do it, if anyone could. Cassidy felt a sense of relief as she turned down the driveway to home, to Slate.

As she pulled up to the ranch house at the Double O, she did a double take. There were two sheriff's cars and a black Cadillac parked in front of the house. As she got closer, she was shocked to see Rusty Jones sitting on her front porch.

She got out of the truck slowly and started toward the house. In the distance she could see the ranch hands gathering at the barns. Something was definitely up. Two deputies were walking toward her, coming from the weanling barn.

"Cassidy," Rusty said, stepping forward. "I hate like hell to do this, but you're going to have to come with us." As the sheriff, Noll Owens, walked across the porch toward her, Rusty waved him back. "Let's not make this worse than it has to be," he said softly.

"What?" Cassidy looked from the lawman to the prosecutor. "I'm not going anywhere with you." At that moment, she trusted Rusty Jones less than anyone she knew. She glanced at the ranch house, wondering if Slate was inside. Had he returned from filling in the fake grave? If he was inside, would he stay calm?

"On the contrary," the sheriff said as he pulled a pair of cuffs from his belt. "Cassidy O'Neal, you're under arrest for the murder of Lucky Hill. You have the right to remain silent and the right to an attorney. If you can't afford one, the state will provide you with legal representation."

Cassidy heard the words, but she didn't believe what was happening. "The murder of Lucky Hill? He was fine when he left here. Ask my cook. Lucky knocked Kip in the jaw."

"He was alive when he left the Double O, but he's not now," Rusty said, shaking his head.

"Yeah, he's pretty dead," Sheriff Owens added.

Cassidy didn't resist as the sheriff snapped the handcuffs on one wrist. The whole scene was impossible. Even if Lucky was dead, why would anyone think she'd killed him? "What happened?"

"He was shot," Rusty said. He turned to the sheriff. "Is that really necessary?"

"Procedure," the sheriff said, cuffing Cassidy's hands in front of her.

"I'm telling you, Lucky left here this morning without a scratch on him," Cassidy repeated. "You can ask any of the men."

"We talked to your employees. They were reluctant to tell the truth at first, but they talked." Rusty stepped closer. "They finally admitted they heard you threaten to kill Lucky." Rusty went to his car and returned with something in a paper bag. He held it under Cassidy's nose. "Recognize this?"

She looked into the bag and saw the gun that had been stolen from her safe. "That's Slate's—" She stopped herself, afraid that if she said anything else Slate would be implicated.

"Yes, the weapon that was signed over to Slate Walker, and, from what I understand, the gun was put in your care."

"Someone stole it from my safe," she said. She was beginning to get a picture, and it was one she didn't like.

"You never reported the theft," the sheriff pointed out.

"I only discovered it missing this morning," Cassidy said through clenched teeth.

"Where is Slate?" Rusty asked in a casual tone.

"If I knew, I wouldn't tell you." Cassidy was spitting mad. The shock had worn off, and she realized clearly what was happening. She'd been hornswoggled and framed.

"We suspect that Slate was your accomplice in the murder of Lucky Hill. Both of your fingerprints are on the gun, Cassidy."

"That's because I held it when I put it in my safe," she answered, with growing anger.

"Two of your men disclosed the information that you sent them to dig a grave today." Rusty shook his head. "All of these facts add up to one very solid murder charge." Rusty looked around the ranch, focusing on the barns. "I knew when Slate came back to town he'd only bring trouble."

"Slate has nothing to do with Lucky Hill, and neither do I," Cassidy said clearly. "I've been framed."

"That's what you're saying about Slate and the bank robbery, and it was his ticket to five years in prison," the sheriff said, with no little amount of satisfaction. "Murder gets you a lot more time."

"I didn't kill anyone," Cassidy said. Her anger was beginning to crack, and what lay beneath it was raw worry. Someone had stacked the deck against her, and she had to admit it was done with great style. While she and Slate were busy setting their trap, someone had been doing the same thing to her—a far more serious and deadly trap. And she'd stumbled into it headfirst. It didn't matter that there was no real motive for her to kill Lucky. The circumstantial evidence was all against her.

"I'm sorry, Cassidy," Rusty said. "I really am."

"I'll bet you are," she snapped.

The sheriff grasped her arm and started toward the patrol car. "Let's go." He looked at the deputies, who'd rejoined them. "Okay, men, go on down there and put that animal down."

"What animal?" Cassidy tried to jerk free of him, but he held her in a firm grip.

"We have an order from the judge to destroy that bay

stallion. Lucky came into town and filed charges against the horse, saying he was a killer. He said Cole Benson was worried about the horse being on your property and asked Lucky to keep an eye on the situation, and that you'd try to get even with him for what he'd been doing. I guess he didn't expect you to strike so soon. But just because Lucky's dead doesn't negate his complaint."

Cassidy twisted free of the sheriff. "Lucky is a liar. Joker's no killer. He could have stomped Lucky to death, but he didn't harm a hair on him."

"That's not the story Mr. Hill told before he met his untimely end," Rusty said. "The horse is a range stallion. He's not really your property, and since he's a menace, the county has a right to destroy him. The judge had just issued a ruling on the matter when we got the call reporting Lucky's body."

Cassidy felt the panic threaten to spill over. She had to think. She had to act fast. "I'm in possession of the animal, and that makes him mine. He's confined on my property and he's not a threat to anyone. If you do anything to him, I swear the county will be hit with a lawsuit that will bankrupt it. You'd better check your authority in this matter before you take a rash action."

The sheriff looked uncomfortably at the prosecutor.

"Have the deputies call Judge Harwell," Rusty said. "Get a ruling on the matter of possession before you shoot him." He started to his car, then turned back. His light eyes were calculating. "Where is Slate, Cassidy?" he asked again. "I've known you a long time and I can't believe you weren't coerced into this. If you cooperate with us, we'll see about some kind of deal, a reduced sentence, maybe."

"Drop dead," she answered. She turned to the men at the bunkhouse and called out to them. "Don't let them hurt Joker. I'll be back later." She didn't have time to say more, as the sheriff put his hand on the top of her head and forced her into the patrol car.

THE MINUTE THE SHERIFF'S hand touched Cassidy, Slate was ready to bolt across the lawn and deck the law officer. Only the knowledge that he had to be free, at all costs, prevented such rash behavior. Hard as it was to watch, he knew that he was Cassidy's only real hope. As much as he wanted to feel his fists connect with Sheriff Owens and Rusty Jones, he couldn't. The end result would be that he would be locked up beside Cassidy. He shifted deeper into the cover of the shrubs beside the house.

He clenched his hands at his sides in frustration. It seemed that ever since he'd gotten out of prison, his actions had been more restricted than they ever were behind bars.

He watched helplessly as Cassidy was driven away in the back of the sheriff's car. Rusty Jones followed. Only two deputies were left, and Slate watched as they headed inside the ranch house to use the telephone to call the judge.

In a matter of moments, Joker's fate would be sealed. Slate had no doubt the judge would order the stallion to be destroyed. For all of Cassidy's brave threats, Slate knew that range animals were valued at the price per pound a meat packer would pay.

He made his decision and hurried back to the patio where he'd stashed Cutter's saddle and the hackamore bridle. He'd turned the gelding out in the creek pasture as Cassidy had told him. He'd almost left the saddle, but his training had kicked in. A cowboy never left his gear in the dirt. So he'd carried his tack back to the ranch. Now he was going to need it—and a lot of luck.

The plan to pretend he was dead was over. There was no longer time for traps or subterfuge. Cassidy was behind bars, and the prosecutor and law officers were looking for him.

It had become crystal clear to Slate that the person behind his and Cassidy's troubles was a calculating, clever person. He and Cassidy had thought they could match wits with him, but he was always one step ahead of them. Slate realized that if the gunman who'd shot him in the shoulder had wanted him dead, he would be dead. The flesh wound had been deliberate.

Everything that had happened had been deliberate.

Rusty had released the gun to him only to have it stolen and used to frame Cassidy for murder. It seemed no matter what steps he and Cassidy took, they were always playing into the hands of their enemies.

And now Joker had been handed a death sentence.

Slate picked up the saddle and started toward the barn. He had one opportunity, and each tick of the clock narrowed the chances of his potential success.

At the corral fence, he hefted the saddle and hopped over. So far, no one had seen him. The ranch hands had scattered. None of them wanted to be present when Joker was killed—to stand around and allow it to happen would be a crime. To go up against the law would mean a jail sentence. He understood the dilemma they were in.

He walked directly toward the stallion. There was no time for winning Joker's confidence. Slate looked over his shoulder. The deputies weren't headed his way—yet. But it was only a matter of moments.

"If you ever decided to trust a human, you'd better do it now," Slate said to the horse. He'd always believed that an animal—once it slowed down enough to pay attention—could tell when a human meant to help. He had to put his full faith into believing that Joker would trust him, trust him completely.

"This is going to be more than a little strange," he said, slipping the hackamore bridle over Joker's nose. Other than a snort of surprise, Joker seemed willing. He led the horse back to the corral fence and lifted the saddle onto his back.

Joker spooked sideways, but Slate stayed with him and carefully tightened the girth. This was the moment when the horse might explode, but Slate soothed and talked to him as he made the saddle fast and finally put his weight in the stirrup.

It was all happening too quickly. Even the most docile animal would balk at accepting so much at once, and Slate expected Joker to go nuts. Surprisingly, the big bay stood steady as a rock as Slate lifted himself up and into the saddle.

Joker was a strong animal, and Slate felt his power as the horse adjusted to the unfamiliar weight of a human on his back.

"Hey! Hey, you!"

Slate turned to see the deputies running toward him. They were drawing their pistols as they ran.

"I hope to God you can jump," Slate said as he aimed the stallion at the far fence and squeezed his legs tight.

Joker shot forward as if he'd been propelled from a gun. He never hesitated at the five-foot corral fence. He soared over it and landed on the other side in a full gallop.

"Hey! Come back here!" one deputy yelled.

A shot rang out and Slate ducked lower against Joker's flying mane. It didn't seem possible that the animal could run faster, but Joker lengthened his stride and flew over the rocky ground. Slate headed for the rough country. It was dangerous to ride so fast, but it was even more dangerous to slow down.

Slate smiled to himself at the thought of the two law officers trying to catch horses, saddle them and give chase. They'd get no help from the Double O ranch hands.

Joker instinctively headed northwest, and Slate made no attempt to guide him. When they were several miles away from the Double O, Slate slowed him to a walk. He was amazed that Joker responded to him with such obedience.

He patted the stallion's neck and looked around, getting his bearings. The terrain was far too rugged for a vehicle. If pursuit came, it would have to be on horseback, which would take a lot of organization.

Joker was safe, for the moment.

CASSIDY KNEW THAT ALL of the plans she and Slate had made were in ruins as she sat in the back seat of the patrol car and watched the familiar scenery pass. They would take her to the jail where they would hold her until...until they charged her. She would have to somehow make bond.

She had to get word to Nita. And to Slate. She rubbed the knot of tension between her eyes and looked up to find the sheriff staring at her in the rearview mirror.

"I'm perfectly willing to believe that your part in Lucky's murder came about because of Slate Walker," Sheriff Owens said carefully. "You've always been a law-abiding citizen, Cassidy. I can't help but believe Slate got you into this mess."

"Slate didn't get me into anything," she said. "Here's a fact for you. Last night, someone shot Slate." She thought she saw a flicker of surprise in the sheriff's eyes, but she couldn't be certain. "There *is* someone out there shooting people and killing them, but it isn't me or Slate."

"Your prints are on the gun," the sheriff said.

"And it was found conveniently near the body, right?" She knew the scenario, and it made her furious that Sheriff Owens was so stupid he never questioned it. "Like I'd drop the murder weapon and leave it, with my fingerprints. What else did you find, my checkbook, maybe a piece of family jewelry?"

His gaze dropped from the mirror.

"What? Was there another piece of evidence?"

The sheriff cleared his throat. "We did, uh, find a ring. A wedding band with an inscription."

Cassidy knew instantly which ring he'd found. "It read 'With all my love, forever, Slate.'"

"Then you admit it's your ring?"

"It *was* to be my wedding ring. But Slate went to prison. We never married. I gave the ring to Mary, for safekeeping."

"And the last time you saw it?" the sheriff asked.

Cassidy regarded her options. The truth would not incriminate her or Slate. She leaned against the mesh grill that separated the front seat from the back. "The last time I saw that ring was the day Slate was convicted of attempted armed robbery."

"Then how did it get to the scene of a murder?" the sheriff asked.

"The same way the gun got there. Someone is framing me." She lowered her voice. "If you don't listen to me, innocent people are going to suffer."

"Is that a threat?" he asked angrily.

"I'm not in a position to threaten anyone." She held up her cuffed hands. "If you're not a part of this, then you're being used, Sheriff," she said, sitting back.

Her dealings with Sheriff Owens had been few and far between. He wasn't the brightest man she'd ever met, but until recently she'd never doubted his honesty. It was possible that he was simply being used by someone...like Rusty Jones.

"You honestly expect me to believe the gun with your prints and the ring you admit was to be your wedding ring were deliberately left at the murder scene?"

Cassidy felt her pulse increase. Owens was playing like he didn't believe her, but there was doubt in his voice. Real doubt. "Think about it. Would I accidentally leave *two* items that would tie me to a murder? That's too much care-lessness even for an idiot.''

In the rearview mirror, she saw his eyes narrow. ''Who would frame you for murder?'' he asked.

''The same person who framed Slate for attempted bank robbery.'' She saw that she was losing him. His eyes went from interested to bored in an instant. ''Don't dismiss me,'' she said urgently. It was time for a choice, and one she couldn't back away from. ''I have a witness who says that Slate was framed.'' How far was she willing to trust the sheriff? Cassidy swallowed.

''The state had two witnesses who put Slate in that bank with a gun. They testified under oath.''

''And one is recanting,'' Cassidy whispered. ''Amanda admitted to me this morning that she lied under oath.''

Owens tipped up the brim of his hat and wiped his hot forehead. ''You better not be fooling around with me,'' he said, as he drove into the sheriff's parking lot. ''I'm not in the mood to be made a fool of.''

''Believe me, Sheriff, I'm not in the mood to kid around.''

When he opened the back door, she sprang out. ''I need to use the phone,'' she said. ''You've got to stop them from shooting my horse.''

Owens looked at his watch. ''I don't know...the horse doesn't have anything to do with this.''

''Of course he does. This is all part of—'' She held out her hands. ''I don't have time to explain. You have to believe me.''

''I don't know.''

Cassidy grasped his forearm. ''I am begging you to listen to me. That horse didn't hurt anyone. At least postpone this until all the issues can be sorted through. That isn't asking a lot.'' She wanted to threaten, but she knew that would be the wrong tactic. ''Please, Sheriff.''

"Okay." He unlocked the cuffs and led the way into the courthouse. He picked up the first phone he saw and dialed the number Cassidy gave him. In a moment he had one of the deputies on the line.

"Hold off on shooting the horse," he said. He paused. "Yeah, is that right?" He looked at Cassidy. "I thought you said Slate had been shot."

"In the shoulder."

"Well, he wasn't hurt bad. He just took off on that stallion. Roscoe said he was headed for the ravines."

"Thank God," Cassidy said, more relieved than she could say.

"See if you can get a lead on where Walker might be taking that stud horse. It's not the animal we're interested in now, it's Slate Walker. He's still wanted as an accessory to murder," the sheriff said before he hung up the phone.

He looked at Cassidy. "Now, tell me about that false testimony," he said, settling back into a chair. "I've got the rest of the afternoon and you're not going anywhere."

SLATE HAD TWO immediate options, and he liked neither of them. He could turn Joker loose and hope the stallion didn't stray over onto Blue Vista land, or he could try to confine the horse in the small arroyo near Sycamore Ridge. But that would mean Joker would be a sitting duck if anyone came after him.

Slate got off the horse and removed the saddle. He led Joker with the hackamore bridle, but it might as well have been a silk string. Joker followed as if he were the best-trained animal in Texas.

Slate stopped at the arroyo and made up his mind. Joker would be safer there, at least overnight. They'd stopped for water when they crossed Raging Creek, and Joker would have to make do with the grass that was foragable. "You'll be fine," Slate told him as he unbridled him and went about blocking off the entrance. If Joker was determined, he could easily escape. Slate didn't have the time or material to construct a solid fence.

It was a good three-mile walk back to the ranch, and Slate took off at a brisk pace. His shoulder throbbed, but it hadn't started bleeding. Worse than his physical pain was his worry over Cassidy. She'd been framed for Lucky Hill's murder. The first thing Slate had to do was find out what had really happened.

Forty minutes later he was walking across the back lawn of the ranch. He noticed that Nita was back with Lindsey, but he bypassed the ranch house and went to the bunkhouse.

"Slate!" Randy Patrick nearly dropped the bridle he was cleaning as Slate walked in the door.

"What happened with Lucky? I need the details, if you have any," Slate said.

There was a moment of silence before Randy spoke up. "Best we can tell he was shot on Highway 51. That's the talk, anyway. He'd gone into town and filed a complaint against Joker, and he was headed west when he was killed." Randy shrugged. "The sheriff is saying that Miss Cassidy killed him."

"That's hogwash and you know it," Slate answered angrily.

"I know," Randy said, gathering the nodding approval of three other hands. "Miss Cassidy wouldn't hurt a fly. So what did you do with Joker?" Randy's grin reflected everyone's there. "That was some stunt. We heard you rode him over the fence."

"He's safe enough." Slate looked at the men. "I need your help."

He saw the shifting of gazes. They didn't trust him. They didn't know him. But if he was going to help Cassidy, he needed them.

Slate had done a lot of thinking on his walk back to the Double O, and he had come to several conclusions. Amanda and Dray Tyree had been in on his frame-up. Clyde Barlow had also been involved in some manner. The wild card was the man he'd seen in Dray's office.

In all of the trial testimony, there had been no mention of the stranger. Even with his memory returning, Slate had only a glimpse of the back of his head, covered by a cowboy hat. It wasn't much to go on, but Slate was positive this stranger held the key.

"I need Kip to take Nita and Lindsey to the sheriff's office and make bond for Cassidy. Clay, you and two other men follow them in a separate vehicle. Take your guns, and if anyone threatens Cassidy or that little girl, I expect you to defend them."

He felt the tension in the room. The ranch hands had no reason to trust him. He was a convicted felon, a man who had been publicly convicted of a crime, but he knew they would come to Cassidy's aid.

"I need a couple of men to go up and guard Joker. He's in a dry gulch near Sycamore Ridge."

"I know the place," Randy said. "I'll go."

"Me, too," another hand volunteered.

"The rest of you keep your weapons ready and watch out for the ranch. Ride the boundaries. I don't know who's doing this, but there's every chance they'll strike while Cassidy is down."

The remaining hands nodded.

"I'm ready," Kip said, walking to the gun rack on the wall and hefting a shotgun. "If anyone tries to harm a hair on Cassidy's head, they'll answer to me."

Chapter Fifteen

In the truck he'd borrowed from Clay, Slate headed for the Tyree home. Expecting roadblocks as the sheriff began a search for him, Slate knew that he would not allow anyone to stop him. He would find the person responsible for Lucky's death, and he would prevent Cassidy from standing trial in a mockery of justice. He knew too well how it felt to be unjustly accused.

The garage door of the Tyree house was open, and Slate saw that both cars were gone. He'd expected Dray to be at the bank, but Amanda was another issue. His jaw tightened. He didn't have time to wait for her to return. He needed to talk to her now!

He parked around a curve in the street and made his way through backyards to the house. It was a simple matter to slip into the garage. Halfway across the cement floor, he stopped. The back door was open.

Dread crept over Slate. Folks didn't drive off and leave their houses wide open. Unless there was an emergency.

Moving carefully, he slipped inside and stopped at the kitchen doorway. The house was a wreck. Dishes had been pulled out of the cabinets and smashed on the floor. It looked as if someone had thrown a tantrum and destroyed everything in his path.

Slate followed the destruction through the house. With

each room he left behind, his dread grew. In the back of his mind, he feared Amanda was dead. He didn't want to find her body. He didn't want to witness another scene of ugly violence. But he had to know.

As he entered the bedroom, he found the destruction more selective. It appeared that only expensive items had been trashed. Clothes were ripped from the closet and thrown to the floor. A cloying mixture of scents came from what was obviously Amanda's dressing room, and when Slate peered into the elegantly furnished room, he found bottle after bottle of expensive perfume smashed on the marble floor.

The demolition of the house was clearly personal. Amanda had deeply angered someone, and they had struck back.

But where was Amanda?

That was the question that propelled Slate through the rest of the house. As he finished his search of the second floor, he was relieved to find the house empty. Somehow, Amanda had escaped. Or been taken.

He was headed down the stairs when he heard the sirens and knew the police were headed for the Tyree home. Perhaps a neighbor had tipped the law about someone in the house.

He tried to remember if he'd touched any surface, left any fingerprints, but it was too late. Two sheriff's cars skidded to a halt in the driveway, and through the lace kitchen curtains that were spattered with ketchup, Slate saw four deputies get out of the cars and crouch behind the open car doors, pistols trained on the house.

Slate opened a window in the dining room and dropped to the ground outside. He was halfway down the block before he slowed enough to turn around.

Somehow he'd gotten a break. He'd escaped without anyone seeing him.

He got into the borrowed truck and headed to the Comfort Ranch Bank. Dray Tyree was next on his list.

CASSIDY HAD CONVINCED the sheriff to send units to Amanda's house to bring her in for questioning. Sheriff Owens, with alarm evident in his face, had listened to the tape that Cassidy had made of her conversation with Amanda. Owens had also sent a car to the Comfort Ranch Bank to see if Dray Tyree was indeed missing.

As Cassidy helplessly waited, the radio on the dispatcher's desk crackled to life.

"This is car eleven. We need the fingerprint team at the Tyree residence. The house has been ransacked and there is no sign of Mrs. Tyree. I repeat, Mrs. Tyree is missing from the premises and the house has been thoroughly trashed."

"I'll send the investigators right away," Owens answered. "Search the area. Question the neighbors."

He stood up and walked to Cassidy. When he stood in front of her, his eyes narrowed. "You wouldn't know anything about that, now, would you?"

"I told you, Sheriff. Amanda promised to wait there. She was worried about her husband, and I promised I would try to help her."

"You should have reported all of this to me the minute you knew about it."

She could see that he was getting angry. "I didn't know if I could trust you," she answered simply. "As I told you, Slate and I aren't certain who we can trust."

"I'm in the same predicament," he said. "Every time something around here goes wrong, I find that you or Slate have been there. It isn't exactly a situation that builds my trust in you."

Cassidy saw his point. "I talked with Amanda. She was fine and the house was fine when I left."

"How do I know you weren't threatening Mrs. Tyree to get her to say all of those things on that tape? How do I know you didn't take her somewhere?"

"It's in my best interest for Amanda to be found safe. I know that tape isn't admissible as evidence that Slate was framed," Cassidy countered. She lifted her chin. "How do I know you and Rusty Jones didn't plant that replica gun at the bank?"

Owens stared into her eyes, unflinching. "It looks like a standoff."

"Maybe." But Cassidy felt the first real hope she'd had since talking to Amanda. She didn't know who'd framed Slate for the bank robbery, but her gut instinct told her that Sheriff Owens had not been involved. At least not wittingly.

Across the room, the dispatcher called out to the sheriff. Cassidy followed him over to the desk and listened to the deputy from the bank call in.

"Dray Tyree is missing. Mr. Barlow said Dray went to lunch and never returned. They're worried about him."

"Start canvassing the town," the sheriff said. "I'll be out there to give you a hand." He turned back to Cassidy. "You're going to have to wait in a holding cell, I'm afraid."

The door to the sheriff's office opened and Cassidy heard her daughter's voice.

"Mama! Are they going to put you in jail?"

She turned toward Lindsey and held out her arms. As she caught her daughter tightly to her chest, she heard Kip's angry voice.

"We've come for Miss Cassidy, and we're not leaving here without her."

"Well I'll be damned," Sheriff Owens said in exasperation. "I don't need this right now."

SLATE DROVE the speed limit to the Comfort Ranch Bank. The one thing he didn't want to do was attract attention from the law. He was glad of his precautions when he turned the corner and saw the brown-and-tan patrol car parked in the lot. As he watched, two deputies came out of the bank and split up. One headed toward town and the other walked to the nearby businesses.

They were canvassing the area.

Slate parked and made his way on foot to the back of the bank. The Comfort Ranch Bank had once been an old general store, and though it offered a lot of history and was highly touted by the Texas Preservation Society, the old structure had a number of weaknesses as a bank.

It occurred to Slate, not for the first time, that anyone hell-bent on robbing the place would have been a lot smarter to wait until the bank was closed and break into the back. A frontal robbery, in broad daylight while the employees were in the bank, didn't make good sense.

He found the window that gave him a glimpse of Clyde Barlow's office. When he peeped inside he saw Barlow pacing the room. Seated in front of his desk was Karlie Mason, sobbing as if her heart would break.

Slate watched in fascination as Clyde went to his secretary and pulled her into his arms. The comfort Clyde was giving Karlie was a lot more than employee-employer. Slate leaned his forehead against the bulletproof glass of the window.

At last he understood.

Slate shifted to the corner of the building, checked for the deputies, and when the coast was clear he walked in the front door. The young blond woman behind the counter smiled at him and started to call out a greeting. It was almost a rerun of the sequence of events that had happened five years before. Slate saw her expression shift from welcoming to one of alarm, but he kept going past her and entered Clyde Barlow's private office.

He swept past Karlie's desk and pushed open the inner office door. Clyde stepped away from Karlie as if he'd been scalded. Guilt turned to anger as he recognized Slate.

"How dare you—"

"I dare because you lied." Slate kept his voice low, but there was no hiding the anger that permeated each syllable. "You lied to cover your own butt." His gaze drilled into Clyde. The banker looked helplessly at Karlie, then he sank back into his chair.

"Yes, I lied."

"Clyde!" Karlie's voice was a cry of protest.

"I can't lie anymore, Karlie. Whatever we've done that's wrong, none of it is worse than the lies I told about Slate." He covered his eyes with his hand.

"Why?" Slate demanded. "Why me?"

Clyde lowered his hand and met Slate's gaze. "Believe it or not, it didn't have a thing to do with you. You were just the luckless bastard who got caught up in it."

"I lost five years. I had a daughter and didn't know it. My mother died while I was in prison, and I didn't even know enough to grieve for her." Slate felt as if the hot, angry words would tear his throat. He saw Karlie cower and sink down in her chair, her sobs steady and hopeless.

"I can't undo any of what I've done, Slate. But don't ever think that I haven't suffered for it."

"Not nearly as much as you're going to suffer."

Clyde's smile was thin. "My wife is dying of cancer. I had hoped to give her the last of her life in peace. I thought I was doing a kindness by not asking for a divorce, by keeping my true feelings hidden." He got up and went to Karlie and put his hand on her shoulder. "I can see that I haven't been kind to anyone. Only cowardly. The result is that I've managed to hurt everyone I love, and even acquaintances.''

Clyde's words were so completely hopeless that Slate felt his anger lessen. It didn't seem possible, but he actually felt sorry for the banker. "Who put you up to lying about me?"

Instead of answering, Clyde walked to the door. He closed it gently. "Don't ask me that, Slate. Dray is missing. I'm afraid something terrible has happened to him."

"You were all in on it. You and Amanda and Dray. And you, too, Karlie."

"No," Clyde said. "Karlie didn't know a thing. I swear that."

"As if I'd believe anything you swore to," Slate answered sarcastically. "You took an oath in that courtroom."

"Yes I did," Clyde asserted. "Every word I said was the truth. I didn't see what happened in the front of the bank." He lowered his gaze. "I made it a point not to look."

"Oh, Clyde." Karlie went to him and put her arms around him.

The anger had slipped away from Slate and he felt only bitterness. "Who told you not to look?" he asked.

"Dray," Clyde answered in a voice that broke. "Dray said he was in serious trouble, that he'd gotten the bank into trouble. He said that if what he'd done was discovered, I would go down, too, because I hadn't done my job. And he said that he'd have to tell about Karlie."

"And Dray told you to make the appointment for me at noon on that day?"

"Yes, he was very specific about the time."

Slate took a few steps closer to Clyde. "Who was in that office with Dray?"

"I don't know," Clyde said. "There wasn't supposed to be anyone else in the bank."

"Think," Slate demanded. "I saw him, the back of his head. There was someone in there with Dray."

"I didn't come out of my office. I told Amanda to keep you in the bank lobby, like Dray said. The door was half open, but I never looked out."

Slate believed Clyde was telling the truth, but it wasn't good enough. "Dray is missing, and so is Amanda. Someone ransacked their house. There's a good chance that the man in Dray's office is the man who has both of them. Think, Clyde. And think hard."

SHERIFF OWENS PICKED UP the telephone. "I'm calling Rusty," he said.

Cassidy was across the space and put her hand on the switch hook. "No," she said as calmly as she could.

"I have to..." He let the sentence die as he stared at her. "You think it might have been Rusty?"

"He knew Slate's father's gun had been thrown into the pond. He knew there was no way the gun at the trial could be Slate's." She took her time. "He knew this and yet he prosecuted Slate."

"I don't know," the sheriff said slowly. "Rusty never struck me as a man who'd do something like that."

"Did Slate strike you as the kind of man who'd rob a bank? Do I strike you as the kind of woman who'd kill Lucky Hill?" She nodded. "You arrested both of us, remember?"

Sheriff Owens replaced the phone. "Okay, you're free to go with your family. But go straight out to the Double O and stay there until we find the Tyrees."

Cassidy hugged Lindsey to her.

"You're not going to jail?" Lindsey asked in a whisper loud enough for everyone to hear.

"Not today," Cassidy answered, smiling. She looked up at Kip and Nita. "Thanks for coming to the rescue."

"We weren't necessary," Nita pointed out. "But where is Slate?"

Cassidy saw the sheriff's interest pick up immediately. "I'm sure he's out on the range somewhere with Joker." She gathered her purse and the tape recorder. "We'll head home."

"Be sure that's where you go," Sheriff Owens said.

"Let us know the minute you hear anything," Cassidy said. She carried her daughter out of the sheriff's office and into the sunshine. When she had Lindsey safely buckled in her seat in the back of the car, she turned to Kip. "Where is Slate?" she asked, unable to hide her worry any longer.

"He didn't say where he was going," Kip said.

"I have to find him." Cassidy tried to figure where he'd go. Perhaps to Amanda's. "Drive through Comfort," she told Kip. "Go by the bank."

IT WAS JUST A HUNCH, but Cassidy knew that Slate would take action. Dray was the logical step. She sat in the back seat, holding her daughter's hand and answering the million and one questions Lindsey asked with such passion. Several times Nita looked back at her, a question in her eyes.

"I'm fine," Cassidy assured her as she gritted her teeth against the slow passage of each mile. Kip was driving the speed limit, but Cassidy wanted to move with hypersonic velocity.

As soon as the bank appeared, Cassidy saw the patrol car. Soon Sheriff Owens would be there, and he would be aware that she hadn't stuck to the letter of her agreement to go back to the ranch.

"Let me out here," she said.

"Cassidy, I don't think this is a good idea." Nita reached

over the back seat and touched Cassidy's arm. "Think about it. This could be dangerous."

Cassidy looked at her daughter. Lindsey was the most important thing in her life. And Slate was her father. He was also the man she loved, the only man she would ever love. She'd accepted that five long years before.

What she was about to do was dangerous. There was no hiding from that truth. Her reasons were many. She wanted justice for Slate, and for herself. She wanted to be with Slate, to be at his side, because they would protect each other.

Also, in a strange way, she felt responsible for what had happened to Amanda. She had no evidence, but she felt it was probable that someone had followed her to Amanda's house. When she'd left, they'd snatched Amanda and destroyed the house.

But Lindsey was the primary reason she was going into the bank. Lindsey deserved to know the truth about her father. Lindsey needed his love, and his presence in her life.

Cassidy leaned across the seat and kissed Lindsey. She turned to Kip and Nita. "Keep her safe for me. Don't let anyone near her, except me or Slate."

Nita grasped her hand. "You can count on us."

Kip nodded. "We'll be at the ranch, waiting for you."

Blinking back tears, Cassidy closed the car door and began walking to the bank.

The minute she entered, she knew something was wrong. The teller's face was strained with distress, and she made no attempt to stop Cassidy as she went into Clyde Barlow's office.

Slate was the first thing Cassidy saw when she entered, and she went to him with a soft cry of relief.

With his arm still around her, Slate turned to Clyde. "Who was the man in Dray's office? Was it Rusty?"

Karlie had managed to gain control of her emotions, and she stood up. "I don't know who was in the bank five years ago, but today, just before lunch, Dray was talking on the telephone with someone. He was upset." She brushed a tear away. "I heard him say that he'd kept up his end of the bargain, and he was angry. But I could tell he was scared, too. He was arguing. I didn't know what it was about, but he was going out to meet someone. He wrote something down on the pad in his office."

Slate didn't give her a chance to finish. He was out of Clyde's office and into Dray's, searching for the notepad. Cassidy was on his heels. Slate found the pad and examined the blank top page. "It's an old trick," he said, searching the desk until he found a pencil. Turning the lead sideways, he gently colored the page.

The words created by the indentation in the pad were faint, but they were there. "Highway 51, near the junction." Slate read them aloud and turned to Cassidy.

"That's where Lucky Hill was murdered," Cassidy said. She had a terrible feeling that Dray's body, too, was somewhere near that location.

"Let's go." Slate handed the notepad to Clyde, who'd followed them into the office. "You should give this to the deputies."

"You should wait for them," Clyde said.

"Amanda and Dray may still be alive," Cassidy answered. "Even if I didn't care what happened to them, Slate and I need their testimony to clear his name."

She felt Slate's fingers close over her hand, and they ran out of the bank and into the slanting afternoon light. It was summer and the days were long, but darkness wasn't too far away. Cassidy stretched her legs to keep up with Slate as they ran to the pickup.

IT WASN'T FAR to the place where Lucky had been killed, and Cassidy filled Slate in about her conversation with

Amanda as they drove.

His emotions vacillated from pride in Cassidy's courage to fear at the realization that she could have been hurt. He kept her hand in his, wanting to force her to stay behind in Comfort, to be someplace safe. But he knew better than to bring up that issue. No place was really safe for either of them, until his name was cleared and the guilty parties arrested.

"Why Highway 51?" Cassidy asked softly as she intently stared out the front windshield. "The side of a highway is a strange meeting place. And Highway 51 is sort of a local dead end."

"It is," Slate agreed. Unless it was specifically set up for a drive-by shooting. Highway 51 was isolated, leading toward the Guadalupe River and rugged terrain where hiding places were plentiful. It had once been an important local road, but the interstate had destroyed its importance.

As Slate and Cassidy bumped along it, Slate noted that the county was no longer even maintaining it.

Lucky's truck marked the spot. Slate noted that the sheriff hadn't had time to send a tow truck out to remove the vehicle. Surely they'd searched it, but he and Cassidy had to try for themselves. Slate pulled up in front of it and they got out, walking slowly toward the place where Lucky's blood still marked the dry summer grass.

"He wasn't my favorite cowhand, but I hate this," Cassidy said as she skirted the area and went to examine the truck. Slate searched the bed of the vehicle while Cassidy took the cab.

Lucky's saddle was there, untouched, and Slate guessed it was because no one had happened along on the road. Highway 51 was that deserted. There were empty drink cans, a bedroll and a few tools, but nothing of significance.

"What about it?" he called to Cassidy.

She held up a fistful of papers. "Receipts for meals and things from the tack store." She shrugged. "Nothing helpful."

Slate jumped to the ground and looked at the tires. He could find nothing embedded in the treads that gave him any leads. It looked hopeless.

Cassidy leaned dejectedly against the bumper. "I'm worried sick about Amanda and Dray. There's nothing we can do, it seems."

"I know." Slate stood beside her, pulling her against him for comfort. "I keep trying to figure it out. Lucky left the ranch and probably went straight to the sheriff's office to file the complaint about Joker. And then he went somewhere else—"

"Or he could have telephoned someone," Cassidy pointed out.

"Someone who told him to come out here." Slate swept his hand around the scrub-cedar-dotted fields that showed outcroppings of rock. "Someone who set up this meeting."

"And then killed him." Cassidy turned to Slate. "It would have to be someone in the vicinity." She stared at him. "Slate, it has to be Rusty. His office is right by the courthouse."

"I'm afraid you're right." Slate agreed.

"Then Rusty knows where Amanda and Dray are." Cassidy's voice had taken on a note of excitement. "Surely he wouldn't do anything to them."

"A man who's killed once..." Slate didn't want her to get her hopes up.

"Let's go," Cassidy said, already moving toward the truck. "Let's go to his office and see if we can make him talk."

Slate was right behind her when his eye caught something bright on the ground. He bent to pick it up, only to discover it was a piece of tin, a tab from a drink can.

"What is it?" Cassidy had stopped and turned around to watch him.

"It's no—" He bent closer to the ground. The tire impression was hard to distinguish, but once Slate made it out in the grass, he knew what it was. He straightened slowly.

"This old road, does Cole Benson still own property on it?"

He could see his question had caught Cassidy by surprise. She shook her head. "I don't know. When he bought Blue Vista, he never mentioned the old Benson place again. The land was poor. I assumed he sold it. Why?"

"I may be jumping to conclusions, Cassidy, but the tracks here are from a dual. I know plenty of ranchers own them, but Cole Benson also has one."

Cassidy hurried back and bent to examine the grass that had been crushed down by the double-wheeled vehicle. "My God, Slate."

"Is it possible?" he asked her.

Cassidy took a deep breath. "I had thought of Cole earlier, in regard to the bank robbery. But it just seemed so unlikely."

"That he would frame me to get me out of the way so he could win the rodeo purse?"

"But there was no guarantee he would win, even if you were out of the competition."

"But he did."

"Yes, he did."

He steadied Cassidy against his side. Cole had become her neighbor, and in some ways a close friend. She would also know that Cole's machinations had been directed not only at money and the ranch land, but also at having her.

"Lucky was working for Cole, wasn't he," she said tonelessly. "He *did* set the rock slide, and he must have seen me putting the gun in the safe. He was the one who shot at Joker, and at you. He wasn't trying to kill you, he was trying to drive you away."

"Cole knew that once we joined forces and began poking at the bank robbery, we'd eventually figure it out. Or my memory would come back and I'd remember that he was in the bank with Dray the day of the attempted robbery." Slate was certain now that it had been Cole Benson in Dray's office. When the truth was told, it would probably be Cole who shot him, not Dray.

"He was?" Cassidy asked. "You never said."

"I didn't remember everything until earlier today. There was a man in Dray's office. I saw only the back of his head." Slate's smile was a bitter twist. "Even now, when I can remember it perfectly, I can't say that it was Cole because I never saw his face. It was him, though. I'm certain of it."

Cassidy thought for a moment. "Cole has no way of knowing what you saw. I'm sure he thought if he could get you out of town, you'd move on, make a life where old memories weren't important. Even if your memory did come back, if you'd started a new life, you wouldn't be inclined to come back to Comfort and dig up the past."

"And when I didn't leave, he decided to take care of me another way." Slate thought of the near misses that had occurred in the last week. "And you got caught in the backlash. Cole never meant to frame you for Lucky's murder. It was my gun, and the wedding ring should have been in my possession since we never married. He'd planned it carefully, but it didn't work right."

Cassidy suddenly pushed away from the truck. "If Cole still owns the property out here, there's a chance that might be where he's holding Amanda and Dray."

Slate caught her excitement. "You're right." But his enthusiasm was immediately dampened by another thought. "If he has Dray and Amanda out here, he's going to be armed. And this time he won't care if he kills us."

Chapter Sixteen

Cassidy could tell that Slate was chomping at the bit, but they'd both agreed that they had to wait for Sheriff Owens and the deputies. She could hear the sirens in the distance, and she knew that Clyde Barlow and Karlie had sent the lawmen out to the murder scene.

The old Benson house was well fortified, and if their suspicions were correct, Cole had already killed one man. Cornered, Cole might not hesitate to kill again. If he was holding Dray and Amanda as hostages, there were too many risks involved in trying to rush the small log house tucked against the side of a cliff.

Cassidy remembered the house well. It was a regular fortress. In her opinion, only a show of great force would convince Cole to give himself up and release Amanda and Dray. With lawmen surrounding the house, he might realize that escape was hopeless. That was the scenario she prayed would happen.

Sheriff Owens shot her a black look as he walked up, but he had no time to argue with her——Slate bombarded the lawman with the facts they'd uncovered.

Leaning against the truck, Cassidy listened as Slate and the sheriff went over the fine details of the past events. Cassidy chose to stand back and let Slate handle it. It was, essentially, his story to tell. He'd suffered the five years in prison, unjustly accused and convicted.

A strong wave of love washed over her as she heard Sheriff Owens's apology and his admission that he'd been easily led to pin the blame on Slate. But it was the way Slate stuck out his hand and shook with the sheriff that made her feel she might truly burst with love and pride. A lesser man would have been petty and aggrieved. Not Slate.

She walked over to them. "Well," she said, "what's the plan?"

Owens looked at Slate. "Your hus…Slate, here, says he'll slip in the back of the cabin if my men and I can divert Cole's attention to the front. I'm hoping Cole will see reason and surrender, but if he doesn't, then Slate can try to get the hostages out. I think it's a good plan."

Cassidy thought otherwise, but she nodded. "Okay. I think we'd better get a move on it." She glanced pointedly at the sun, which was hanging in the tops of the cedars.

"Let's go." The sheriff signaled his men and they caravanned to the small side road that disappeared around a curve between rocky land that was covered in dense cedar growth.

"Slate, I'll go with you," Cassidy said.

He almost refused her, but he nodded, handing her the gun the sheriff had given him.

"I don't like this," Owens said, handing Slate another automatic. "She should stay here with me."

"I'll stay behind a tree," Cassidy reassured him. Only she knew the truth about the back of Cole's cabin. The back door was bolted from the inside with a stout wooden bar. The only way in was a small bathroom window, and Slate was too broad-shouldered to fit through it. If anyone got into the back of the house, it was going to be her.

"Keep her out of bullet range," Owens warned Slate.

Cassidy smiled and reached for Slate's hand. Together

they ran west, then north, cutting through the trees and moving as fast as they could. Sheriff Owens had given them fifteen minutes to get into position before he alerted the occupants of the cabin that they were surrounded.

As they darted and slipped through the woods, Cassidy finally accepted that Slate's name would be cleared. No one could give him back the five years, but Sheriff Owens had agreed to do everything in his power to set the record straight.

Cassidy saw the dim outline of the cabin before Slate did, and she put out a halting hand to still him. The dark wood and stone seemed to be a part of the cliff. The trees surrounding it were so thick that she could move within ten feet of the house and still retain good cover.

She waited for Slate to notice the way the house was built.

"There's only one window," he said angrily. "It's so small I can't—"

"That's why I came," she said.

Slate turned to her. "You knew!"

"I used to come out here sometimes to work with Cole's mother's mare. It was before I started at Three Sisters. I remembered how odd it was that the house had only that small back window. It opens into the bathroom. There is a back door, but they have it bolted with a four-by-four. You could never break it down."

"But you think you can get in the window and open the back door for me?"

She could see Slate wasn't impressed. "I can. And I intend to."

"Cassidy, you can't. It's too dangerous."

She let him finish, and then she went to him. She placed her hand against his jaw and felt the slight roughness of his beard. "I have to, Slate. And I know you understand why. Amanda was once my very good friend. If there's a chance I can help her, I have to try."

Before Slate could respond, the sheriff's amplified voice came from the front of the small cabin. "Cole Benson! This is Sheriff Owens!"

"We don't have time to argue," Cassidy said. "You can boost me up to the window. That would be a big help." She didn't wait for his answer but closed the distance to the house. When she felt his hands around her waist, lifting her so that she could push the window open and grasp the sill, she knew that whatever faced them in life, they'd work together as a team.

Straddling the sill, she smiled down at him. "I'll open the door," she mouthed, and disappeared into the house.

The small bathroom was dimly lit by the setting sun, but as Cassidy inched the door open, the hallway was dark as a cave. She listened carefully but heard no sound of occupancy. For the first time she seriously considered that they'd miscalculated. Perhaps Cole wasn't involved. Perhaps if it was him, he'd taken Amanda and Dray somewhere else. Perhaps they were dead.

That last thought threatened to paralyze her, but she forced herself forward into the hallway, closing the door behind her. Now she had only memory and what she could feel with her hands to guide her.

She remembered the layout of the house. It was small and compact, and, four steps along the hall, she felt the door to the den. Opposite was the kitchen. Or she could continue straight ahead to one of the two bedrooms. As she remembered the furnishings, she thought the bigger bedroom was the smartest choice. If Amanda and Dray were confined, that would be the easiest place to restrain them.

It also put her near the back door.

Testing each step before she put her whole weight on it, she eased along. Her fingers found the solid four-by-four timber that was used to bolt the door. Very carefully she started to lift it.

The wood was wedged tightly, and Cassidy gritted her teeth, using all of her strength. At last she felt it begin to move.

She didn't hear the footsteps behind her or see the dark figure that stood in the hallway watching.

"Who's waiting outside the door?" Cole asked softly.

Cassidy felt a jolt of fear so intense she thought she might die, but her heart continued beating and she turned to confront the man who'd been her neighbor, someone she'd considered a friend.

"Where's Amanda?" she asked as calmly as she could.

"I can't believe you're so concerned about someone who betrayed you, who lied and ruined your life. It was Amanda's greed that gave me the opportunity to set Slate up. She embezzled, and Dray tried to cover for her."

Cassidy saw the gun in his hand. It was dark and deadly, and she could hear the threat in his voice. Her own gun was tucked in the back of her waist, but to reach for it might be a deadly mistake. "The sheriff is outside, Cole. We can all talk this through. The past is over and done. No one can give Slate back the time he spent in prison. We can talk it all out."

"No amount of talk can give Lucky Hill back his life." Cole smiled. "He thought he could blackmail me. I knew he was a greedy fool, but I didn't think he was that stupid."

"There's no escape for you, Cole," Cassidy said. She had to be strong. She couldn't afford to show how frightened she was.

"I have hostages. Enough to spare in case I have to kill one or two."

"Then Amanda and Dray are still alive?" It was the first hopeful thing she'd heard from him. "Where are they? Can I see them?"

"See them? You'll be joining them shortly." His voice turned bitter. "This could all have ended differently. You were coming around. You were beginning to care for me. I worked to make you care, and you were beginning to. You owe it to me. I won. I beat Slate in the bronc riding. I bought the land that you loved. Everything that you wanted. I became everything the people in Comfort honored. If Slate hadn't come back, you would have loved me. I deserve love. No matter what anyone said, I deserve to be loved."

Cassidy had only her instincts. "I could never have loved you that way, Cole. Whether Slate came back or not, I would have always loved him."

"You were getting over him. If he hadn't come back—" He angrily bit off the last of the sentence. "He's out there, isn't he? He's the one outside the door, waiting to come in." An edge of cleverness seeped into his tone. "So we'll open the door and let him in. I might not get away, but I'll have the satisfaction of taking him to hell with me."

Before Cassidy could stop him, he swept the timber out of the way and pulled the back door open. Cassidy started to cry out, but Cole grabbed her, his hand covering her mouth. "One word and I'll go in there and put a bullet in Amanda's head. You understand?"

Cassidy could barely breathe, but she managed a nod. Cole held her in front of him with his arm around her throat, and he loosened his grip enough for her to breathe and talk. He had given her a clue into his thinking. "You deserve love, Cole. But love is given. You can't force someone to love you."

"Not even my own mother," he said, his angry voice growing loud. "I was never good enough. Never smart enough. No matter how hard I tried."

Cassidy started to deny it, but thought better of such a move. She changed directions. "You blackmailed Amanda and Dray. You even blackmailed Clyde Barlow. And you pulled Clyde deeper into it by helping him sell Three Sisters and skimming off part of the profits. You are very smart, Cole. There's no doubt about that.''

''Living in a small town has its advantages. If you watch closely enough, you can learn people's innermost secrets.''

He was proud of his actions. Cassidy felt disgust. She'd seen the hard edge of Cole before, with his workers, with his attitude toward the range horses. But she'd never dreamed how deep his cruelty ran.

''Look!'' He forced her to look out into the night. To her horror, she saw Slate moving from tree to tree. He was nothing but a black shadow, but she recognized him. ''Should we wait until he comes inside? I want him to see you in my arms.''

Cassidy twisted, trying to free herself, but it only made Cole tighten his hold. She forced herself to relax. She had one chance. The hallway was so dark that Cole hadn't noticed the gun in her jeans. She eased her hand behind her back and gripped the handle. The waistband of her jeans prevented her finding the trigger, and she moved her fingers millimeter by millimeter, trying desperately not to alert Cole to what she was doing.

His attention was focused on Slate. Cassidy struggled to find the gun's trigger as she watched the man she loved draw ever closer to his death. She started to call out, but Cole's arm was brutally clamped on her throat, almost choking her into unconsciousness.

''Watch, Cassidy,'' Cole said.

Her finger found the trigger just as Slate shifted from the last tree and started toward the open door. He assumed it was safe to enter, that she'd opened the door for him. She could see that his gun was drawn but aimed at the ground.

She had no choice. Angling the gun barrel away from her own body, Cassidy pulled the trigger. The gunshot was so loud, she wasn't certain if she'd hit Cole or not. The repercussion had snagged the weapon deeper in her jeans, but she felt Cole's grip loosen and she took the opportunity and jerked free.

Whirling around and drawing the gun, she aimed at Cole only to see him stagger and fall back against the wall. Then Slate was beside her, his own weapon trained on Cole as he pulled her against his side and held her.

"Drop it," he ordered Cole.

"Damn you both," Cole answered as he let his pistol clatter to the floor.

"Come on, Sheriff," Slate called out.

The front door burst open and lawmen swarmed the house. They found Amanda and Dray, tied and gagged in the big double bed, and released them. Someone hit a light switch and Cassidy found herself staring at Cole, who leaned against the wall. A bullet wound in his left thigh bled profusely, but he made no attempt to staunch the flow. One of the deputies applied a tourniquet and forced him to sit.

"Good work," Sheriff Owens said as he motioned for Dray and Amananda to be cuffed and taken to one of the patrol cars.

As the couple passed Cassidy and Slate, they stopped. "We're sorry," Amanda said. "I know that doesn't undo what we did to you, but you'll never understand how sorry we are."

Cassidy found that, at the moment, she had nothing to say. Maybe later, when the pain was less raw.

Shaking Slate's hand and patting Cassidy on the shoulder, Sheriff Owens said, "You two should head home. Come by the office in the morning and I'll have Rusty there. We'll begin the process of clearing your name, Slate. Make it at nine."

"We'll be there," Slate said.

NITA CLAMPED THE LAST garland of flowers around the porch railing and stood back. "Magnificent," she said.

Cassidy nodded, smiling but a little teary. She'd done this once before with a woman she'd loved like a mother. At that thought, she looked out at Slate, who was coming in from feeding the weanlings, and talking to Joker over the fence. They'd brought the stallion home, and so far, Joker had taken a rare delight in tormenting all of the ranch hands. But Slate loved him.

And she loved Slate.

"You're not supposed to come up here," Nita admonished Slate as he put one booted foot on the steps. "You can't see your bride on her wedding day."

Cassidy and Slate both laughed. This was one day Cassidy didn't intend to let Slate out of her sight.

The front door burst open and a blur of blond hair and a white lace dress flew across the porch. Lindsey never paused, she simply launched herself into midair, trusting that Slate would catch her. And he did.

"I'm the flower girl." She held out a white wicker basket that was empty of the rose petals that had been there earlier.

"You're the prettiest thing I ever saw," Slate said, kissing her as he winked at Cassidy.

Nita looked at her watch. "Slate, Cassidy, you have an hour until show time. Now, scoot!" She took the flowers from Cassidy's hands. "I realize this is a horse farm, but I want both of you in the shower and dressed before the minister gets here."

Holding Lindsey between them, Slate and Cassidy headed into the house.

At her bedroom door, Slate stopped. He bent to kiss Lindsey, and then pulled Cassidy into his arms. "This is better than I ever hoped," he said.

"It's odd, but I knew it would be this way. Even when

you had no memory of me, I could still see a future for us." She had never felt such peace and contentment. Beneath it was excitement at her wedding, but her love for Slate was so sure, so strong, that a public commitment was not necessary. It was icing on the cake.

"I love you both," Lindsey said, drawing their attention back to her.

Laughing, Slate bent down. "Now, help your mommy get dressed. We don't want to be late for our own wedding."

"I'm ready," Lindsey said, holding out her dress.

Cassidy checked her watch. "See you in forty-eight minutes," she said to Slate. "On the porch."

She closed the bedroom door, knowing that Slate would never again be on the other side of it.

She chatted with Lindsey while she bathed and put on the simple white dress she'd chosen for her wedding five years before. Slate had made her a garland of roses from the flowers in her garden, and the scent reminded her of Mary Walker as she placed it in her hair. But today was a day of happiness. Mary would have been ecstatic, and Cassidy held that thought as she took her daughter's hands and walked to the porch to the cheers and applause of more than a hundred people who had come to wish her well. And then Slate had stepped onto the porch, and she forgot everyone else.

The ceremony was a simple one. They exchanged the traditional vows, and Cassidy found herself in Slate's arms as his wife. She had never felt happier.

Slate bent to whisper in her ear. "Whatever memories I may have lost, I'll never forget this moment. We'll build new memories together, Cassidy. For the rest of our lives."

They were surrounded by well-wishers and pelted with rice as they ran down the steps and hurried into the rose garden, where a reception had been set up.

Cassidy had turned to join a cluster of ranch wives who'd been stout friends during the past five years, when Rusty came up to her and Slate. His face slightly flushed. "I wanted to tell you personally that I made a serious mistake. I assumed that Slate and his father had retrieved the gun long ago. It never occurred to me that someone had created such a complicated frame-up, involving a duplicate weapon." His flush intensified. "You didn't have a memory so you couldn't have rebutted the testimony. But I should have known better. I should have questioned the evidence and gone into that pond to see if I could find a gun. I can only say, Slate, that in the future I'll be more careful. I'll remember that a person accused deserves every chance to prove he's innocent."

Slate started to say something, but Rusty wasn't finished. "Last night Cole admitted that Dray was supposed to kill you in the bank. Dray was reluctant and his aim was off. It was a fluke of fate that you hit your head and lost your memory. Otherwise, Cole's plan would have been foiled right then and there. I'm sorry, Slate, Cassidy. Sorrier than you'll ever know."

Cassidy could find no hard feelings for the past on her wedding day. She squeezed Rusty's hand. And Slate shook it. "The past is over and done," Slate said. "We're looking to the future here at the Double O."

Cassidy heard the honking of a car horn and stepped out of the rose garden to see who had arrived with such fanfare. The big black truck bore the sign of Ramsur Rodeo on its side as it stopped.

"I hear tell you have a prize bucking stallion here," the man driving said. "I'm T. R. Ramsur, and I want to buy the horse you call Joker."

Cassidy shook her head. "He's not for sale."

"Ma'am, I've been left short of stock due to a bad deal with one of your neighbors. I need that horse."

"Joker's not for sale," Cassidy repeated, aware that Hook'em had stepped up to her side. "He's going to have a good life as a performance horse," she said. "Besides, my husband has ridden him. He isn't the bronc folks say he is."

"That's not what I hear." Ramsur's dark blue eyes lightened. "I hear he's got more fire than Mr. Twist."

"You ain't never seen an animal that can twist and buck like Joker," Hook'em put in.

"He can buck," Cassidy agreed. "But he's not for sale. At any price."

T.R. opened the truck door and stepped out. He was a small man wearing a bolo tie clipped with a gold image of a bucking horse. "I heard you wouldn't sell him. But consider this. I'm set for a big rodeo event up in Fort Worth. And I need a star. The news about this horse is all over the circuit. How about you let me borrow him for one event."

Cassidy saw Slate coming toward them. She explained Ramsur's offer, sure that Slate, too, would refuse.

"Sorry," Slate said. "We're gentling Joker. He has no future in rodeoing."

Ramsure grinned. "One event. Three-hundred-thousand-dollar purse. And you can compete."

Slate laughed. "But I've ridden him."

"I hear he likes bucking," Ramsur insisted.

Cassidy hadn't seen Clay and Randy join them, but Randy spoke up. "That horse loves to buck. Sometimes when he's out in the corral he does it just to get us to come and watch him. He's a ham bone, Slate. You should give it a try. Joker will love hearing the crowds."

Hook'em cleared his throat. "He is a ham, Slate. Set up your rules. No spurs, no strap, nothing to make him buck. Either he bucks or not. He's smart enough to know it's a show. Hell, he was down there puttin' one on for me not two hours ago."

"I can't," Slate said. "I've already ridden him. It wouldn't be fair."

Ramsur laughed. "Let me worry about fair. Walker, your reputation is still well known in Texas. There's a young cowboy, Dillard West, from out of Waco, who claims he can ride better than you. I want a match between you two on that stallion." He pointed down the drive to Joker, who seemed to know the gist of their conversation. As they watched, he jumped, arched, spun and crow-hopped a complete circuit around the corral. "Even if you don't win, I'll give you five thousand just for bringing the horse to Fort Worth."

Slate looked at Cassidy. "What do you think?"

Cassidy considered. Joker was an actor. And he *was* a ham bone. He was good when he needed to be, but mostly enjoyed being wild. There was also the matter that the three hundred thousand would give Slate a chance to buy back his mother's ranch. With Cole headed for prison, the land would be up for sale. "It's up to you," she said.

"Three hundred thousand, no spurs, and you know I've already ridden him once?" Slate confirmed.

"Winner take all."

"What if he doesn't buck when I get on him?" Slate asked.

"Then you're the luckiest man I know," Ramsur said with a grin. "No one believes a horse is smart enough to know when to buck and when not to." He tipped his hat. "See you tomorrow in Fort Worth, folks. It's going to be one helluva day."

SLATE GRINNED as Dillard West picked himself out of the dust. He'd lasted seven seconds on Joker's back before he'd found himself sailing through the air and falling in a tangle of chaps and dirt. As Slate watched, Dillard bent to pick up his hat and dusted it against his legs. Joker eased up behind him and pushed him hard with his nose. Dillard sprawled facedown in the arena to the roar of the crowd.

"My God, he is a ham, isn't he?" Cassidy asked. She straightened Slate's kerchief and kissed his cheek. "Are you sure you can ride him?"

"Nope," Slate said, grinning. "That's what makes it fun."

The announcer opened the microphone. "We're giving Joker a small rest before Slate Walker tries to hang on. You folks remember Slate. He almost made it to the top five years ago, and this is his comeback ride on the buckingest horse I've ever seen."

There were cheers and whistles, and Slate had the crazy sense that he was closing the door on a part of his life. Rodeoing had once been a way to show his skill and make money. But he no longer needed the thrill or the test of his courage. This was his last ride, and he only hoped that Joker wouldn't break his bones.

"You're up," the gate handler called to Slate.

Slate approached the chute where Joker seemed to be waiting with the patience of an old cart horse. But Slate saw the fire in the stallion's eyes. "Remember, I'm the one who feeds you," Slate said as he climbed the side of the chute and settled his legs around the stallion.

He could feel Joker bunch beneath him, and Slate knew that the stallion would give him no quarter. This was going to be a ride.

In the distance he heard the announcer, the gate opened, and he was out.

Slate concentrated on holding on, on keeping his hand in the air and his hat on his head as the screaming faces around the arena became a blur of color and noise. Slate had never ridden anything as twisty as Joker, and he knew the horse was putting his heart into the performance. And it was a performance.

At the eight-second buzzer, Slate freed his hand and jumped clear of Joker's flashing hooves. The ride was over and he'd won. He felt a friendly muzzle in his back and turned to find Joker standing docilely behind him. He turned to wave at the crowd, his grin wide. He was completely unprepared for the giant push Joker gave him.

Slate felt himself falling hard, and then there was the taste of dirt in his mouth. For Joker, the crowd gave a standing ovation.

"ARE YOU SURE ABOUT THIS?" Cassidy asked as she leaned on the rail and watched Lindsey riding around the corral on the big bay stallion.

"Joker loves her. He'd kill anyone who tried to hurt her. And she's a fine rider. Good balance, good instincts." Slate leaned across the rail and kissed Cassidy. "They're fine, Cassidy. Don't worry."

Cassidy grinned. She wasn't worried. She was in heaven. "As soon as she's finished riding, send her up to the house. Nita is waiting for her."

"How about a ride?" Slate asked. "I thought we'd go down to the swimming hole. Take a dip." His smile said there other things on his mind.

"In the middle of the day. In the open. We're an old married couple," Cassidy answered, unable to hide her own grin.

"And it's time we took advantage of the privileges," Slate responded, his hand moving up her arm to gently brush across her breast.

Cassidy felt the familiar rush of desire that Slate always evoked. "Ten minutes," she said softly. "I'll get some towels."

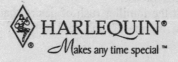

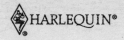

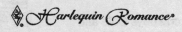

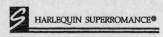

The Gifts of

Christmas

**Join three of your favorite historical romance
authors as they celebrate the festive season
in their own special style!**

Mary Balogh
Merline Lovelace &
Suzanne Barclay

**bring you a captivating collection
of historical romances.**

Indulge in the seasonal delights of Regency and
medieval England and share in the discovery of
unforgettable love with *The Gifts of Christmas*.

Available in November 1998,
at your favorite retail store.

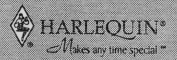

HARLEQUIN®
Makes any time special ™

COMING NEXT MONTH

#489 SOMEBODY'S BABY by Amanda Stevens
Lost & Found
Nina Fairchild's accusations were almost too incredible to believe—
but as Grant Chambers stared into her haunted eyes, something in her
gaze touched his soul. He had to uncover the truth, for Nina claimed
someone had stolen her baby—that Grant's new nephew was hers....

#490 NEVER LET HER GO by Gayle Wilson
A bullet took undercover agent Nick Deandro's sight and his
memories. But it couldn't erase the feeling that he knew Abby Sterling,
his temporary bodyguard, from somewhere....Could he remember in
time to protect *her?*

#491 SPENCER'S SECRET by Laura Gordon
The Spencer Brothers
Logan Spencer was back in town to find his best friend's killer. But
he hadn't expected his passion for his friend's widow to resurface—or
that her secrets had kept him from being a father to his own child....

#492 UNDER THE MIDNIGHT SUN by Marilyn Cunningham
A lonely stretch of frozen tundra, a stranger's body buried in the
snow—and Brian Kennedy's life became enmeshed with the life of
beautiful Malinche Adams. She needed his help to solve her brother's
murder.... But if he helped, would he risk losing his bachelor's heart?

AVAILABLE THIS MONTH:

#485 REMEMBER ME,
COWBOY
Caroline Burnes

#486 SEND ME A HERO
Rita Herron

#487 MYSTERY DAD
Leona Karr

#488 THE ARMS OF THE
LAW
Jenna Ryan

Look us up on-line at: http://www.romance.net